Caffeine Nights Publishing

Cool Water

Pete Haynes

Fiction aimed at the heart
and the head…

Published by Caffeine Nights Publishing 2014

Published in Great Britain by Caffeine Nights Publishing

www.caffeine-nights.com

British Library Cataloguing in Publication Data.
A CIP catalogue record for this book is available from the British Library

ISBN: 978-1-907565-76-2

Cover by

Mark (Wills) Williams

Everything else by
Default, Luck and Accident

The meek will inherit the earth –
if it's okay with everyone else.'

Dave Haynes

In memory of my brother, Dave

Thanks to Brendan Loughlin, John King and Garry Bushell for their help and support

Pete Haynes

Pete was born in West London and became interested in writing at an early age. He began writing plays after success as the drummer in the punk group The Lurkers.

An early work, Thank Your Lucky Stars, was performed at the Edinburgh Fringe, running for three weeks to excellent reviews and he has recently had a short play produced at The Bush Theatre in London.

Pete left school at fourteen and did a variety of jobs, mainly working on building sites, but he has also worked in a crematorium and amusement arcades. After drumming in the group – including appearances on Top of the Pops and other television shows, he made several albums and toured Europe and the USA – Pete went to university. He has worked as a Support worker for many years in the community with people with learning disabilities and mental health difficulties. For a while Pete lived in West Belfast, where he worked as a project worker in a victim's group; he worked with people living with trauma caused because of the conflict in Ireland.

Cool Water is a work of fiction for adults that falls into social/political realism, but the detailed insights given to the psychological make-up of the main character make it an original piece of work.

Pete Haynes
E-mail: esso@petehaynes.co.uk
www.petehaynes.co.uk

One

It is the sound of a city waking itself in an early morning light under low heavy clouds. The hum of traffic is momentarily ruptured by a screech of brakes and a blast on a horn. Bottles smash and break as they are thrown into the back of a dustcart, but above all the sounds is one that repeats itself and is distinct from the accompanying noise of an urban early morning overture. The sound is coming from an area that is a vast construction site. Holes, half-filled with water and debris, litter the site and stacks of timber and steel lie heavy and silent, as if sleeping.

The construction site is boarded off and one side of it is a massive hoarding. Written across the hoarding in a multiple of colours and smiling faces, intended to depict all members of the community, are the words, BELFAST IS CHANGING. Further along the hoarding written in bright letters is the date, 2000.

The sound can now be recognised as the early morning call of a cockerel. It is a thin tinny sound, repeating itself and the call of the miniature cockerel grows louder. It is coming from a blue, plastic watch. On the face of the watch are the initials R. N. I. B. The watch repeats its synthetic crowing call. It is strapped to the wrist of a man who is lying face down in the shattered terrain of churned mud and concrete. The man is naked. His left leg has been crudely severed above the knee. The handle of a pool cue is rammed into his buttocks.

The sound of the cockerel call repeats itself, over and over.

Two

There was a lively and fun atmosphere in a West Belfast youth club. Philip Alexander stood by the doorway. He worked voluntarily at the club as a steward. His stature and demeanour was more adult than those around him. Detached from the youth activities, his interest and concern was of security and adherence to the rules. He was alert as he monitored the comings and goings around the doorway, and his body language showed that he was ready for potential action. Philip Alexander stood with his arms folded, every now and then checking the time on his wristwatch as if the evening was planned to meticulous detail.

A few feet inside the doorway was a table that had a large book on it for members to sign themselves or guests in. Next to the table was a doorway that led into the club itself where loud music was playing. Behind the table was an empty chair. The chair's normal occupant was an elderly man who was not at the club that evening, and his days were numbered for how long he would be able to work there in the future. He had been at the club for years, signing youngsters in, checking their dues were paid and seeing that there was no misbehaviour. Things had changed in youth work as the incoming professionals were now managing the affairs of young people and legalities, policies and procedures had to be observed. Three young girls of about fourteen years of age stood by the table, pushing at one another and laughing. They were all dressed in Bay City Roller outfits.

Edward Scriver, a young man of seventeen, emerged from the club carrying a large papier mâché skull. The girls giggled and then laughed as they pointed at the skull. One of the girls said, 'Oh, that's nice Edward, you've found yourself a girlfriend.'

They all laughed at Edward, although it was done in fun rather than with malice. Edward dismissed them as immature and turned in a circle looking for somewhere to put the sculpture down. He eventually gave up and returned through the doorway into the club. The girls watched him leave and laughed some more.

Three young men appeared at the doorway outside the club, each one of them holding a large bottle of cider. One of the young men was Donny Campbell. He, like Philip Alexander, was eighteen years of age. Donny stood in front of the other two and stared at Philip Alexander, but he remained resolute, blocking their entry to the club.

The girls became quiet, their good-humoured play now gone as they watched the scene in the doorway.

Donny looked at Philip with a faint sneer showing in his face as he said, 'Fuck me, it's Philip Alexander, soon to be a snide copper – and has always been a slimy cunt.'

The two youths with him laughed. Donny added, 'What are you doing, chucking people out who drop a sweetie wrapper?'

Philip Alexander stood his ground, bracing himself for a confrontation. He pushed his chin forward and spoke firmly.

'Turn around Campbell, and take your friends with you – you're not allowed in here.'

Donny did not move, and the expression on his face did not change. One of the young men standing behind him sensed some action and fun. He leant forward and belched loudly before saying, 'Go on Donny, give the copper shite some bother.'

Donny looked over his shoulder and grinned at his friend, and at the same time he stepped over the doorway into the club.

Philip stepped forward, placing his hand on Donny's shoulder he said, 'Out! Come on – on your way.'

Donny stared at Philip and pushed him backwards. The young man standing behind Donny sneered, 'That's it D C, let him have it.'

The girls moved away from the table and Edward rushed into the hallway from the club, his arms extended in an appeal for a truce as he tried to calm the situation. 'Now, let's stop it, let's stop it now – everyone take a step back and think about it.'

Philip turned to look at Edward, and at that moment Donny stepped forward and smashed the bottle he was holding into the side of Philip's face. Philip dropped to the floor and the girls screamed. They were terrified, but Philip was unconscious and could not hear their screaming. Edward was visibly shocked by the amount of blood gushing from the flabby wound in Philip's face. Donny stood over Philip and smiled. He looked at Edward and said, 'I just had a "think about it," as you said – thanks for the advice.'

Donny turned to his friends and laughed as he held out his hand. One of them gave Donny his bottle and the two friends also laughed, although surprised at the sudden ferocity of the attack they do not let it show. Donny raised the bottle to his mouth as he walked through the doorway and out of the club. His two friends embraced his shoulders and laughed. Edward watched them as they left. He looked around himself as the girls continued to scream, and for some reason Edward noticed the amount of tears running down the face of one of the girls. People came through the doorway from the club to see what had happened. Edward was flustered as he looked around helplessly.

'Tiger Feet' by Mud was playing inside the club.

Three

Three months later Donny Campbell was standing in the dock of a crowded courtroom. The judge looked down at Donny. Taking his glasses from the bridge of his nose, he inspected, with a distasteful air, a small group of young men in the public gallery who were there to support Donny. Adopting a swagger in his stance Donny rolled his shoulders and grinned as he looked up at the young men. It was a stance that showed his defiance to his position of being prosecuted in the dock of a courtroom. An middle-aged woman was sitting by herself behind Donny. Her shoulders hunched and her face bearing deep scars from worry and hardship. A scarf, which had been bought for her from a street market five years earlier as a Christmas present, covered her head and was tied in a knot under her chin. Her hands were roughened through the drudgery of scouring and washing, doing cleaning work where abrasive chemicals age and misshape the hands of many women, and in doing so bringing a premature arthritis to the joints that become weak and trembling before their time.

Donny bought the scarf when he was thirteen years old, and the woman with the washed bone complexion was his mother. She was the only member of the family that had shown up at the courtroom. Philip Alexander sat to the side of the dock. A deep scar that had a reddish outline to blue gristle showed clearly on the side of his face. Philip was wearing a suit and tie. He sat upright, as did the large military looking man sitting behind him. The man was Philip's father, and sitting next to him was his mother, a smartly dressed woman with strong features. The anger that she felt was clearly evident in her face.

The judge settled himself as he prepared for the summing up. He looked from his notes to Donny, and regarding him gravely, an ominous shadow passed across his face before he spoke.

'This is not the first time that you have stood where you find yourself at this moment, Campbell.

'Decent, ordinary, hard-working people live in dread of people like you. The things that they have worked for, and things that they cherish and have been brought up to respect, are the ideals and values of decent people wanting to live in a decent society. The likes of you do not share those values.'

Mrs Campbell's body twitched, her narrow beaten shoulders giving slightly to yet another blow that had followed many in her life. She was a woman with a meek nature, fearful of those in authority and had always abided by the law. Her life had been lived secondary to people she had contact with, from childhood and then into a marriage and having a family. The need for making firm rules and giving stable guidance was beyond her capabilities. Her weak face flinched at the words of the judge. She had been bullied all her life, and her face reflected the pain and disappointment she had felt from the actions of others, whether it be from her family, or as in this case the damning words of a man exerting his authority.

The judge continued. 'You are slack in moral fibre – yours is a course that brings destruction to the things honest members of society strive for.

'You, and those like you, do not make any amends for your behaviour, neither do you and your type want to make a contribution so that others may benefit.

'Whatever the modern analysis of your kind and your behaviour might be, I see it as selfish, bullying and cruel. I am representing the views and values of the lawmakers in this country of ours, people who strive to make our country fair and work against criminals. They work to create a wholesome society – to banish inequity and give all honest and innocent people in this country a land for them to be proud of and raise children in peace – but the likes of you do not respect these values.

'You will serve a sentence, for you need to be removed from a society that has suffered because of your presence.'

Donny looked impassively at the judge, a sneer appearing on his face the more he looked at the elderly man. Some of the young men in the public gallery laughed at a remark one of them had made. The judge looked at them and then to the court policemen before continuing.

'The law, the courts of this country, are here to see through a course of justice, and in doing so, remove the likes of you from the streets of this God fearing, law abiding society.'

Four

A few weeks later Donny was sitting with three other young men around a table in the recreational area in borstal. A table tennis table and some chairs took up most of the floor space. The other young men in the area were playing cards, board games or just talking. A few officers supervised behaviour and swapped the odd line of banter with the boys. The officers were smug and basked in the comfort that their status afforded them. Their manner was patronising and they were aware of the fact that they had little power outside of the system in which they were employed, but within the confines of the building where they worked it was a different matter. Their conceit was present in nearly every interaction that they had with the boys.

A young man called Malc was holding court at Donny's table, enjoying the feeling of being the dominant person in the group. Malc had been talking for a while about his exploits and the names of people that he knew, names that were known for being associated with violence and gang warfare. He had been inside for only a few days and was testing the water to see where he swam in it all. Malc continually glanced at Donny as he spoke. He felt confident that he had impressed the other two and gained their respect, but was worried about Donny, who did not show any signs of fearing him. The two other youths nodded and smiled at the permitted time, but Donny did not. He just watched Malc with a blank expression.

Malc pointed at one of the youths.

'Flash the ash – I'm right out.'

The youth pulled a tin from his pocket and Malc continued talking with his hand held out waiting for the cigarette.

'Yeah – I take no shit from any fucker in here. I haven't seen anyone who is able to bother me anyway.'

The youth handed him a rolled cigarette from his tin and Malc took it without acknowledging him. He put the cigarette in his mouth and leant forward in a gesture for the same youth to light it, which he did, dutifully. Malc leant back in his chair and said, 'Yeah. I'd be able to deal with any shit in here – no bother.'

The two youths watched him, remaining silent while Malc looked around the recreation area, nodding, as if at a suggestion he had made to himself. His conviction in asserting himself was growing. He spat out a loose strand of tobacco, sucked his teeth and spoke in a manner that sounded like he might have said it to himself many times before.

'In all honesty, I can say that I don't need to use a weapon.'

He paused, waiting for a response. Satisfied nobody had said anything he continued.

'I reckon I get it from my brother – yeah, oh yeah – Johnny.'

He said the name proudly and with a reverence that he felt should be shared by the others.

'Johnny Ferguson – he knows anyone worth knowing. Nobody upsets him – if you don't want to get your hole kicked across the street.'

Malc placed his foot against the table and rocked himself.

'Some people say I'm just as mad, cos when I get them down I won't leave it – I kick the fucker till he's a piece of shit.

'Some say it's over the top – but it's a warning to others.

'Don't mess – don't fucking mess, boy. Yeah.'

He was relaxing, revelling in his belief that he was in control. The only fly in his ointment was Donny. He had not said anything, but he could feel that Donny was not as compliant as the other two. Malc looked at the faces around the table in turn. The other two youths watched Malc as young railway enthusiasts might watch and consider when at a meeting for trainee engineers. But Donny did not share their eagerness to please him and the indifference he felt towards Malc was clearly shown.

Malc carried on, 'I must get that from my brother – that's what he always told me, "Let them know you mean business, so they don't fuck you about again."'

He stopped and looked at each one in turn around the table before continuing.

'Oh yeah, my brother Johnny, he'll muller them so bad, and no one, and I mean no fucking one ever gets away with anything with Johnny.

'Cos my brother has a reputation see, and it's Johnny's thing. He'll always get you back. You'll do nothing to Johnny Ferguson and get away with it. Never. He'll always get you back. That's what puts the shite up people – see?'

He nodded at one of the youths to confirm what he had just said, and the youth nodded back in agreement.

Malc went on, 'Yeah, Johnny knows this place well – he's told me the rules and who and what to steer clear of.'

He looked around the recreation area before returning his attention to the table, enjoying the authority he was establishing. Malc felt he had to show an example of some kind that will support his bragging. His gaze settled on Donny who had been watching him lazily. Malc had decided to confront Donny, having lost patience with him for not being attentive enough or showing respect. He looked at Donny with a puzzled expression. An awkward silence fell upon the table.

Donny shrugged and said, 'What?'

Malc did not reply. He smirked at Donny and nodded accusingly at him.

'You get them all in here.'

He stared at Donny. Donny held his gaze. Malc raised his head and looking down his nose at Donny he steadied himself as he made his move.

'I think we'll have to watch this one – he looked a bit too long at my dick the other day when I was having a slash.'

The look in his eyes threatened.

'You know what I'm saying?'

Donny stared at Malc. Malc knew he had tested the ground, and although Donny's stare did not falter, Malc felt he had come through. He turned to the others.

'As I say, you get them all in here.'

As Malc finished his sentence, Donny jumped up, grabbed him around his neck and smashed his head down onto the table a few times, and while holding him he repeatedly drove his knee into his face. Donny picked up Malc's cigarette from the table, and after checking to see if it was still alight he rammed it into Malc's ear before smashing his head down onto the table again. Donny fell on top of Malc.

Chaos broke out in the recreational area. Officers closed in and grabbed Donny, but they had difficulty dragging him off Malc. Several officers were needed to pull Donny away, and as they did so one of them stepped back quickly on seeing Donny's face. It was heavily blooded and there was a large piece of Malc's cheek in his mouth. Donny looked around at them and then spat the flesh and blood down at Malc.

Five

Donny was sitting on the side of a bed in a cell staring down at the floor. An officer was standing in the open doorway looking at Donny. He was a grimy man. Everything about him was unwholesome. His uniform hung from his body, it was probably the smartest piece of clothing that he had ever owned. The white collar would have been as discoloured as his teeth if it were not for the rules that stated uniforms had to be regularly washed. His hair was greasy and his face showed that he had drunk too much over the last couple of years. The man leered at Donny as his eyes flickered at a memory that would have got him sacked if he had been found out. He took a deep breath, as if at the effort of speaking.

'Oi, Campbell.'

Donny waited a few seconds before looking up at him.

'When you give someone a wee peck on their cheek, don't get so carried away.'

Donny did not respond. He just stared at him. The officer sneered.

'This place, and other places like this, will be seeing a lot of you in the time you spend on this planet.'

He considered Donny slyly. 'I'll be putting the word round.'

The man nodded, his mouth showing excitement at a future prospect.

'Just keep going like you are, sonny, and they'll be queuing up to take a piece out of you.'

Donny looked down at the floor. The man stared at Donny for a last unsavoury moment before stepping backwards and slamming the door shut. Donny listened to the sound of the large key turning in the heavy lock and the barrel shifting as the steel grated into place. A vacuum more than a silence filled the cell. An occasional shout or the sound of footsteps passing was all that could be heard.

Donny exhaled deeply. Checking his bitten down nails, he bit at the quick under the nail of one finger. Spitting out what he had caught between his teeth he stared at the opposite wall, but his solemn gaze was looking at more than the wall in front of him. Donny was turning his mind back to a memory. His bottom lip dropped slightly because what he had recalled was painful. Sounds from his past filtered into his mind and filled his head. Music was clear and loud. It was Nazi march music. The music gave way to the voice of Adolf Hitler giving a speech at a rally. Donny lifted his head in an effort to escape from the voice and the music and the images that were playing in the theatre in his mind. He was fully immersed in the scene, as he always was when having the flashbacks. The smells and feelings were what he experienced as a young child, with fear being the overriding emotion, and as always he felt a twisting burn in his stomach.

He returned to the bedroom of a small terraced house where his uncle lived, a place that he went to many times as a child in the early 1960s. In his mind he saw himself as a child sitting on the bed. Donny's uncle Alan was then in his forties. He was standing next to a film projector. A tapping sound was heard as the reels turned, playing footage of a Nazi rally onto a white sheet that was pinned on the wall. Donny looked from the flickering images on the wall to his uncle, but only for a moment because he had to watch the film being played. His uncle wore a shirt with no collar and the sleeves were turned up a couple of times. His eyes glared with severity as he fingered a small moustache that was clipped neatly over his lip. He looked down at Donny as he spoke.

'You will have to listen to your uncle, young Donald Campbell, if you want to learn the very important things that I know.'

He watched Donny, as if waiting for a response. Donny twitched his head to one side uncomfortably, but that was not the reaction his uncle was looking for. Donny shrugged, not knowing what else to do. His uncle nearly smiled as he said, 'They're all liars.' He nodded at the images on the wall, watching the Nazi troops marching in lines, 'But not them, oh no, not them, every single one of them is a real man.'

He pointed at Adolf Hitler. 'And he, was a great man.' He watched and listened to Hitler give his speech before turning to Donny. 'People round here are brainwashed, they say I am mad for loving this man,' he nodded at Hitler, 'but they don't know

21

what they're thinking – they're scared. Don't listen to the lies of the weak ones. They're everywhere.'

'Teachers – homosexuals and the like. Filthy liars. Negroes, Americans, making us weak with their lies – because they know that we are right.'

He stopped talking, finding it hard to breathe as his anger grew. He took a step towards Donny.

Donny flinched as his uncle began to speak.

'Look at you – weak and being made weaker by Americans and Jews.

'The food you eat – the language you speak – the stupid music – all the rubbish and lies on the television. Look at you!

'The way you are dressed.'

Donny was dressed in ragged clothes, as was the norm for a poor youngster coming from that area in those times. His uncle lost his temper and lunged at Donny who cowered and held his arm up to protect himself. Donny lost his balance as he evaded his uncle's grasp and fell backwards onto the bed. Donny pressed the side of his face against the wall, maybe in a vain effort to escape from his situation, and also because the coolness of the wall brought him some comfort. He pressed his head hard against its surface, feeling its coldness against his cheek.

The pattern on the wallpaper was of little pools of water with tiny palm trees in the middle of them. Donny had looked at them many times before, in times just like this. While holding his face against the wall he would look at the clumsily painted little pools of blue water, and even though his uncle raged at him, he imagined where they were meant to be, knowing they were in some far-off place he would never have heard of, and the word paradise always came to his mind. It was a word he had heard, and his eyes would linger on the pools of water with the soothing coolness of the wall against his face.

'You know it makes your uncle angry. You – you...'

His uncle said through gritted teeth as he stood over Donny.

Donny waited to be hit, but his uncle turned to a chest of drawers, opened one of them and took out a Luger pistol. He held the gun in the air as he nodded at the images on the wall. His mood calmed as he spoke quietly.

'A great gun, used by a great people. If only you would listen, Donald.

'If only you would listen to me.

'But you won't. You can't.'

Lowering the gun he let his hand drop to his side and he walked over to the projector. He turned it off and looked down at the floor, shaking his head as if defeated. After a short while he had settled himself. Smiling grimly, he talked to Donny while looking down at the floor.

'I know what you want. I know what you want to hear.'

He placed the gun on top of the chest of drawers next to an old record player and cued up a record. He looked at Donny in a way as if he was buying him a treat at the seaside.

'You want to hear my cowboy songs, don't you?

'That's what you really came round here for – to listen to my cowboy songs.'

'The Streets of Laredo' by Marty Robbins played. Donny's uncle watched him.

'You wee scamp, you. Listen to the words, Donald.

'Listen to what the man is telling us.'

Donny was frightened, but having experienced all this before he was resigned to what was happening to him. He watched his uncle as he became increasingly agitated. Finally, he snapped at Donny.

'Come on, come on – you're not listening – not really listening – but then, you don't listen to your uncle when he's trying to teach you – and give you guidance.'

He stepped towards the bed, scowling, feeling that his patience had been tried too far.

'Get up, get up – you, insolent boy,' he growled.

Donny was reluctant to move, but seeing the look on his uncle's face he jumped down from the bed.

'Come on – come on – quickly,' his uncle said, 'Dance then – dance. Dance that jig I showed you.'

His speech became more aggressive as anger burned inside him.

'Dance – dance you little fucker, you.'

He lost control and grabbing hold of Donny he shook him violently before pushing him onto the bed. The voice of Marty

23

Robbins became warped and the words collapsed into one another.

The scene in Donny's memory theatre slowed down, and the voice of his uncle had an echo to it as he stood in front of Donny with his penis in his hand masturbating frantically.

'You naughty, naughty boy – bad boy. Bad, bad boy – making your uncle do disgusting things he doesn't want to do.

'Happy now? Happy now that you've upset your uncle?

'I'll beat some decency into you, boy – that's what I have to do.'

His uncle loosened his trousers and let them drop to his knees while his penis rested on top of his underpants.

'You vile, dirty child, you,' he said, and spit from his mouth landed on Donny's face as he pulled him close to his own sweating face. Donny noticed the stains and thick viscous waste around the roots of his brown and broken teeth. His uncle sat on the bed, dragged Donny across his lap and pulled down his khaki shorts. Donny was wearing a snake belt, which was elasticised with a coiled silver buckle that had the pattern of a snake on it. Donny looked at the belt, remembering how he chose it when he was with his mother in Woolworth's. All the boys at that time wore them. It was a rare treat having the belt bought for him and he liked wearing something that was seen as modern.

His uncle slapped him, and although Donny cried he beat him harder while holding his other hand over Donny's mouth to quieten the noise of him crying out.

The sounds of his uncle grunting and slapping him pounded in his head as Donny sat in the cell trying to pull away from the memory. He tried to control his breathing, now back to his present reality sitting on the bed in the cell. Donny stared at the wall opposite him, sweating and breathing deeply. He shook his head violently in an effort to remove the dying strains of 'The Streets of Laredo.'

Six

Donny studied his reflection in a full-length mirror, looking at his very muscular body, his shaven head and the tight fitting capped-sleeved tee shirt he was wearing that showed his heavily tattooed arms. The mirror was set in an old fashioned wardrobe, but then all the furniture in the bedroom and in the rest of the small terraced house was old. The curtain was almost drawn, allowing just a narrow shaft of remaining daylight to enter the room. Holding a loaded syringe with a hypodermic needle in one hand he unbuckled his belt, pulled down his trousers, jabbed the needle into his buttock and injected the contents of the syringe. Donny dropped the empty syringe onto a table, pulled up his trousers and buckled his belt, all the while checking his reflection in the mirror. He picked up a child's backpack from the table and looked at it, written across the fabric of the bag in bright primary colours were the words, Learning Is Fun. He pulled a sawn-off pump action shotgun out of it and placed the bag onto the table. Donny looked into the mirror and struck a pose with the gun to his side. He smiled at his reflection, pleased with what he was looking at.

The sound of a ball kicked repeatedly on the outside wall of the house caused Donny to drop the pose. The voices of two boys talking could be heard from outside in the street. Donny walked over to the window and with one finger pushed the curtain to the side. Taking care not to be seen he peered down at the boys and listened to what they were saying. One of the boys said, 'I'm telling you – what me ma says – it's best to get out of here – people think they've made it if they marry someone with a job and have a wedding reception down the Ranger's club bar. I'm telling you – I'm going to America when I leave school – our Craig lives there – and he says it's one big place.'

The other boy said, 'When your da gets out of prison, maybe he'll take you.'

'Nah,' the first boy replied, 'He says he's already built us a canoe – and even the paddles to go with it – he says he's not going to fucking paddle it for us as well.'

After a pause the same boy continued. 'Yeah – right now, our Stevie is in the same wing as our da.'

There was a morose expression on Donny's face. He let the curtain fall back into place, walked over to a sound system and switched the radio on. Donny lay down on the bed, holding the gun to his chest. He stayed on the bed for a long time just looking up at the ceiling. The light in the room faded, and the young boys had long gone with their ball. It became dark except for a ray of light coming from a street light outside that shone like a torch through a gap in the curtains. Donny continued to lie on the bed with his eyes open, his right hand gently stroking the barrel of the gun in an absent manner, as one might stroke a cat while relaxing in an armchair.

Donny listened as a newsreader told of a robbery that had taken place, his eyes vacant and distant.

'Police think that it might be connected to a similar robbery earlier this month when three men were also involved and a sawn-off pump action shotgun was used.'

Donny was not really listening to the radio. The news finished and a quiz show came on, but Donny could not hear it, he had fallen asleep holding the gun to his chest. The participants in the quiz show competed with each other to get the biggest laugh from the studio audience. Their rapid talking babbled over one another in efforts to deliver their lines, and a muffled laughter exploded every now and then, rising and falling as if turned by a dial.

Seven

Loud music and unruly noise broke out of The Royal Bar every time the door opened. The people leaving the bar rushed because a fierce rain was beating down on the streets of west Belfast. The Royal Barwas on the corner of a busy main road and a quiet side street that was barely lit by a street light. Through the darkness and rain a fine aura could be seen quite clearly encircling the light.

A car was parked in the quiet side street. It was a Range Rover, and sitting inside it were three people. Donny Campbell was in the front passenger seat. He was looking over the back of his seat at a sly looking youth of about sixteen. The youth was very nervous and his bottom lip had been trembling throughout the whole time he had been in the car. In between short dry coughs of fear he licked his lips. His eyes did not leave Donny's face, and although blinking continually his eyes remained dry. The man sitting in the driver's seat was the same age as Donny. His name was Dougie.

Nothing was said. The sound of rain hammered a speedy thudding beat on the roof of the car. Donny tossed a small package into the youth's lap. He snatched at it, fumbling the package around in his thin shaking fingers. Donny watched him as Dougie talked to the youth's reflection in the rear view mirror.

'And remember now, don't go playing the big shot by opening your mouth.'

He let his words sink in.

'You're earning well. You're doing good for yourself.'

The youth looked from the package to Donny, who was staring at him. Unable to look at Donny he glanced out of the window. He was uncomfortable and felt trapped. Donny maintained his threatening gaze and the youth nodded, as if Donny had said something to him. The youth fidgeted and looked about himself, at the windows, down at the seat, at the floor, at Donny, and then through the window next to him. Dougie was watching him carefully in the mirror. He spoke to the youth.

'You've done good work for us – let's not ruin it – you're one of the lucky ones.'

The youth breathed heavily as his eyes flitted up to the back of Dougie's head, all the while trying not to meet Donny's stare.

Dougie continued. 'No, so use your head – because you're never going to have what's called a job. So – don't just blow it.'

The youth looked down at his lap, and taking a deep breath he slowly looked up, and his eyes met Donny's stare, which was devoid of reason. Donny began to speak. 'Yeah – get out there and enjoy yourself.'

He watched the boy for a few seconds.

'And take a good look at the next dustcart you see. Go round the back of it and watch the crusher for a while.'

The youth ventured a slight nod. Donny continued. 'Anyone fits in there.'

The youth nodded slowly, licking his lips he looked down at the package in his hands. The car was silent. The youth looked through the side window at the rain outside. He watched the rain as it formed large globules on the top of the window and how they became smaller as they began to slide down. His eyes caught the path of one drop as it landed, and staying where it was for a couple of seconds before moving down gradually in a straight line. It rolled from one side to the other, deviating a crooked passage as it made contact with other drops, and then sliding down quickly until its path was blocked by a small ridge of water that caused it to run along in a horizontal line. It finally made its descent as it spilled from the ridge, trickling a miniature zig zagging all of its own until it reached the bottom of the window and was lost in the amalgam of water. It was now indistinguishable from the other drops. The youth tensed up as he tried to keep its form in sight, but the drop had melted within the mass of water.

Donny was watching him.

Eight

It was a busy night in The Royal Bar, there was karaoke entertainment and the atmosphere was rowdy. A stage was set up in front of the speakers, which was no higher than six inches and at a push just large enough for four people. It was packed at the counter and all the tables were stuffed with glasses.

Harsh, attacking laughter blasted in short volleys. One man was held back by three other men from reaching another man who stood with his arms by his sides in a sign of not wanting to fight. The man being held was determined to make his point, his fists were tightened and spit flew from his mouth as words of hate and threat growled through his gritted teeth. Nobody around them was taking any notice. A man gave them a little space at the bar while he waited to be served, but no more than shoulder room as he did not want to miss his turn to be served.

A young man and woman were locked in a full embrace against the wall that led to the toilets. One of his hands was inside the young woman's top and his other hand was pushed down the back of her jeans. Their mouths sucked around each other's and their heads weaved. The girl suddenly pulled away and took a draw on a cigarette as she shoved her other hand down the front of the young man's jeans. A youth walked passed them and gave the young man a congratulatory nod, but he was too far gone, his eyes were heavy and any sheen of craving had dissolved into a narcotic and alcohol fusion that deadened his gaze. The young man's pupils were dilated and his face was the colour of sour milk. A large television was hanging from the wall above the couple on three heavy chains, and although it was turned on it could not be heard above the raging noise in the bar.

Three men and a woman were working behind the bar and it was hard going. Orders for drinks were fired from all directions and diplomacy was needed to placate the impatient. One of the barmen was young and dressed in relatively fashionable clothing of the day, while the other two men looked like they had been caught in a time warp, wearing white shirts with ties, black

29

trousers and shoes. The younger of the other two had a quiff in his hair. Sweat was running down his face and neck, and the back of his shirt was stuck to his skin. He took quick snatches of wiping his brow with the back of his hand as he held glasses under beer taps and gestured to an empathising patron at the bar about how hot it was and how rushed they were. But maybe the patron was not empathising at all, and maybe he just wanted to catch the barman's attention and get on his good side so that he would be served quickly.

That was what the other older barman was thinking as he looked at the patron. He had no eye contact with the customers. His approach was strictly no-nonsense. Serving beer was serious business. The bones in his cheek worked themselves into a ball and were clearly visible in the side of his face as he went about checking and wiping surfaces, pointing at a person to let him know that he was next, his look telling the customer not to hesitate with the order because there just was not time for that kind of amateur behaviour. The overly drunk who falter with their order were immediately passed over as the barman raised his eyes at having had his time wasted. The tattoos on his wrist told a story of a young man who had entered the armed services, the ink now thick and crude. On his other forearm, amongst other tattoos, was one bearing the name of a girl, but the look on his face said all that happened years ago and life now was about pulling drinks, cleaning up and keeping men from hitting one another.

The woman who worked behind the bar was about thirty years of age and had salon-tanned skin and wore clothes that were totally inapt for the work she was doing, although pleasing to a drink fuelled eye, but not functional for physical work. She constantly tugged at her low cut dress, putting it in place after bending down or reaching up for a glass, and her shoes had thin high heels, making walking on the beer soaked floor a precarious effort. She had a bouncy personality and her motor driven voice raised itself above any noise that the bar could throw out. She looked like a middleweight boxer who was out of training, but had a pleasant face and a straight, honest look. Her hands were quite large and square and the shackle of rings and bracelets she was wearing glinted beneath the lights. Her thick boned nose was pushed a little to the side, showing that it might have been broken at one time. The woman's hair was an explosion of streaks, and she combed at it every few seconds with her large pink nails. She raised her eyes at remarks made to her by some of the men. She playfully pointed a threatening finger at the men and showed a smile that revealed brilliant white teeth. The warmth in her beaming face seemed to make up for all the broken down people in The Royal Bar as they struggled with their fears, pettiness and defeat.

Two fat girls left the stage after finishing their song. They were embarrassed and giggling and only one person offered a tired yet loyal clap, but then one of the girls lost her footing as her ankle turned, her knee gave way and she landed on the floor. Her friend took her arm and helped her up, and this caused them to laugh all the more. Nobody took any notice of the girls.

The man who was in charge of the karaoke system looked over his speakers, inspecting them as a pilot might check the propellers on his plane. He had heavily greased, dyed black hair that had thinned so much he moulded what was left of it into a shape he imagined being passable as fashionably acceptable. The man's appearance was dishevelled, having a look from the early 1970s that had been unconsciously maintained and exhausted to a point of falling apart. He struck a pose of concentration as he signalled to a young couple, who were holding hands for support and trying not to laugh, that their song was ready, but they were stopped from getting on the stage by a man with a shaven head who jumped up in front of them and grabbed the microphone.

The man was drunk and he was cheered on by a rowdy group seated around a table near the stage. He was wearing paramilitary trousers tucked into high boots, a tee shirt and a pair of cut-off leather mittens. His arms and neck were covered with tattoos. He reeled about the small stage, bending into the microphone to give greater emphasis to his rage as he sung to no recognisable tune. It was a rambling shout accompanied to a marching clap from his friends who got to their feet because they were stirred up by the man's song. He shook his fist as he delivered his lines, slurring into the microphone he twisted his mouth around his tuneless words.

'So I grabbed this Taig, and I shot the cunt – and then I watched the cunt die...'

The group cheered loudly and the man growled as he clenched his fist. He stood upright, raising his fist above his head as his mouth hung open, looking slack and broken, but then it tightened as he incited aggression for his attack.

'I'll fuck any fucker who wants to fucking fuck with me.'

A loud cheer broke out from his group. The man intended to replace the microphone on its stand, but it fell to the floor with an amplified thump. Without bothering to pick it up he made his way back to his group with lurching steps. Arms were thrown around him and beer sprayed from their table as it was knocked to the side.

The man in charge of the karaoke hurried over to the stage, picked up the microphone and checked to see if it was working by shouting, 'One, two,' into it before replacing it on the stand. The man's manner and actions were camp. He turned his eyes upwards as he checked the microphone in a way that intended to convey an appearance of being a professional and that the people in the bar would not understand his art and expertise. His face carried a heavy weariness that reflected his dissatisfied life. For years he had told people that things were once different when he was at the top of his profession and mixed with big names in the entertainment industry. It was not true, but had said it so many times he now believed it himself. He had only ever worked in small bars and did modest birthdays and weddings. There had been the occasional booking for a person who might have known someone who knew someone who was on the television, but that was as far as it went. The aspirations that he had as a young man to break through in the music industry had come to nothing. All those years of sending off tapes of himself deejaying to local radio stations have now passed. It has been many years since he realised that he was out of time and too old.

He continued to slog away in the face of constant rejections. His mother would hear of his plans, sitting in the cramped kitchen of their small terraced house, listening to his ideas and frustrations, of how he was let down, listening to him talk of how people were not interested in talent and knowledge, but just facile gimmicks and a pretty face.

She would sit there with a tea towel in her hands, careful not to interrupt him and mindful to concentrate on remembering the

32

names that he would talk about or he would lose his temper. Those late nights went on for years. When he came in after playing 'a gig' or a 'booking,' she made a chip supper and watched him carry his records and equipment through the front door, usually cursing the rain. It had been just the two of them for a number of years, his mother listening to his hopes, of the people who were going to get back to him, those having contacts with names that she had heard on the radio. It went on and on, and she saw him become more isolated the older he became, and she felt for him.

He grew bitter, and she became frail. Her strength could no longer fulfil her will to carry on and see through a hope she had of seeing her son happy, or settled before she died. But it was not to be. Her illness rendered her very weak, and she suffered badly in those last few months, and still she could hear her son lump his musical equipment through the door at a late hour. She heard his sighs, his frustrations, at another uneventful night, and she would weep for her son's dissatisfaction. The time came when she died, and she reached out at the pain of no longer being able to keep a watchful eye on her son.

Her life had passed. A small woman in physical stature, but her heart held a love that was the greatest power on this earth.

As the man fiddled with the microphone, and silently cursed the man who let it drop to the floor, he looked over at the door. He was watching Donny Campbell enter the bar. They were the same age and went to the same school. His eyes did not leave Donny as he slyly watched him walk up to the counter, but he then he swore out loud because the music had faded and the volume of the television was turned up. He was irritated because the bar staff had meddled with the sound system without asking his permission to do so. After all, as he kept reminding them, he was in charge of the music.

There were calls for hush and for the volume of the television to be turned up as a photograph of a known paramilitary figure who had recently been shot, appeared on the screen.

A newsreader sat at a desk that had a slim computer on it, and behind him was an office setting that appeared to be buzzing with activity. There were men and women rushing quickly from one computer to another, passing pieces of paper in a way that looked as if the contents of the messages were pressing and important. There were over a dozen desks in the office scene, with earnest young people sitting behind them, gazing intently at computer screens and then standing up quickly and hurrying to another person who was looking at a computer screen and handing over a piece of paper. The scene was a place of energy and urgency as they coped with the breaking news that was apparently rushing in.

The newsreader's voice could be heard clearly. 'There are questions being asked in the House of Lords regarding the acceptance of self-styled community leaders such as Donny Campbell.'

A loud cheer erupted in the bar, with some people looking over at Donny and raising their fists. Donny nodded modestly.

The newsreader continued. 'The Province appears to have slipped, ethically. There is a tolerance shown towards those having no regard for the law as they now have a function, albeit a negative one, in that they have gained notoriety and are fast becoming popular role models for youngsters starting out in life with few opportunities.'

A roar of approval broke out, which turned into clapping and chanting and the newsreader's voice disappeared under the noise. The music was turned up and a sign was given to continue with the karaoke.

One of the older barmen, the serious one, walked over to Donny and spoke as if he was bringing grim news.

'Here, Donny, you have one in, and that fellow over there wants to buy you a drink.' He nodded at a man who was looking over and smiling ingratiatingly. Donny acknowledged the man and the barman placed a bottle in front of him. Donny picked up the bottle, took a sip and faced the counter, detached from what was going on around him. He looked around the bar, but found nothing of interest so returned to looking directly in front of him.

His gaze settled on a mirror behind a row of optics. Donny stared at his reflection. He could not hear the music, the raised voices or the laughter and the shouting. As he looked deeper into the reflection of his face the sounds in the bar did not exist. He studied certain features and scars on his head and face as he thought of the history behind them. His mind went back to a time when he was a child, a time that Donny often thought of, returning to his infancy and the incidents that were stuck in his memory. His mind filled with sounds of voices and music echoing in a wooden church hall. He was back in the church hall he went to in the mid-1960s. A man barked in a nasal voice that sounded like a factory siren above the noise of youngsters shouting and playing musical instruments.

A young Donny was facing the wall, away from the rest of the boys. He was standing very close to the wall with a drum strapped over his shoulder and holding long drumsticks that looked out of proportion to his small frame. Most of the other boys were facing the man with the barking voice. He was in his early twenties, having greasy hair, a pale complexion and deep pockmarks in the skin of his face, left from bouts of severe acne. The man stared at the boys through the lenses of thick, black framed glasses. He was wearing a white shirt and black tie and had the sash of a band across his chest. The man was working himself up as he spoke with growing excitement, and in doing so showing that most of his teeth were missing.

'So I say, remember those brave men. Our heritage, sixteen hundred and ninety – the battle, and our bravery lives on within us.

'We have a brave history, and we thank our loyalist brothers for our freedom – and we are responsible for our future, especially in these times of communists and troublemakers – and evil, and the like.

'Boys – men, I should say, we have our part to play in our glorious future.

'When we march, our lines will be straight, our uniforms will be smart, gleaming and shining – and we will be the envy of every band.

'And, I will personally buy the sweeties of my choice for the best turned out junior soldier.

'We will, as always, conduct ourselves in a manner befitting a loyalist regiment, and in doing so, gain the respect of everyone.'

The man finished his speech and told the boys to pack up and get themselves ready to go home. Donny returned to facing the wall, banging the drum a couple of times as if at an imaginary enemy he was advancing upon, because in his mind he was in a battle. People were shot as they marched in line, bodies were gouged with bayonets, men tried to escape from their victors but their throats were slashed. There was screaming and the stabbing and beating was vivid in his mind as marched through a scene where soldiers were burning down houses and buildings where people lived. Women and small children were dragged from their homes and thrown to the ground. No mercy was shown as children were shot in the head and the bodies of dead women were kicked. Some men were torturing women that were still alive, ripping off their clothes and stabbing at their naked bodies with long knives, all the while laughing wildly at their screams of pain and for mercy. And Donny continued to march through the slaughter, playing his drum.

Donny felt a sensation run through his body. He looked around the hall, checking to see if anyone was watching him because he had slipped into what he had been told was one of his daydreams. He turned to the wall and contorted his face in hatred.

The echoes from that hall all those years ago faded as Donny found himself staring into the mirror behind the bar counter in The Royal Bar with music thumping out around him. And Donny continued to look at his reflection, noticing the unhappiness in his face.

Nine

The sounds of weights clanking filled the small training room as they were dropped onto the hard matted floor. There was not any sophisticated hi-tech equipment, it was mainly free weights and a couple of basic machines. Mirrors were fixed to the ceiling and on the walls, and there was background music playing that was intended to be relaxing.

Donny was sitting on the end of a bench finishing some reps with a barbell. He was dressed in tracksuit bottoms and a tight tee shirt. A man in his late fifties, who was wearing a tracksuit, was standing next to Donny. He placed his hand on Donny's shoulder and looked into his face.

'Looking good, Donny,' he said. 'It's a clear mind and healthy diet.'

He laughed at the irony of what he had just said. Donny looked up at the man with no change in his expression, and without acknowledging him he looked at his reflection in the mirror. The man watched Donny closely. He shook his head slowly and smiled, but found it difficult to show the affection he wanted to. He spoke quietly.

'You're building your own kingdom, Donny. Precise, designed and dedicated, to yourself.'

He laughed and rubbed his hand on Donny's head as if he had hair.

'And why not?' he went on, his cheerfulness fading.

'No fucker will give you anything.'

He watched Donny proudly, in a way one would imagine a father looks at his son. The man continued to look at Donny, but the mood was broken by the voice of another man who was standing at the other end of the bench.

The man spoke with a soft tone.

'Are you arms or shoulders today, Donny?'

Neither Donny nor the older man looked at him. The older man suddenly laughed and slapped Donny's back.

'Look at you. All those years ago, when you came to me for advice, and I gave you guidance for building a body – and here we are, "arms or shoulders," indeed – sakes man.'

He placed his hands on Donny's shoulders and leaning close to him spoke excitedly.

'Yes, oh yes, Donny boy – snap a man's neck with those arms – a back to drive steel rods through the Black Mountain – shoulders like an oak door and hands that can deliver that killer blow.'

Donny continued to look at his reflection. He was listening to what the man was saying, but was isolated in his thoughts as he looked at himself.

The other man spoke again in his soft voice.

'Donny, shall we do forearms and bi's together – Donny?'

Donny looked up slowly at the man's face. It was hideously deformed and deeply scared. Donny did not answer, but just looked at him. As they looked at each other a fourth man approached the bench and wrapped his arm around the neck of the man with the disfigured face. He pulled his head close to him and pointed two fingers, as if they were the barrel of a gun, into the side of his face and laughed as he made gunshot sounds. The disfigured man tried to shrug him off and they grappled with each other before falling to the floor. Donny nonchalantly watched the two men writhe around the floor having a mock fight. The older man laughed uncontrollably, holding his sides he pointed at the men on the floor urging them on. Veins stood out on the side of his head and his face was deep red as blood pumped through his neck showing sinews that looked as if they were going to snap.

Donny joined the men in their mock fight, and with the help of the disfigured man held the other man down. The disfigured man took a bottle of amyl nitrite from the pocket of his shorts, unscrewed the cap and forced it under the man's nose. He struggled, but was held in place. All three of them laughed boisterously, which made the older man laugh all the more. He looked like he was having a seizure as he bent over laughing with his hands on his knees. The man with the deformed face grabbed the older man, and although the older man tried to break free, he dragged him onto the floor amongst their bodies.

The older man spluttered, 'Oh, you're good lads – you're good lads.'

In between their shouting and laughing, a smooth, slushing sound of the sea breaking gently onto rocks and lapping the shore could be heard from the CD player.

Ten

A soft, golden halo hovered and moved a shivering dance above the flame of a slim candle that burned gently and true. It lit, but only faintly, the figure of a man sitting on a chair. He was bound and gagged with his head resting on a table. The man was wearing glasses with very thick lenses, and sitting on a chair just away from the table was another man who was also bound and gagged. The outline of three men could be made out standing next to the two bound men. It was the same bedroom that Donny Campbell was in before. The three men were wearing Snow White masks. Donny Campbell revealed himself by taking off his mask, and the other two followed by taking off theirs. Donny threw his mask onto the bed and looked from the two bound men to his accomplices.

'You go now. I have to be with them alone.'

They looked from Donny to the two gagged men, and as they turned to open the door they were stopped by the sound of a cockerel calling. It had a thin artificial sound. It called again. They looked at Donny and then down at the man slumped over the table. And again the electronically measured cry of the cockerel call sounded. The man looked at them through the thick lenses of his glasses. All three of them looked at the man. The cockerel sound was coming from a plastic watch on his wrist. The two accomplices looked at Donny. He nodded towards the door, gesturing for them to leave, and as they did one of the men stole a last look at the man wearing the glasses and the watch on his wrist.

Donny checked the contents of a hypodermic syringe. He walked over to the man who was seated away from the table and stood behind him.

The man was silent. He had been beaten and was resigned to his fate. He jolted forward as Donny shoved the needle into the back of his neck. The man winced in pain. Donny leant over him and looked into his face as he spoke.

'Ten seconds and counting.'

The man gasped quietly and gurgled before lurching forward as he fought for breath. He spluttered, but gave in as his death came swiftly.

Donny turned to the other man, who was watching him with eyes that were hardly visible behind the thick lenses. Donny dropped the syringe onto the table and picked up a knife that had a long thin blade. The man was sweating heavily and his mouth worked against the gag that restricted movement and muffled words he was trying to form.

Donny stood behind him, and leaning close to the man's face he spoke into his ear in an even tone.

'Now, if you did not wear those glasses of yours, you wouldn't be here...'

Donny looked around the room.

'Here, in my boudoir.' Donny stopped talking and looked at the man. The room was still. Donny nodded at the other man as he said, 'You see, you and your friend, Mary, over there, are a couple of queens who should know better. I can't allow any talk, which would cause a break in security.

'Too many people – too many questions.'

He turned and flicked a switch on the sound system. 'River Deep Mountain High' by Ike and Tina Turner began to play. Donny raised his voice over the music.

'Good song, isn't it?'

The man did not respond. His weak eyes stared forward at a place people can only guess about.

Donny spoke quietly. 'Maybe you should take your glasses off?'

The man breathed desperately.

Donny continued in an even tone. 'You could pretend I was someone else. Your mother, maybe?'

He rammed the knife into the side of the man's neck. The man propelled himself across the table, but immediately weakened.

Donny watched him die and then turned up the volume on the sound system that was on an old chest of drawers. Donny looked quickly from the two dead men to the chest of drawers as if suddenly remembering something. He opened one of the drawers and carefully took out a video camera. He inspected it, weighing it in his hands as if it was a very precious thing to him, like a guarded secret that only he knew about. He placed the camera on the table and pulled at the man who was slumped across it, shifting him into a seated position. Donny took a knife from his pocket, flicked it open and cut at the flex that bound the man's arms and the gag in his mouth.

The gag fell away and Donny looked impassively at the thin bladed knife sticking out of the man's neck, taking a detailed note of the blood that had gathered around the handle and how it had run in a small stream down his neck and over the collar of his shirt. A fine spay of blood had shot out when the knife was pushed in, leaving small flecks on the side of the man's neck, over his jaw and up that side of his face, peppering the frames of his glasses and completely covering one of the lenses.

Donny put his fingers into the man's mouth and pulled out a golf ball. He examined the ball before putting it in his own mouth. Donny smiled as he picked up a remote control and turned to a small television that had a built-in video. He picked up the camera from the table and pointed it at the man. The man's face appeared on the television's screen. Donny leant forward so that his own face also appeared on the screen. Letting the golf ball drop from his mouth onto the table he watched the image of his face and the ball bouncing.

Donny put the camera on the table and cut the flex that bound the other man. He dragged the dead men into sitting positions against the table with their heads resting on one another's shoulders. They looked like two drunken friends sleeping off the effects of a heavy night on the tiles. Donny positioned the man's glasses on the bridge of his nose and stepped back to inspect the two men. He looked at the knife in the man's neck and the frozen expression of pain and anguish set in a final response to the man's time here on earth.

Donny tucked a plastic sheet that he had previously spread out on the floor under the two men. He took a torch from under the bed and shone it in the men's faces, looking closely at the wound around the knife and the expression on the other man's face. He picked up the camera and filmed with one hand while shining the torch with the other, and all the while the image of what he was filming played on the screen over his shoulder. He held the torch in various positions and at different angles, trying to capture a grotesque portrayal of what he had created.

Donny played a selection of music, but mostly from a CD of disco love songs from the 1970s and 1980s that came free with a newspaper he had bought.

After satisfying himself he turned the music off, fell onto the bed and pointed the remote control at the television.

Donny lowered the volume as the music started and a flurry of images lit up the room. He watched the screen with an intensity of a research academic filing new information, but the objective scrutiny gave way to lust as he pushed his hand down the front of his trousers and masturbated while watching a collection of images he had taped over a period of time in the room. The first one was of Donny standing behind a man who was dead and slumped in a chair. Donny was stripped to his waist holding a cheese wire around the man's neck. Pumping up his body he pulled on the ends of the wire with all his might, rocking the wire deeper into the flesh and finally into the bone. For a short while the only sound was a grunting noise made by Donny in his efforts to severe the man's head before the music began to play, which was 'Feels Like I'm In Love' by Kelly Marie. The music changed to a children's song that was once popular at wedding receptions as it brought all age groups to their feet and dance the familiar steps in time with the simple song.

The dead man's head was almost severed from his body, and then it dropped forward held only by strands of flesh, veins and sinew. Donny stepped back, striking a bodybuilder's pose he flexed the muscles in his arms. The picture on the screen dissolved and lines flickered before another image took its place. Donny frowned as he tried to remember the night he had filmed it. A young man was sitting upright on the floor with his hands tied behind his back. He was still alive, but only just. The shot changed to a close up of the young man's face, and then a hand came into view holding a severed penis with blood running from where it had been cut. The penis was forced into the man's mouth and a few seconds later a lit cigarette was pushed into the penis.

Donny looked at the image as The Beach Boy's song, 'You're so Good to Me' played. He continued to watch the screen with a transfixed stare as the music changed to The Real Thing's, 'You to Me are Everything.'

Donny fast-forwarded the videotape to the most recent recording, stopping it as the two men on the floor in front of him appeared on the screen. 'Feel the Need in Me' by the Detroit Emeralds was playing. Donny dropped the remote control and picked up a pair of pliers. He gripped the lobe of his left ear between the teeth of the pliers and masturbated furiously, and just as he came he let out a roar of pain and pleasure as the steel make contact through the flesh of his ear. He jumped from the bed, pulling his jeans together and holding his ear. Looking down at the blood on his hand he kicked the dead men, but his energy was spent. He sat on the bed taking deep breaths as he cupped the bloodied ear to the side of his head.

Donny leant back against the wall with his eyes tightly shut. Turning his face he pushed his cheek against the wall and whined as he held his ear.

He slowly opened his eyes. They were flat and extinguished, but they opened a little wider as he looked at the pattern on the wallpaper, studying the little blue pools of water in the separate little islands. The wallpaper was old and stained, with the white having browned over the years and the blue faded to a pale shade of its former colour. It was the same paper Donny looked at as a child, because it was the same room he visited when he was a child. After his uncle died Donny bought the house from the Housing Executive and left everything pretty much as it was, especially the bedroom. He did not live in the house, but it was a place he came to for various reasons, either to get away from things or to bring people back for his pleasure.

Tonight he had his pleasure, and now he would go through the feelings that he always did and think about himself and his life. He did not feel fear, but there was an unpleasant sensation that was a constant and it made him feel uncomfortable. His breathing calmed and his eyes focused more clearly. His ear throbbed and he touched it lightly with his fingertips. Donny slid down the wall with his face pressed against it, feeling relief and comfort from its coolness. It soothed him as he looked at the little blue pools of water and the clumsily painted little islands that were replicated in the print of the aged paper.

Eleven

A banquet had just taken place in the Conference Room in the city hall. Those taking part were junior politicians, employees from the council, the police, journalists, religious bodies, community groups and others from the business community. They had descended upon the hall with their ideas on matters such as resolving conflicts, creating a more open society and expounding the benefits of why people should invest in the area. The stage was now empty except for a row of chairs resting idle and empty. Written on a banner above the stage were the words, BELFAST IS CHANGING.

The Conference Room was full of people sitting around tables or standing in small groups engaged in discussions. Three men were sitting at one of the tables. One of the men was wearing a police uniform, it was Philip Alexander, now in his forties he had risen in the ranks of the police to the position of Acting Assistant Chief Constable. The man who held the post before him was killed in a car accident and the circumstances surrounding the incident were reported as 'suspicious.' Philip Alexander took the vacant post after being encouraged to do so and had been given the nod that if things went well he would have the job on a permanent basis. Sitting next to him was Edward Scriver. He was dressed in casual clothing although acceptable for formal occasions. The other man was Chief Constable Murray. Murray was in his late fifties, and he was out of patience as he regarded Edward Scriver in a tired fashion. Philip Alexander had also heard enough of what Edward was saying as he tossed his napkin onto the table and leant towards Edward.

'Don't tell me about "bridge building," "initiatives," "sensitive, collaborative approaches."'

He continued to look at Edward as he said, 'And the excitement of twinning conflicting cultures.'

His eyes narrowed as he tried to reach Edward.

'What was it you said? The "creation of a positive forum for future development?"'

45

Philip Alexander shot Edward a penetrative look that bored through many men, young and old, who had stood in his way. Murray watched Philip and glanced at Edward with a sarcastic smile. Philip shook his head in despair as he looked at Edward, and his face hardened before speaking.

'Ed – Edward – I remember you from the youth club days.'

He turned his face showing a deep scar on his cheek.

'You were there on the night when our good friend, Mr Donald Campbell expressed his approach to understanding, rules and respect.'

His eyes searched deeper into Edward.

'Donny, the self-styled community leader, who gets more respect than you or I could ever hope to achieve.'

Murray watched Edward incredulously as Philip Alexander spoke.

'I'll tell you what Ed, I'm reminded every time I look in the mirror, that the scum out there survive very well, earning more than the three of us put together.'

Edward breathed in deeply before speaking.

'I know, I know – I've heard all this many times, but, Philip, you know that isn't the whole story. It's symbolic behaviour, in detriment to positive progression.'

Philip Alexander looked down, dismissing what Edward was saying.

Edward stared at him with his hands held theatrically out to his sides. Philip Alexander treated Edward with a patience that he did not show to others of Edward's ilk. He lowered his voice in an attempt for Edward to understand him.

'You and I have grown up dealing with people, from when we were young. I took cadet training and became a police officer, and you, as I remember from those days – you wanted to become an actor, or something.'

Edward's face flinched at his words, 'you wanted to become an actor or something,' and his reaction did not go unnoticed by Philip Alexander. Edward thought about the way Philip Alexander threw the line away, as if it did not matter, when it was the most important thing in his life.

The work that Edward did at the youth club was on a voluntary basis and part of a project that he was doing at school before

46

going to university to study drama and art. He came from a middle class area and the club was in a poor part of Belfast that was notorious for violence during the Troubles. After his time at university he struggled to find work that was fulfilling, there were no jobs he found interesting or held any excitement for him. Edward felt that his creativity was repressed, he wanted to be an actor and London was calling with the promise of a life offering stimulation and possible recognition of his talent.

Edward was always a bit of a loner and had been seen by some as maybe a little strange, but that might have been no more than the intensity Edward had at pursuing what he felt was the most important thing in his life, which was to be a successful actor or artist. He felt that the environment where he lived in Ireland did not provide the opportunities that he needed. There were not the theatres, film companies, agents and other artists. He had rows with his mother and father, telling them that he did not fit in, but they had heard this from him for years. They hoped he would grow out of it and that his feet would eventually land on the ground. He could then get on with his life, and maybe, meet a nice girl and get married. But he grew morose and frustrated at what he felt was being denied to him. His circle of friends became smaller. The ones he knew who went to university either returned to where they came from, set up home and took a job befitting a graduate, or went to find work in England, and a few travelled further to the United States of America or some other land far away.

Edward moved to England and secured a place in a drama college, although he had to pay with money he borrowed from his father. It was a one year course and he made contacts that led to him getting small parts in lesser known repertory venues. He made a few acquaintances and chased, to a point of harassing, a fellow female student who did not reciprocate the depth of feelings that he had for her. When the course finished he spent most of the following year applying to companies and agents and trying to meet people in the hope of gaining a contact that would open a door for him.

He had no success whatsoever and his father felt that he had subsidised Edward long enough. Time went by with no luck in attaining anything that could secure him subsistence above evading rent and asking favours to get by. Work, in the other sense of the word, had to be pursued at the expense of following his dream and heartfelt ambition. He taught art for a few hours a week at night classes and did bank work for a local authority with young people in youth clubs.

He was encouraged to study for a teaching qualification in youth work, which meant he could earn more money and have a recognised qualification to fall back on. But Edward, as many people, could not commit himself to a job. It got in the way of what he wanted to do and saw himself as being, and although people would say things like he did 'valuable' and 'meaningful' work, unlike theirs that was concerned with materialistic values, it did not mean much to Edward because he saw the work as just a means to earn some money. His words sounded hollow when he listened to himself telling people what he did for a living. He felt a fraud, accepting accolades from others for doing commendable work when his intentions were set firmly on self-interests. Although he did more and more youth work and the acting began to fade. He contacted other agencies that dealt in social work, getting a few evenings here and there, and then a full week's work, which progressed to a month's work with options of a further six months. Except Edward did not see having more of the work as a progression, because it was not what he really wanted to do.

Edward brought an artistic approach to the work he did with the young people, and although he was often praised for what he did, he felt his energy was wasted and remained dissatisfied and resentful as he saw others he knew at drama college get on in an area of work that he wanted to succeed in, while he became known as the person who 'works with kids.' He began searching for something, a thing that was more than merely an interest, wanting to find something that held a deeper spiritual meaning. He dabbled with Eastern religion, but in his heart he knew that it was really more to do with trying to gain the affections of a young woman he had met at an audition who went to meditation classes.

Edward accompanied her to retreats where a visiting guru would expound on philosophy through an eclectic mix of Eastern religious thought. Rows of white middle class young men and woman would be in attendance, nearly all of them under thirty years of age, sitting cross-legged on the floor in a large manor house. It was barren, basic, a stifled austerity, an antithesis of the material aspirations of their parents, sitting there, laughing at remarks that criticised their own culture. They listened attentively as the guru spoke of wisdom and pointed a crooked finger at the unsolved mysteries that exist. They embraced a diet of food and perceptions that challenged their backgrounds, and spent hours listening to smiling gurus present one-dimensional lectures to the guilt-ridden strays sitting before them.

Edward failed to gain the attention of the young woman he had trailed behind for over two years. She settled down and married a young man who also went to the retreats, but had got himself into the rapidly evolving and financially rewarding work of computers. So, Edward went to India to prove to her how honest his commitment was to embrace an alternative philosophy. Just before he left for Delhi he dropped round their house they had recently mortgaged, wearing a sackcloth shirt and shapeless trousers made from a rough weave in a co-operative community industry in a part of the world suffering poverty and beleaguered by multinational companies.

In later years Edward felt embarrassed when thinking back to those days, at what a fool he made of himself and shuddered when thinking how pathetic he must have seemed. That Indian trip lasted a year and ended with him becoming ill without any insurance and the ashram he was staying at did not have the medical care needed to treat him, so his father had to pay. It was a lot of money, and with the insistence and pleading from his mother, Edward returned, but not to his home in Ireland. He went to London where things carried on much the same as they were before.

People in England did not really know what was going on in Ireland, and Edward felt Belfast was a place that had never offered him anything that satisfied his creative desire. It made him feel sick when he thought of where he came from. He saw it as drab and limited by bigotry. He hated the narrow-minded rigidity of thought, the restrictions and fear, the paranoid watching and judgmental thinking, all played out in a dismal post-industrial landscape, soaked from the seemingly persistent

49

rain, peppered with housing estates that reside under heavy laden clouds with exit and entry roads designed by military specialists in security, observation and control.

Time had moved on and Edward was not the young interesting guy from the troubled area of Ireland anymore. He was now in his thirties, and acting parts for intense young men battling against their physical and mental environments were going to young men ten or so years younger than him. The political scene was changing in Belfast and it was opening up to the outside world. The camera, tourists and businesses were invited to the land that once spelt danger. A media driven rush had turned a light on a country that had previously stagnated in darkness. The image of Belfast was changing.

Edward finally took the social work qualification in youth work, applied for a job in Ireland, and having got the job returned to the area that he came from in Belfast. He had written a pamphlet titled, 'Valuing People,' and had hopes of extending it to a book. He secretly harboured desires to find some personal fame as a person who was known as a leading campaigner for a state where there was no inequity and opportunities are afforded to everyone.

Edward had settled for a world of policy and procedure, working for a local authority he pontificated about people and society. People whom he once believed he connected with through his art and acting, people he felt that he represented, empathising with their desires and dreams, believing that he could counter an authority that designed the type of society whereby a person felt that it was torture to live in it. He felt that his artwork and acting offered hope and understanding and was a symbolic gesture in sympathising with their plight.

But all those grand ideals had now gone. He contributed to the doctrine that sets boundaries of cultural appropriateness, and denied the ball that twisted in his stomach as he gave speeches on honesty and purpose, knowing he once felt that he had a spirit straining at the leash, but now, all was tepid, and he was conscious that he was following a path, as many others do, to find a sense of strength that was given through security.

Not long ago he looked into the mirror and felt fear coursing through him, but he pushed the feeling aside. He now accepted the rewards that his work offered him while nursing a feeling of emptiness inside. It was a void, that when roused bled a poisonous resentment towards those who he regarded as really creating something of worth in a society that he tinkered with on the sidelines, in safety.

Edward's attention had drifted. Philip Alexander's comment about him wanting to be an actor had stirred deep emotions that blocked out everything around him. But Edward was now back to the noise and smells in the city hall, sharing a table with Murray and his uncompromising brusque manner, and Philip Alexander's face was right in front of him. Edward knew that Murray would not be surprised by his momentary absence, because it would be the kind of behaviour he would expect from those coming from social work.

Philip Alexander continued. 'You dabbled in youth work, and have now made a career in social work. I remember your talks on expression through dance and drama, and people exploring themselves.'

His manner became firm as he swallowed what he really thought and chose words he saw as diplomatic.

'My hope is of building protection for ordinary people from those that do harm – those who make no worthwhile contribution to the society in which they live. I want to see people go about the business of running their lives without the intrusion of selfish criminals...'

Edward cut in, speaking quickly with a delivery that was rehearsed.

'We all have to work towards gaining an understanding – ignorance divides people.'

Murray tutted, but Edward persisted, he had not finished reciting his script and turned in his chair to face Murray.

'As tough as you might find it, we all fall short...'

But Philip Alexander was not going to listen. 'All this social engineering,' he said, as his face creased in loathing, 'when it comes down to it some seeds will produce, and some will not.'

Edward said, 'Depends how the soil is prepared.'

Murray and Philip Alexander swapped tired glances, seeing Edward's philosophy as adolescent. Murray cleared his throat before speaking and looked at Edward in a fatherly manner.

'Your values are our values. Please do not try to steal the moral high ground, Mr Scriver. This is not a competition. We all have our part to play.'

He smiled condescendingly as he touched Edward's sleeve with his finger.

'You are younger than I am, you are up with the new language and terminology, but I have the experience, learned from years of policing. I represent valuable, esteemed members of our society.'

He grinned slyly as he looked at Philip Alexander.

'No, it is not a matter of scoring points – a game of who can reach down to the gutter, pick up a piece of crap and then try to sell it as a valuable jewel.'

His manner hardened as his voice lowered.

'Social work, all work, has its place – I hope and trust that we can work alongside one another.'

An insincere, thin smile showed on Philip Alexander's face, which slowly faded as he levelled an unwavering dark gaze at Edward. He said, 'There are those out there that we have nothing in common with. We could never work together with them – I am pleased to say.'

Edward looked from Philip Alexander to Murray. Nothing was said.

Twelve

Across from the new civic centre was the newly built part of the pedestrian shopping centre. The retail industry was growing, consumers and businesses were encouraged to gather in the city centre as restrictions of entry were relaxing and fear of explosions were less. For many there was a positive mood swing.

In a branch of a well-known building society three young women could be seen through the window sitting behind their desks. They were dressed in their company uniforms that looked like how a futuristic style of dress might have been depicted in a 1960s science fiction film.

One of the young women was Katie Preston. She was twenty-one years of age. Katie was engaged to be married and wanted to buy her own house with plans to take advantage of her company's incentive to get a subsidised mortgage. She kept a studious eye on the booming prices in the property market, but at present she lived at home with her mum and dad, her sister, who was a year younger than her, and her younger brother. Katie had recently joined a fitness club, even though her mother told her it was too much money, seeing as she was saving for a mortgage, and although Katie agreed with her mother she felt she owed it to herself to have an indulgence. After all, she had read about treating oneself well. She had read that in one of the self-improvement books she was interested in reading. The books gave examples of positive thinking and people who are seen as role models, people who have achieved the success that they aspired to and gained happiness or whatever they wanted in their lives. Katie had started to read them when she was seventeen, liking the idea of taking control of one's life she felt it lifted the grey sky that seemed to hover above the city where she was born and grew up. When she was younger she saw Belfast as small, depleted and in decline. She wanted to stand aside from the damp, gloom and darkness and not be swallowed up in a place where many people limit any possibilities that are seen as different from the ingrained habits and routines. Katie felt the pessimism of it all dictated a predictable and often bleak future.

Katie liked the way the books were written and felt inspired by strategies of breaking free from past events, situations and present ties that bind and hinder development of an individual driven freedom. What she read breathed vitality, of having a new life with exciting prospects. She enjoyed writing down the various plans to 'realise one's possibilities' – 'utilising motivation' to make a 'new you' and to break through the grey clouds into a world of blue skies with an optimism for a future where one's desires and 'goals' are realised. She loved the images that the books presented, and although knowing she was not going to run planet Earth, she looked forward to her future in getting what she wanted.

Katie did not drink or smoke and she saw buying the membership of the health club as a 'reward,' telling herself she 'deserved it' for the effort she put into her life. She enjoyed the pampering of the jacuzzi, sauna and tanning facilities after a workout in an aerobics class or after a gruelling session in the gym.

Katie was engaged to David who was twenty two years of age and had been going out with Katie since she was sixteen. At that time the seventeen-year-old David, who had already left school one year, was seen as a mature young man to the serious thinking young Katie.

Although coming from the same area David's family were different from Katie's. His father was a bit of a drifter, not destined for the park bench, but never very good at holding down a job to provide for his family. David's mother had lost control of his two older brothers when they were very young, and the difference between his two brothers and him was plain to see from when they were children. One of David's brothers was Ian McClelland, who like his other brother had got involved in street gang culture where taking drugs and serving spells in youth custodial centres was the norm. David was not a weakling or a coward, but his interests were different. He liked sport and hated the heavy drinking and drug culture that pervaded the area where he lived. After leaving school he worked for a local builder doing general labouring work, he then attended a computer course at college under the direction of Katie and her mother, with intentions to secure a 'better future.' But he lasted only two months. He knew it was not for him. The immediate need for wanting money at the end of the week redirected David to get a job with another builder, a small concern, but giving him the opportunity to learn different skills. He had not yet decided on what trade to specialise in, but had ideas of setting up his own business one day.

At first, Katie's mother was not that pleased with her daughter going with David. He was seen as not good enough, and his family did not help, but her mind changed as she saw that he was a hard worker, polite and devoted to her daughter. Katie's family would not be called middle class, but her mother had aspirations for her children to do well, and although neither of her two daughters went to university, they were settled in jobs taking full advantage of training schemes and making the most of what was on offer. Her youngest child was an eleven-year-old boy. His teenage years looked as if they would be different from those who were older than himself, in that he would not be seeing the armoured cars, tanks and army having a heavy presence in the streets where he lived.

David was getting on with his life and committed to the relationship that he had with Katie, but he was constantly worried about his older brother Ian because of his involvement with criminals. Katie was looking forward to a rosy future with David, he had proven himself as a good person, and she knew that with her help and support they would do well together. She was content and excited at their prospects.

Thirteen

Donny's face appeared misshapen and hardly recognisable in the reflection of a little brass ornament. He looked at his distorted image, pulling his head slightly away and then moving it closer, altering the strange looking features. The ornament was on the mantelpiece above a fireplace that had been blocked off years ago, an electric fire now in its place with imitation coal and logs and a red light beneath the facade that when turned on gave a glowing effect. Donny was standing in the front room of a small terraced house in west Belfast. He was wearing a white short sleeved shirt and a black tie. The small room was crowded with people who had just returned from a funeral. The house had the furnishings and feel of an old person's home. There was a spirit of pride against the odds. A highly polished old ornate clock stood on a little table. It was an esteemed family possession, probably handed down a generation. The room had a homely feel, but the filler and paint on the door could not hide the repair done it after a fist in a fit of temper had punched into it. The house had accommodated a family that had grown up and left, leaving only an echo of their struggles, personal joys, victories and losses that some people say they can feel, hear or see.

A black ribbon joined two photographs that were hanging on the wall. They were taken thirty years ago. One was of a ten-year-old boy, the other of a man in his early forties. A card pinned to the wall beneath them read, 'Robbie. Rest In Peace.' Some of the people in the room were holding cans of beer, some small glasses and others cups of tea. It was a sober affair. A man in his seventies stood next to Donny. Placing a cup and saucer on the mantelpiece he studied the side of Donny's face. Donny knew that the man was looking at him, but did not turn to face him. The man nodded at the photographs. 'I was a young man then, didn't think I was, but I was. And he,' the man gestured to the young boy in the photograph, 'my youngest – it's a good thing we can't see into the future.'

The man's expression became grave as he looked at Donny. Donny gave him a brief nod. The man continued. 'Another tragedy, which should never have happened.'

Donny did not respond. A growing contempt showed in the man's face.

'About your age, wasn't he, Donny?

His tone carried blame. Donny turned slowly, facing the man he spoke dispassionately.

'If you can't do the time...' He let the words hang, but they had no effect on the man who watched Donny carefully before responding.

'Oh, I've heard that before, and too many times of late – unfortunately.'

He fixed Donny a sharp look. Several seconds passed as Donny looked around the room in a casual manner, ignoring the man who continued to look at him. Finally, he spoke without looking at the man.

'Well then, you should be getting used to it.'

The man shook his head slowly.

'No, I am not getting used to it. As old as I am, I hope and pray to God that I will never get used to it.' His expression crossed from sad to sour.

'He wasn't the type to be mixed up with drugs – given the opportunity offered in a decent place, he would have led a normal life – as others do elsewhere.'

He gestured bitterly through the window.

'But not here – not now.'

He looked up at a sash and a Boy's Brigade hat that was pinned onto the wall. His gaze fell onto Donny as he spoke, his voice becoming firm.

'It was no bullet from a nationalist – the threat is from within.'

Donny looked at the man without any emotion. The man carried on, needing to say what was on his mind.

'And some are more acclimatised than others to live and thrive in a cesspool that has the values of fear, corruption and deceit as the accepted norm.

'The young applaud the gangster, the hoods, with their violence, principles of immediacy, interests of self, and to accommodate practices that are unknown to the great majority of people who were born and brought up here before little guttersnipes were given a pedestal.

'History and country have no place in the young minds of those who gather in our streets – they are sullied and warped by those that walk tall, showing their arrogance with a conceited pride.

'Those above, in their positions of authority and power have always been hypocrites, and now it's being made easier for them.'

Donny was unmoved, and as he spoke his tone was flat and distant.

'Have you finished now? Because I want to get myself a sandwich from the kitchen.'

But the man went on, 'I remember your face when you were a boy – as a child, always dirty and in need of a good scrubbing.

'Your smile always crooked – in one grubby hand you held the wrapper of another child's sweetie, your other hand held behind your back against the holes in your ragged jumper, holding a dagger made from a lollypop stick.

'Wee bugger you were, Donny.'

He gave a short derisive laugh.

'The child – a little angel, the picture of sweet innocence – kiss my arse it was.'

He took a plastic coin bag from his pocket that had white powder in it, and his eyes were unfaltering as he looked steadily into Donny's face and said, 'Things do not really change son. This is your candy now, and it's an expensive sherbet dab in many ways.'

Donny looked from the powder to the man. The man shook the bag as he said, 'Take it with you. It was in his room – we've never had anything to do with this kind of thing – it's all gone towards killing his mother, the worry and all.

'You will never be welcome here in my home. Put that stuff in your pocket and leave – and never return to this house.'

They looked at each other. Donny smirked, looking down at the bag he turned without taking it and walked towards the door.

Two men were standing in the doorway. One of them was about Donny's age, the other ten years younger. The older man turned on seeing Donny.

'How is it, Donny?'

'Not too bad,' Donny said and shook the man's hand.

The man nodded at the old man by the fireplace.

'Bit of a shock, Robbie being plugged an' all. His da's taking it bad.'

He watched the old man who was looking down at the carpet and putting the plastic bag into his pocket. Donny nodded indifferently. The man looked at Donny.

'I hope the favour will be returned – can't trust the cops, they're never loyal.'

Donny spoke, ignoring what he said.

'I'm off to England tomorrow.'

'What, you driving over?' the younger man asked.

Donny stared at him before saying, 'Why?'

'You know,' the younger man went on uneasily, 'give you a bit of freedom with luggage.'

Donny did not answer him. He turned to the other man and said, 'I have a couple of contacts, a bit of business.'

They looked at each other for a few seconds and then Donny continued. 'Yeah, London. Some of their people have been over here – return the compliment.'

Donny and the man nodded at one another at an agreed understanding. Donny turned to leave, 'Right then,' he said. The man offered his hand and Donny shook it, and as he left he gave a short nod to the younger man. They watched Donny as he left the room without saying anything to anyone, but his departure was watched by nearly every pair of eyes in the room.

The older of the two men in the doorway checked around to see if it was safe to talk.

'You know Donny to speak to then?'

The younger man shook his head. 'No, not really – he's not the easiest to get to know, and doesn't seem to want to talk to anyone.'

The older man looked at him for a few seconds.

'I've known him since we were kids.'

'Oh aye, aye I know that,' the younger man said.

The older man continued, double-checking around the room before he spoke.

'But nobody really gets to know Donny.'

He grinned before continuing, 'Yeah, and don't ask Donny about driving – it nearly turned into a national joke. He can't drive.'

The younger man frowned. 'But he's got three Range Rovers that I know of.'

The older man shook his head. 'I know, I know, but he never learned.'

They looked at each other, saying nothing, as if pondering this fact.

The older man went on, 'As you know, I've been on some jobs with Donny, he has always given it more than anyone else – you've read and been told about his style – and interests.'

This was not said as a question, but as a statement and the younger man nodded. The older man continued, conscious all the while to be mindful of who was standing near him.

'A few years back we were given names and addresses of Taigs – and we were fired up to carry out those executions. Sometimes, two, three or four of us would go. There were times we would touch lucky, like the front fucking door would be left open – you could get in all quiet like, do the execution and get out. Stupid Taig fucker made it easy for us – but this didn't please Donny, it took the fun out of it for him – Donny would make hard work of it – smash the door down, even if it was unlocked.

'He'd do weird stuff – singing a song, reciting nursery rhymes – it was like, I don't know, it was like, a show for him – he'd go into a world of his own – take things onto a different level.'

The man stopped talking and checked to see if anyone was looking at him. He was taking a risk, one that would have dangerous consequences for him if it was found out that he was telling the story, but he felt that he had to tell it. He leant close to the younger man's face.

'But as I say, I've known Donny a long time.'

He looked at the younger man, as if unsure whether to carry on, but he did, and the story he told had remained clear in his mind even after many years. He returned to the mid-1970s when he and Donny were youths, describing how the two of them approached a large house in the country. They had heard that a professional couple lived there, they were catholic, 'High-stepping Taig bastards,' he whispered to Donny as they surveyed the outside of

60

the house in its remote surroundings. They were drunk, had stolen a car in the city and driven out into the blackness of the countryside to seek out excitement, both having vague expectations and driven by urgent demands. It was Christmas Eve and they figured it would be a good time to burgle the house, believing it would be empty with the occupants out at a party, visiting relatives or away on holiday.

They broke into the kitchen at the back of the house, smashing the lock on the door and when inside turning on the light. There were Christmas decorations on the walls of the large kitchen, and on a table were some cakes and two glasses of sherry with a card that had written on it, 'Presents For Santa And Rudolf.' They drank the sherry and suppressed their laughter, even though they thought they were alone in the house. Donny opened the oven and took out an uncooked turkey. He sat on a chair hardly able to contain himself with his penis out and started to fuck the turkey. Donny said, 'I've gotta have a shite,' and that he was going to do 'a little dirty protest of my own' as he smeared faeces on the wall and in the oven.

After finishing in the kitchen they decided to search the house, and just as they left the kitchen to go into the hallway they were met by a man and woman dressed in their bedclothes. They almost bumped into each other. Donny pulled an iron spike from inside his jacket and the other youth took a small jemmy bar from the inside of his coat. The woman screamed as they were attacked with the weapons, and the man's resistance was futile as the first blow from Donny connected hard on the side of his head, so hard in fact that the man would never have proper speech again or the full use of his left arm. Donny followed him to the ground, beating him with the spike. The woman held her face as the turned end of the jemmy bar tore into her skin, breaking the bones in her cheek. In his fury, the youth attempted to knock her unconscious, but it proved more difficult than he expected. Her will to remain conscious to protect her children, who were upstairs, motivated her to fight. But inevitably, the cracking blows to her head pounded her senseless and to a place where she would never return from, to a world where she could not communicate any more with other people. Her story was followed in the press as she left a general ward of a hospital only to enter a psychiatric wing of another.

Screams from two children, a boy and a girl, on the stairs stopped the beating. Donny scaled the stairs, screaming at them not to look at him or the other youth. He bundled them up the stairs, pushing the girl into one bedroom and taking the boy into another room. The other youth was stopped from joining Donny in the bedroom with the boy. Donny gestured for him to wait outside, which he did, but unknown to Donny he watched what was going on through the crack in the door. What he saw shocked him. Donny threw the boy face down onto the bed and clambered on top of him. The youth went to move away from his position of spying through the crack in the door, but was drawn back to watch, disbelief fixed him rigid. He moved away from the door as Donny came out of the bedroom. Donny laughed as he said, 'Did you see the wee bastard's face when he thought I was going to drill him up his wee hole?'

The man's memory turned off and flicked through the years to the present, back to standing in the front room of the little house in west Belfast. He looked at the younger man and said, 'But he did.'

There was a brief silence, distancing himself from his thoughts and memories the man altered the mood as he changed his tone.

'And I can tell you this, as a God fearing man – I hear talk from these nationalist, faggy, lefty do good shit, scum – assertions, myths, suggestions that there was something connected with perversion – a sexual gratification with what we have done in our past activities – they try to undermine our history, our purpose – and us.

'We – nearly all of us, are family men – might go over the top sometimes, with high spirits, but, to call us disgusting words that imply a sexual involvement, only goes to show that it is those who say those things who are in fact the sick ones – they are depraved and lack morals that apply to decent family life.'

He looked at the younger man. Nothing was said. Finally, the younger man spoke. 'I hear Donny has a room – it's called the lounge of fear.'

The older man looked down slowly, and then around the room.

Fourteen

A shaft of light pierced through a tiny hole in the curtain, providing the only light there was in the dark room. Three men were standing in front of a man who was slumped in a chair in the bedroom of Donny's house. Donny was with two other men. One of them was Johnny Ferguson, a man having a large, bony frame. He was in his mid-forties. His face carried scars and an expression that epitomised his life. Many of the tattoos inscribed into his skin were collected as a youngster in institutions of detention, the thick, crudely drawn outlines showing an amateur hand in comparison to the others that were done in a tattoo salon. The man standing next to him was quite a few years younger that Johnny Ferguson. His solid frame was rooted to the spot as he looked at the body in the chair.

Johnny Ferguson reached forward and pushed the head of the man in the chair. 'He's gone. He's dead – we'll have no more fun out of this one.'

Donny stood to the side of the chair holding his arm out across the dead man's body, as if protecting it.

'Leave him now,' he said. Donny gestured for them to leave by nodding towards the door. They looked from the body to Donny and turned to leave the room. Donny leant close to the man and examined a thin line of blood running around the man's neck and across his throat. Johnny Ferguson opened the door, but stopped in the doorway. Both men watched Donny. Donny looked up at them and said, 'You go now. I'll deal with the stiff.' He then looked down at the dead man's face, and as the two men turned to leave the room Johnny Ferguson whispered into the other man's ear, 'Yeah, he'll deal with "the stiff," and the one he's got in his trousers.' The other man smiled slyly and they smirked at each other before finally leaving.

Donny looked at the door, checking to see if it has been closed and then turned his attention to the dead man. He picked up a pair of pliers from the table, snapping them open and shut in front of the dead man's eyes. Taking the man's hand he positioned the teeth of the pliers around one of the fingers, leaning close to the man he squeezed the pliers until he heard the sound of bone snapping. He pulled the pliers away from the hand, tugging at it to free the strands of tissue binding the finger to the hand. He let the finger drop down and looked closely into the man's face, speaking evenly.

'I'm not gonna let you take these to the other world – you might want to start pointing your finger at me, you shite you. Nah – you won't be able to point these creepy little fingers of yours at Donny boy – oh no, I've thought of everything – Donny's got it all covered – no worries.'

He studied the man's face, pushing a finger between the teeth of the pliers he said, 'You were a teacher,' Donny exerted pressure on the pliers until the bone snapped, 'weren't you?'

Again, he pulled at the finger, freeing it from the remaining tissue before letting it drop onto the floor.

'A teacher, eh?

'I didn't like teachers – and their type – and they didn't like me – one rule for one and one rule for another – sitting in judgement and deciding what fate they think someone deserves – liking the idea of having sway over someone's future. Well – you didn't see this happening.'

He looked deeply into the man's eyes for a while before continuing to speak in a voice that was quiet and holding no feeling.

'Mind if I kiss teach on his cheek?'

Donny dropped the pliers on the table and went over to the video recorder that was on top of the television. He pointed the camera at the man, trying different angles until he found one he was satisfied with. Before turning the sound system on he slapped his arms to get blood moving in them. Setting the camera to record he lifted the man from the chair and cradling him in his arms he walked in small circles in front of the television. Music began to play. It was 'Don't Leave Me this Way' by the Communards. Donny moved in a circle, performing a slow dance, watching his image on the television screen. He danced for most of the song and then lowered the man onto the floor and stood over him.

Donny stared at the man, turned to the camera and adjusted its angle until he saw the man's image on the television screen. Lying down by the man's side he pulled down his trousers and pants and held his penis. 'Stand by Me' by Ben E. King played as Donny masturbated, all the while watching himself on the television.

Fifteen

When Johnny Ferguson and the other man had left Donny they got into a car and drove off to what was known as a 'safe house' in the nearby countryside, once there they watched videos played cards. They had to burn some time, probably a few hours before returning to pick up the dead man's body, and then they might have to dispose of it, this was the usual routine. A lime grave was Donny's preferred method, or sometimes he wanted the bodies to be found, so they would be left in ditches outside of town and were usually discovered within days.

The two men had bored themselves in the house to the point of falling asleep. A few hours had passed so they decided to go for a slow drive back. They sat mostly in silence, both brooding over their own concerns as the car slowly made its way nearer to the city, which was indicated by the interior of the car being lit by the halogen stare of oncoming cars and an orange glow of street lighting.

The silence in the car was only just broken by a barely audible sound coming from the radio that was turned very low. Johnny Ferguson was sitting in the passenger seat. He looked from the rain soaked streets outside of the passenger window to the other man. Johnny Ferguson was troubled. He said, 'What do you think? Donny, I mean – he enjoys his sessions in his lounge of fear, as he calls it.'

The other man looked ahead. He was thoughtful, his eyes holding an insipid stare into sporadic glares of light that whitened his face. A whisper of a smile moved the corner of his mouth as he spoke. 'Donny's "fun room." It's his playroom – where he gets his kicks. I've heard things – but God knows what goes on in there.'

He did not look away from the course he was driving. The car was silent. Johnny Ferguson looked into the side of the other man's face. 'You know my brother Malcolm was killed a few months back?'

66

The other man nodded, but only slightly to acknowledge what had been said to him, not wanting to engage in any conversation about Donny's past and Johnny's brother. Johnny Ferguson continued.

'Well, Malcolm was inside with Donny, when they were kids.

'Malcolm pulled him about being suspect back then.'

The other man did not respond. He stared ahead. The car was silent. Johnny Ferguson studied the man next to him for a few seconds and he also looked out ahead, but still troubled. Looking into the distance he spoke in a voice that was as distracted as his look.

'He stubbed a cigarette out in Malcolm's ear.'

Nothing was said. The two men sat in silence, staring ahead, both engrossed with an internal intent, oblivious to what was happening outside of the car. All noise and movement of traffic was a detached blur.

Johnny Ferguson muttered under his breath.

'The bastard.'

The other man glanced quickly across at Johnny Ferguson, and returned to staring out ahead, but his expression had been marked by his remark. He changed the subject.

'Best see what the state of play is – get rid of the body – or what's left of it.'

He looked at Johnny Ferguson as he said, 'Donny's got to get his beauty sleep –he's off to England tomorrow.'

The man steered the car from the stilted concrete roads where they had been driving and away from the brightly lit city centre area into the densely housed districts with narrow streets until they came to their destination. The man turned the engine off a little way from the house, letting the car roll silently to a slow stop outside the small terraced house. The two men looked at the house. It was seemingly innocuous in that it was the same as the other houses in the street. A tomcat that was passing Donny's door stopped momentarily and looked up at it, and as he did so immediately lowered himself to a crouched position and sped quickly away, looking back at the door as he went. The man sitting behind the steering wheel looked closely at the door and saw that there was not a blue drawing pin pressed in the wood over the knocker, for that was the signal that they used. Donny would press the pin into the door when he had finished, letting them know that he had left the house. As it was not there the man knew Donny was still in the house. The man thought about this. Donny would not have forgotten the drawing pin if he had left. Maybe he had fallen asleep, or maybe he had overdosed on some chemical concoction, and that thought, involuntarily, brought what could be considered to be the beginning of a smile on his lips. The two men decided to drive off and give it more time. They drove away with only a little more noise than when they had arrived.

Upstairs, in the room of the house, Donny was leaning over the dead man who was now naked. He was forcing the handle of a pool cue up the man's backside. The image was showing on the television screen a few feet away. Music started to play and Donny moved to the rhythm of the song, which was K. C. and the Sunshine Band's, 'That's the Way I Like it.'

Sixteen

The next day Donny started out on his trip to England. He had travelled to England before, a couple of times, but that was the only travel overseas he had done. When he had been to England before he had gone by boat, travelling in a car with others, but this time he was going alone and had decided to fly.

He was stopped at customs and asked why he was travelling to England. They asked him what he was going to do when he got there and where he would be staying. The farce of it all made Donny smirk inwardly because he was aware that the British state knew more about himself than he did, and here he was going along with the game acted out by a minnow representative of the state in a £30 uniform.

On arriving he would face more questions about his reasons for going to England. But it had all been planned well in advance, the addresses, names, phone numbers and reasons for travelling to England. He told customs he was going to stay with a friend and there was a possibility of getting a job with his friend in the company where he worked. Donny was given clearance and allowed to enter.

It was the first time that he had flown. It did not bother him. He looked out of the window and imagined what it was like for pilots in the Second World War, going on bombing raids across the sea to destroy coastal installations and then to the towns inland. He thought about the programmes he saw on television when he was a child. That old black and white footage showing an aerial shot in daytime, looking down from the plane to the targets below as the bombs tumbled effortlessly out of the plane towards the ground. There were the films of night-time bombings. Donny found them more interesting. The towns with all their houses and buildings were seen as just little pinpricks of light. And after the bombs were discharged from the aircraft there was a time of waiting before the bright eruptions of light showed on the ground below. Donny would think of all the people, hiding, hearing the planes above them, and then that could be it.

As Donny sat on the plane he reflected on the bombing raids and other war footage. Those television programmes were on at a time in the evening just before he went to bed. He had clear memories of armies marching through towns, women holding out their hands for any food that might be offered to them, old men who were useless, too weak and feeble to offer resistance against the invading soldiers, and so they stood to the side with women and children watching the victorious army of men march through their town. Buildings that were once the homes of people, or grand civic buildings once having great significance to the place and people, now lay in embers or as broken roots, smashed uneven into the ground, reminding Donny of stumps of teeth shattered into the gum of a mouth.

There were scenes of the soldiers in their uniforms laughing and dragging women by their hair as they separated them from loved ones. It could have been a husband, brother or son maybe. The people were kicked and the soldiers enjoyed the control they had as they pulled women and children onto the carriages of trains. Donny remembered one scene where a grinning soldier was forcing the butt of a whip under the chin and into the throat of an old lady. Men, skinny and stripped to their waists, stood blindfolded next to holes in the ground, their heads bowed, and then there was a volley of gunshots and they fell into the holes, collapsing like paper dolls. Some of them dropped to the ground and a soldier stepped forward and kicked the bodies into the holes. Some of the men pleaded for mercy, their hands stretched to their sides, their faces gaunt, dark and unshaven, their mouths working quickly, but the words they were saying were not heard or heeded. A revolver was put to the side of a man's head, and as the gun jolted backwards the man dropped, his eyes staring as if startled, his mouth no longer moving, it was all too late and finished with, his expression was one that we will all face in our own way.

The music used in the programme played clearly in Donny's mind as he sat on the plane, as clearly as if he was listening to a recording through headphones. He followed passages of the sombre music, interested in where it took him, not having thought about the music for years, but it was embedded deep into his memory and flowed on its own volition as if playing live next to him. And Donny thought of the sights, sounds and smells that were in the small front room of his home as he watched the worn newsreels, with the upper class accents of the newsreaders giving details of events and the names of foreign towns. He thought of his brothers, one older than him and one younger, and his sister. Sometimes his dad was there, and his mum, darning socks, sowing on buttons, taking in or up trousers as they would be passed from brother to brother. A cramped room with the small black and white television in the corner, and in front of the grate was a tin tub that he was scrubbed and washed in when he was very young, sometimes with his younger brother, in the tub together, and the soap, stinging his eyes and his mum kept rubbing the coarse flannel across the back of his neck and digging deep into his ears.

He pulled away from the thoughts of bath night, but stayed in the room, feeling its claustrophobic tightness, remembering the punches and kicks he got from his older brother for speaking out of turn and the uproar that ensued. He paid back his older brother for those kicks and punches in later life. His younger brother left home barely on school leaving age to join the army, but he ended up a chronic alcoholic filtering methylated spirits through slices of bread on a park bench somewhere in Glasgow, and dying forty years before the allotted three score and ten. His sister, also younger than him, sitting like a broken toy in the armchair, her legs curled under her body and her arms wrapped around her skinny knees. She would urinate where she sat and then burst into tears as Donny's father dragged her from the room, cursing her and her impeded state of mind, a mind that continued to follow a neurotic development that led to serious mental illness. She spent many long stays in the psychiatric wing of the city hospital, and it worsened. They found a place for her in a mental home out in the country, where she might still be to this day. Donny's older brother moved away when he was eighteen and hardly ever returned, he never phoned or wrote. He started a family and worked at his job. The last Donny heard he was in a new town development thirty miles from the city.

His father would glare, brooding, his rage always near to bursting. He was a small man, stockily built through the heavy labouring work that he did between bouts of unemployment. He was dissatisfied and bitter, smoking thinly rolled cigarettes until they burned his thumb and forefinger. His spleen poisoned by the rough deal he got in going through a world war and then afterwards working for unliveable wages. He got married and had children when he never should have done. Donny's father went to his grave cursing the world and his lot. And his mother was released from her drudgery through her death when Donny was thirty years of age. The authorities would not let him go to the funeral, but then rushed him to the graveside, standing in handcuffs between armed officers. There was hardly anyone there. The only person he recognised was a lady of his mother's age who lived down the road. She had worked with his mother in the hospital, both of them were cleaners. The woman looked over at Donny, but she did not acknowledge him, and he did not acknowledge her.

Donny stared through the small window of the plane, his mind going back to jerky black and white newsreels. Footage of the German army, their uniforms seeming better than those worn by the allied soldiers, their faces angular, chiselled and grim, and the distinctive style of marching. The images were vivid. He thought of how the German grenades were different from the British ones, having stick-like handles, lobbed by a soldier wearing his storm coat and square helmet. The armoured cars and small tanks crushing the remains of houses, and rolling over barbed wire and the corpses of allied soldiers and civilians who had perished in a place that had been turned into hell. The film would cut from screeching aeroplanes to machine gunner advances on the ground, faces contorted in battle hate. A deep feeling rose in Donny. He was getting an erection. It was common for him to do so when going over memories of those images with the sounds amplifying the feelings, the sounds of shouting, screaming and music.

He looked at the other passengers. He felt that his difference was obvious and he looked at a stewardess, thinking that her presentation of a self was taken from a magazine, probably designed by a group of men in a boardroom. He looked at a male steward, thinking how overtly homosexual he was, noticing his manicured nails, his manner tired and irritable, having aspirations greater than serving coffee and box-set food he flicked on the corporate smile as his mean eyes squirreled around the passengers that he despised. Donny looked across at a man and woman, a middle-aged couple. They had a self-satisfied look about them, as if having lived a life where they have been accustomed to being indulged. The woman pointed with her tanned hand at her choice of drink, chunky jewellery taking up most of the skin on her fingers with heavy bracelets sliding along her thick wrists as she pointed her painted false fingernail, her face showing no regard towards the stewardess. The man opened a bag of peanuts and settled back in his seat, letting the female steward unscrew the cap of his mixer. He watched her in a detached, lazy manner, just like the woman next to him. Donny thought how they looked greedy and cruel.

Donny wanted to strip the man and woman naked and roll them on the ground. He wanted to show how disgusting they would look without their trappings. Donny watched the man as he closed his eyes, reminding him of an overfed lizard. He wanted to skin the man's face with a scalpel while he was alive and watch him squirm in agony, and he would prevent the woman from consoling the man, who was most probably her husband. She had most likely been with him for years, watching him get richer and fatter. Donny's plan for dealing with the woman was to break her back, to throw her face down onto the ground and pull her head backwards until her spine snapped. He wanted to smash the front of her face into a pulp, punching it with his knuckleduster and then insert his penis into her ear, wanting his cum to glue up her hair and earring. And then a memory came to Donny, one from when he was a young man, when he had beaten a man severely and had used acid to permanently disfigure him. He had filled a bicycle pump with acid and squirted it into the man's face. It was just the once that he did that, it was something that he had thought about for years, and it worked as he imagined it would. As the man screamed Donny pulled his hands from his face so that he could see the burning and blistered skin. The act helped raise Donny's reputation as he climbed the ranks within the world that he inhabited.

Donny fantasised about pumping acid into the man's face on the plane, stripping away the skin, and the once bloated man who looked like a toad would have a face that looked like the skeleton of a bird's face. Donny did not know why he thought that. His mouth was dry and he became agitated. Donny hated the man and woman for making him feel disturbed.

A stewardess asked Donny if he wanted anything, but he declined and watched her as she pushed a trolley down the aisle, stopping every now and then, reaching around the trolley and bending to pick up whatever she was asked to get from it. He looked at the other passengers, and a feeling of sickness and hatred formed in the pit of his stomach. He felt that he wanted to beat and smash some of the people that he was looking at, seeing them as weak and privileged beyond what they deserved. He had a feeling, but it was hard for him to explain, it was that they should not be doing what they were, that they should not have any rights, that the law should not protect them, because they are not important. He went through thoughts that he had done so many times before, thinking of what use most of them were. He saw them as sheep that had to be told what to do, living in fear and having an existence as reverential slaves. So why should he be bothered about the likes of them? This was what Donny asked himself. He saw them as living off means that they had not created themselves, yet will sit back satisfied, basking, and ignorant of the fact that it was the work and actions of others that had provided it for them. Donny thought that this made them lesser men.

Donny concentrated on the tightness in the pit of his stomach, imagining it as a poisonous energy he could control and knowing that later he was going to discharge it throughout his system. He felt that it gave him strength and that it was a gift, making him different from other people because it gave him greater mental and physical strength. It was the main source from where he got his strength, a power that made him superior to those who are run of the mill. It was something he always did. If he was agitated and had disturbed feelings that were brought about because of the actions, or the suspected actions of others, he would utilise the power of that feeling, mentally control it and then dissolve it in his system, seeing it as a liquid running through his veins and organs. He believed he could use the power of that captured emotion as an energy against others. He gradually calmed himself and controlled his feelings of disgust that he felt towards other people, and he nearly smiled as a warm feeling rose in him.

He turned his attention to looking out of the window and within seconds he was back to his childhood in the small front room of his parent's house with its damp confined feeling. As the young Donny watched the war footage he imagined what it would feel like to drop thunder and fire from the sky onto housing estates. He entered the dark, grainy world through the screen of the small black and white television, feeling the music and the noise, seeing himself as taking part in what he was watching, being on a plane during bombing raids, watching the bombs rain down like shoals of tiny silver fish and then seeing buildings separated from this world as they were ravished in fire and heat. On the ground people were screaming and others rushed to assist them by carrying ladders and aiming hosepipes, while others held their heads and faces in despair as buildings fell around them. They knew all was lost.

And then the smirk that had formed on Donny's face left him as his uncle's voice spoke as clearly as if he was sitting next him on the plane. His uncle's face was close to his own, and Donny felt as helpless as he did when he was a child. He could smell the tobacco on his uncle's breath and saw the dirt in his teeth. He was standing over the young Donny in the bedroom of his house, pointing to photographs in one of his war books that Donny was holding in his lap as he sat on the side of the bed. The photographs were from the Second World War showing a graphic depiction of destruction and methods of torture.

'See the pain? See the pain?' His uncle asked, pointing to the face of a man that was contorted in agony. The torturer stood over the man, his expression a mixture of exultation and empty amusement.

'It has to be done,' Donny's uncle said, 'there are those who have to be slain and taught their place, because it is nature, and to stand in its way will corrupt what is natural. Look at the strength of this man.' He pointed to the torturer, 'He's not there because of luck or good fortune, no, he's there because nature dictates that he takes his place and performs his duty in correcting the deviant misdoing of those like him there,' and he pointed at the man who was being tortured. 'Him – and his type, they will ruin and sully with their immoral ways, using deceit to further their own interests, and that's why it always ends in calling upon the bravery of those that history hides, but nature cannot harness and bridle. From their wrath of superior strength comes a freedom that the weak will enjoy – and the weak will use the natural beast – this man,' he pointed to the torturer, 'to perform what they cannot and what they deny.'

His uncle exploded as he snatched the book from Donny and threw it onto the bed. He picked up a popular magazine, which was a little titillating for its day and known for printing gossip about pop stars and actors. He showed it to Donny, on the cover was a man and woman running on a beach.

'Look what they've made man into.' He snarled, throwing down the magazine. Donny did not understand what he was saying to him, but he was frightened as his uncle became angry and the unpredictability of his behaviour made Donny attentive to every action made and every word that was said. His uncle preached at Donny, as if he was an audience, and he practised different poses as he worked himself into a fury.

Donny pulled away from that scene in the bedroom all those years ago, but the words his uncle said remained with him and he listened intently to them as he went over what it was that his uncle said. As a child he did not understand what his uncle was saying, and as he thought about that his uncle's voice overwhelmed Donny and pulled him back to the scene in the bedroom. His uncle grabbed at the front of his shorts, pulling roughly at his snake belt, his speech now finished he spat insults through gritted teeth. 'And you're going to grow up to be a sissy boy – because you're a naughty boy now, playing with your winkle and looking at your uncle, I should take the skin from your backside for being so vile.'

His anger and lust boiled over as he raged. Losing control he started to beat Donny who tried to get out of his reach, and as he leapt from the bed a couple of heavy blows landed on his head and body.

Donny snatched himself from the scene, and sucking in the reconstituted air inside the plane he travelled through the years, watching and remembering events as they flicked by, and although the years can serve to buffer the experience of his uncle, his memory retained the feeling as if it was the present. He looked from the other passengers to out of the window, breathing deeply and a sour taste filled his mouth.

Donny stood up, pulled down his hand luggage and dropped the holdall onto the empty seat next to his own. He sat down and took a small notepad from his jacket pocket and went through the pages, studying names and addresses that had been written in the pad. The names and addresses were not what they read, it was written in code as a precaution if Donny was pulled in for questioning.

Meetings had been planned in England with intentions of finalising the business that was to take place in the Province since the passing of what had been called the Peace Process. Areas were to be agreed upon within Belfast and other parts of the Province where the setting up of stalls for the emerging market was to be organised. It was considered necessary to make arrangements beforehand so that the different factions knew of their place in the market when it opened up for business. This planning was important in order to deter a free for all. If that was to happen all sides would inevitably lose blood in the fight and profits would be squandered. There was money to be made in security, firearms, accessing property and land, and the belle of the ball that they all wanted to have their dance with was the lucrative drug market. Being in its infancy it was now the time. It was a prime opportunity and had to be organised from the outset.

It was to be carved up between the main players who had been involved in dealings and practices within the Province, and a settlement had to be made in order to prevent any foreign fingers getting into the home-baked pie. It was quite a unique situation in that the establishment who had an ongoing, willing and reciprocal relationship with the illegal groups that operated on the ground had already prepared the foundation.

The people that Donny was going to meet already had links with the so-called paramilitary group that he was a senior figure in. The meetings had been set up by those high up in state affairs and Donny was told that he was to meet one or two of the significant 'shapers' that have forged the links between the different groups in Northern Ireland and the 'mainland.' They are people coming from the Civil Service, the military, the police and politicians.

These were seen as exciting times. There were opportunities normally unforeseen and profits in sums that would not have been believed a few years previous. It was open season for property, commerce and the setting in place of all kinds of businesses, and those who had held positions of influence could now really cream off the forthcoming spoils to be had. The adoption of an attitude and language, which not that long ago would have been unknown in the Province, had been put in place to act as a smokescreen to who was really gaining out of a new emerging society.

Donny was not fully aware of the process, but knew enough of his place within it and was conscious of the raiding parasites swarming around the money pot. He checked the little address book once more before placing it in the inside pocket of his jacket. He fastened his seat belt, after being prompted to do so by a smiley stewardess, and gazed out of the window as the jet airliner broke through the dirty clouds for the final time to an exposed, dreary, flat landscape of patchwork fields and a sewage plant. Roads clogged with traffic scored their way through the land and the plane's engines changed tone as the ground drew closer. With a distant look Donny watched the runway come up, as if to meet the begging wheels of the plane.

Seventeen

Donny arrived at the house of his contact, which was to be just one of the places he was going to stay at during his time in England. It was in London, south of the river, an area that offered no pleasure for his immediate needs and so he decided to go in search for what he wanted. He told the person he was staying with that he was going out alone that first night and took the tube into the West End. Donny visited a sex shop and then trawled a couple of bars until he eventually found what he was looking for. The experience provided the satisfaction he sought, fisting a silver haired man who was most probably something big in the legal profession. He arrived back at the house in south London by cab in the early hours to find that his host was waiting up for him, wanting to introduce Donny to his wife and eldest boy.

Eighteen

The following evening Donny was taken to a meeting above a pub that took place in a long rectangular room that had a bar at one end and a stage at the other. The walls were adorned with neo-fascist flags, posters and regalia. The atmosphere was highly charged with aggression, but good humoured in that it was a gathering of the clan. The meeting was organised by a periphery nationalist organisation whose party status was negligible in mainstream politics, but having a high profile of notoriety. Its image was tarnished as a disgrace because of its policies and the behaviour of some of its members who are known for being violent and racist provocateurs.

Some of the speakers spoke about the organisation in military terms and of the right to be armed while others targeted individuals and groups as their enemy And there were those that spoke of housing, employment and social problems that was the result of immigration, which was instigated by those in power above as a strategy to fragment and destroy a national identity.

Certain speakers roused a chanted support and the raising of arms in the Nazi salute.

The meeting was over and people stood in small groups talking. It was crowded and loud. Donny was introduced by one of the men who took him to the meeting to a man named Richard Piquard, a middle-aged man who was dressed smartly in an expensive suit and tie. Piquard held a wineglass, which seemed out of place with his surroundings, in his manicured hand. He regarded Donny with admiration and respect, and beneath his serious repose the signs of a smile showed as his intensive gaze studied Donny, meticulously breaking down his body parts. He nodded as Donny spoke, as if reading the words and attributing a greater meaning to them than there actually was. He stood back a little from Donny and assumed a non-threatening posture, but squared his shoulders and shrugged them slightly in a movement indicating control.

Donny also looked closely at Richard Piquard. He was told by the man he was staying with that Richard Piquard had pushed for Donny to attend that evening and that he was a very highly placed person with great influence, but because of his position and the nature of the organisation he had to be careful of any overt links between himself and the organisation leaking out.

A tempered smile drew itself across Richard Piquard lips when he and Donny were left alone to speak. 'It's very good of you to make the trip, Donny, or would you prefer Donald?'

Donny told him that it was fine to call him Donny. Richard Piquard released a shallow smile and tapped Donny on his chest.

'I'll tell you what I respect and like about you, and your people over there. It's that the reality of war is outside your front door, literally, in the streets where you live.'

He said this enviously, looking closer at the features in Donny's face. 'People like you are heroes in the war and the struggle against elements that are on course to destroy our culture and traditional way of life. Whatever banner, or headband, they decide to wear, it is the erosive, weak, spineless cloud of communism.'

He looked around himself, surveying the room and the people in a proud and avuncular manner. He turned to Donny, tapped his shoulder and pointed out a man in his mid-forties who was dressed in traditional skinhead clothing.

'That man there, his name is Robert Birch. Robert has been a pioneer in nationalist endeavours for many years. He sets a solid example to younger men who have a passion, conscience and wish to be involved in the fight for what is right for their country and race.'

A song broke out around the bar and some lines of Rule Britannia were chanted. Robert Birch was standing with the crowd who were singing and chanting. A few Nazi salutes were thrown up. Richard Piquard watched them like a satisfied shepherd. He gestured for Robert Birch to join him and as he walked over with another man, Michael Connelly, Piquard told Donny he had to speak to someone and walked off. Robert Birch shook Donny's hand and said, 'Good to see you – heard a lot about you and seen you on the television, of course.'

They continued to shake hands. 'My name's Robert Birch,' he pointed to Michael Connelly, 'and this is Michael, Micky, Connelly.'

Donny was puzzled on hearing his name. He frowned, looking closely at him he said, 'Michael Connelly?'

Connelly nodded and said, 'Yeah. What of it?' Robert Birch broke in, looking at Donny. 'Yeah, my heritage is English, and I'm proud to say so. My wife is English, as is her family and heritage. I don't want our race mongrelised any more than it already fucking is, for fuck's sake, but I respect other people's race and country, I just want people to respect mine – and the people in it – the honest hard working people, paying their due each week – only for a bunch of cunts to land here and take it all – and our own people haven't even got a place to live theirselves – I mean, look at the hospitals, and all that – old people, fucking ill, put into the system all their lives – some of the poor fuckers actually fought in the fucking war, for fuck's sake – and what do they get out of it? Fuck all – that's what. Waiting to die in the corridor of a third world fucking hospital where no cunt speaks English – and it's not only the wogs, cunts and the rest of the shit that come here to steal off us – it's those cunts in the House of Commons, and Lords, and all their mates and family doing well in the law business, with their own companies, and their interests – got their dirty fingers in all their pies – inventing laws that excuse them from paying into the system – and getting up to all kinds of dirty deeds, professionally and personally – they're not patriotic at all, they're only here on the take – and they're all mixing and doing deals with the Jews and Asians – Arabs – and giving the queers all their powers in government – and owning the media – the lot of them – with the Yids. That's why I admire Richard Piquard, he's a solid man, coming from the upper tier like, but putting something back to those that fought and worked for this country, and have had enough of the cunts fucking it up for the decent people – and all the criminals getting away with it – the big and the small – it's a fucking crime – it really is.'

Donny watched Robert Birch, nodding at parts of what he was saying, but all the while his eyes examined him as if he was a foreign object. Robert Birch gave a friendly tap on Donny's shoulder. 'And I respect your people – the Scottish – and I

believe the Irish should be Irish, because that's what they are –
but then, they should fuck off out of this country and leave us
alone.'

Donny nodded impassively, barely able to conceal that he was
not interested in what he was talking about. Robert Birch
continued. 'You've got a Scottish name, ain't ya?'

Donny nodded again in the same blank manner, looking from
him to Michael Connelly who winked at Donny. 'How's
business? Connelly asked, as he stepped in front of Robert Birch.
'We've been told on this side of the puddle that it's all systems
go where you come from and that you are clearing up big time.'

Donny watched Michael Connelly closely as he continued.
'Fair play to you, fair play mate – make hay while the sun's got
his fucking hat on. You'd be missing out if you didn't.' Donny's
expression did not change as he continued to watch Connelly as
he spoke. 'Clubs, raves, parties – you boys have got it all stitched
up – ain't ya? Lucky fuckers – but there's a bit of infighting
going on.'

He tapped Donny's chest, 'But then, you're top dog mate,
being in charge and all that. You're sorting it all out.'

Donny watched him thoughtfully, giving a slight nod of
acknowledgement to what he was saying.

Michael Connelly continued in a more serious and business-
like tone. 'And that's what I'd like to talk to you about – you
need support from this side. We can get the gear, everything,
sniff, smack, smoke the lot – how much you want and whenever,
it'll be there. You send over a few of your boys, help out at doing
security at gigs, parties, whatever, a show of keeping them sweet
like, and me and you can do a bit of business without letting the
rest of your mob getting their maulers on it. Sweet, ain't it?

'It's the long term plan you gotta aim for, if you're smart, and
we've got backing that goes right to the top – you know that, it
don't go no higher – they set the rules for fuck's sake – they are
the big daddy – this is just another gig for them.'

The two men looked at one another. Robert Birch watched
them, looking bovine and confused.

Michael Connelly's eyes intensified as he looked at Donny.

'You're carving it up for yourselves, right? Keep it that way.
What I know about your place, where you come from, is that it's

changing and there's a service to be provided, and you don't want to miss out on it. There ain't no macaroons or Eastern European cunts getting their fingers in there, yet.'

He paused and they looked at one another. Donny looked at Robert Birch as Michael Connelly continued, his speech picking up pace.

'Yeah, you ain't got no coons or any of them over there, have ya? Pakis and all that?

'Fuck me, had bundles of fun as a youngster paki bashing and queer bashing, and all that.'

Donny said, 'We had our bit of fun, don't worry about that.' Michael Connelly went on. 'Yeah, bit of queer bashing – dirty fucking cunts – queer fuckers – how can it be right, having some cunt shoving his hampton right up yer arsehole? It's not proper – natural – up yer dirtbox – is it?

'The old Nazi party had it right, take the cunts for a ride around the block in a van.'

He stepped backwards and laughed, but in a few seconds he had regained his posture and continued to speak. 'Yeah, don't charge the cunts any money – just have a pipe coming from the exhaust through the window. Luvverly – I'd drive the van around the block all day fucking long, and I'd be wearing a pair of boots made out of the skins of their dicks – the dirty fucking, cunting queer cunts.'

He looked squarely at Donny.

'How do you deal with the queer cunts where you come from? Eh? Bet it's great over there, innit? Do what you fucking like – all that hardware and stuff hanging about. Slice a few of the cunts up and make out it's something to do with politics, or some shit. Blame the whole fucking lot on the situation, and all that.

'Bet it goes on big style, don't it?

'Fuck me, it sounds like fucking heaven – a free for all in doing away with queers and stuff like that.'

He pointed at Donny with growing excitement, 'Let the IRA and all those cunts take the blame, and all that shit – yeah, yeah, I bet it all goes on – sounds like fucking paradise – as it should be, you lucky bastards.'

Donny watched him, his face was expressionless but his eyes penetrated into Michael Connelly. Richard Piquard joined them.

He smiled ingratiatingly at Donny. 'Just a word, if you don't mind, Donny?'

He gestured for him to move away from where he was standing. Donny gave a slight shrug and nodded at Robert Birch and Michael Connelly as he followed Piquard.

Richard Piquard turned and guided Donny with his fingertips, gently pushing his elbow until he was satisfied with finding a quiet space. He chose his words carefully after checking Donny with a measured look. 'You're a figure of notoriety, Donny, there are a lot of people who want to meet you.'

He broke his gaze from Donny and looked around the room. His mood had changed, finding it difficult to disguise the repugnance he felt for the people there. He braced himself for what he was about to say and gently waved his hand. Donny noticed his perfectly manicured nails and how clean and soft his hands were.

Piquard said, 'Besides these lads, worthy and honest as they are, there are some very significant members of our society who share a penchant,' he paused as he looked about the room and the people in it, and then added quickly, 'for the attitude and the way of thinking that you have, Donny.'

He looked at Donny for a second before continuing in a more practical manner. 'This is an important part of my life – organising and educating those who are, enlightened.

'However, Donny – I do have another world – there are those from school, old friends, family, and certain dignitaries who…'

He stopped suddenly, looking at Donny, and when he started to speak again he chose his words more cautiously. 'But we are all flesh and blood. Yes, Donny, there are those who are excited at the prospect of meeting you.'

Looking into Donny's eyes he handed him a card. 'Give me a ring later – there are those who I would like you to meet – there is no need to tell any of the people you're staying with about this, little arrangement – just come along by yourself.'

Taking a deep breath he lifted his head and said, 'I know of one person in particular who is very keen to meet you. He takes a great interest in the work that you do and in the way that you operate. There is a party that I would like you to attend, it's top draw and all that. You might find it a bit off-putting, I don't know, but, you should get on, Donny – meet the right people, there are those who want to help you'

He raised his eyebrows at Donny.

Donny watched him and gave a slight nod with the shadow of a smile. He looked down at the little card in his hand and then up at Richard Piquard who was watching him closely. Piquard smiled weakly and tapped Donny on his shoulder. 'Be seeing you – things can really start working out for you.' He gave him a final tap with his manicured fingers, as if pushing home his point.

Donny watched him leave the room as he stopped to shake hands with various people on his way to the exit, Robert Birch and Michael Connelly were among them. Donny looked at the card and then put it in his jeans pocket. He wanted some cocaine and no one had yet seen to his requirements. He tensed and flexed his arms, gripping his hands tightly, knitting them into hard balls. Letting his hands relax he looked down at his forearms, paying attention to the veins and the swell of the thick muscles, flexing the bicep of his right arm he watched it bulge under the sleeve of his tee shirt, and then as if forgetting where he was he looked around to see if anyone was looking at him. He breathed deeply. He felt excited, the elation of an adrenaline rush caught hold of him, and as it did so the conflicting feeling of a nervous sickness came upon him. His legs felt weak so he raised his feet and trod down a few times to get the circulation back into them.

The excited feeling became overwhelming. He looked over at Michael Connelly and wanted to break every bone in his face. He wanted to destroy his body, tear the flesh and smash every bone. His hands and arms had the sensation of swelling at the thought of this, as if he had actually exerted the force. Donny watched Michael Connelly as he talked to Robert Birch, studying his quick movements, his small features, the slight bone structure in his small hands that were noticeably clean, with the nails cut to an even rounded shape, and the way he pointed his finger as he spoke to Robert Birch. The small, slightly built man was doing all the talking, and it made Robert Birch look slow and stupid as he nodded, trying to keep up with what the fast-talking little man was saying.

Donny continued to look at the way Michael Connelly stood, at his relaxed, arrogant posture, in control, pointing into the face of

Robert Birch as he spoke, his voice with a hard-edged whine just audible above the collective noise. Donny wanted to crush him, his stomach gave into a rush of heat, an erection formed in his underpants and pressed against the front of his jeans. He swallowed spittle that formed in his mouth, it tasted like bile, and he did his breathing exercise to release the tension, but he wanted to walk up to the two of them and punch Michael Connelly hard in the side of his head. He was just starting to go through another fantasy of what he was going to do to Michael Connelly when a voice by his side pulled him away from his thoughts.

'You give the impression of being a quiet sort.'

Donny turned and saw a man in his mid-forties staring at him through the thick lenses of his glasses. They were framed in thin gold wire. The man's eyes drilled into Donny with a respect that searched for more information that could be eked out of Donny's face. He was dressed in jeans, a tee shirt with a large Union flag on the front and a cardigan. The man's face was heavily lined before its time and hard calluses on his hands and the broken nails on his fingers gave testimony that hard labour was how this man earned the money to survive. 'Pleased to make your acquaintance,' he said in a deep flat tone, his hand extended to shake. Donny shook the man's hand and nodded obligingly, noticing how the man's eyes changed from being magnified to very small behind the thick lenses.

'Pleasure to have you over here, and at the meeting,' the man said, and Donny nodded, not with indifference, but his mind was elsewhere. The man told him his name, how long he had been a member of the party, what it was like in the 1970s, what he got up to then, what he believed to be best for his class and country, why things are not working out because of immigration and that the country was in need of a strong leader. He then spoke about Ireland, telling Donny what he thought of the situation and what should be done.

Donny watched him quietly, his emotions deadened by the bland rambling of the man and his dull voice. And then the mood shifted as Michael Connelly and another man approached him and interrupted what the man was saying. The man took his leave, holding out his hand for a final shake. It meant a lot to him, and again Donny obliged and watched the man walk away and stand alone near the bar area, holding a soft drink in a small glass that looked childish in his large hand. Michael Connelly smiled at the man's departure as if he was a simpleton.

The man with Michael Connelly was tall and thin with a dark complexion and sunken eyes. He was dressed in a dark suit that looked fashionable and expensive, a heavy gold necklace was on show outside his black turtle necked sweater. Donny noticed that he was not wearing any socks. At first Donny thought that he looked like he was some sort of academic, or maybe a media type of some kind, but the gold capped tooth that flashed when he opened his mouth and the thick gold bracelet and rings he was wearing pitched a different style. Donny studied his body and mannerisms.

'Yeah, Duane Bishop, Donny Campbell.' Michael Connelly introduced them to each other, waving the flat of his hand to make slicing movements in the air. He pointed at Donny. 'He is the man, and you need to meet him, cos there's gonna be some serious business going down and we've got the nod that we're in the frame when it all gets set up, like.'

Duane Bishop held out his hand for Donny to shake as he said, 'Pleasure, pure pleasure – you're one serious dude, man, and I'm just full of respect for you – you know where I'm coming from, yeah?'

Donny shook Duane Bishop's hand, saying nothing, looking from Connelly to Duane Bishop as Bishop spoke. 'I don't wanna say too much, see, I don't want my mouth to run off with anything unto, see? Cos, I know you're the big hitter out there, yeah? Where you come from like, and I respect the fuck out of that man, yeah?'

Donny could not think what to say to him. So he asked him his name, making out that he had forgotten it. He was having difficulty in understanding his accent.

'We're gonna be on this big one,' Duane Bishop said, 'This is big party time, and everything's being done for us, it's like a fucking dream – you're gonna be sitting out on your boat in the Caribbean, or wherever the fuck you want it to be, in a couple of years' time, yeah? And leave this shit hole all behind you – and fair play – too right, cos you're the fucking man alright, your rep is massive man, and what with the backing you're getting from the filth and their masters, I'll tell you man, it's all paved out for you, we're being set up nicely too – so, my friend, doing business with you is gonna be a pleasure – pure pleasure.'

He offered his hand again to shake, and Donny shook it, and gripping it tightly pulled Duane Bishop's hand close to his body, as if gaining some sort of control. Donny smiled and nodded. Duane Bishop also nodded and smiled, showing his teeth in the age old display of offering no threat in that primeval meeting ritual of grinning and not wanting physical confrontation.

Michael Connelly looked on with a crafty smirk on his face, enjoying the power exchange being displayed between the two men in front of his eyes. He was a person who took pleasure in seeing people and beings suffer and struggle, usually against the odds, while he was in a safe position, sheltered from those who are physically more powerful than himself. He liked the feeling of having control over them, of setting them up to perform violent actions that he will benefit from, either materially or for his excitement and pleasure.

There had been a lot of planning and setting up of who would provide what to whom in the general logistics and management of a developing drug trade, along with the profitable opportunities in security and other businesses. Donny's instrumental function was in the business of fear, redirecting those that strayed from the set procedures and boundaries, and as this was a fundamental role in the functioning of the whole system, his reward and status was commensurate with the importance placed on his activities. What he gained in satisfying his personal desires was merely a perk that was allowed to him because of his position.

He had a high profile and it was his image that headed the emerging drug market and the violence that went with it. All that was deemed immoral and corrupt was symbolised in his presence, but that, again, was a principal part of his function.

Donny turned and shook Michael Connelly's hand and as he grinned his eyes tore into his face. It could have been taken as over exuberance, but even in this situation of aggressive friendliness, Michael Connelly could sense that Donny felt aggrieved and that he would take violent revenge against him when the time came. His small, sharp brown eyes met Donny's, and he too presented a smile that broke into a hollow laugh as he

89

checked the strength in the grip that Donny held on his hand. He nodded thoughtfully as he watched Donny's glare and his grin that became maniacal. Michael Connelly's gaze penetrated deep into Donny, and his piercing look continued until he could see clearly what he wanted know. He smiled into Donny's face, having found what he was looking for. He had come to a decision. Shaking his head passively he asked Donny, 'You alright for some sniff, or whatever you want?'

Donny looked at him. 'It's sorted out as I speak,' Michael Connelly said, and he forced his small tight mouth into a smile as his darting eyes danced all over Donny's clumsy presentation of raffish good humour.

Twenty minutes later Donny was in the front passenger seat of a Jaguar car pushing his face into and swallowing an assortment of drugs with a relish that caused the man sitting in the driving seat to regard him with astonishment. Another man sat in the back of the car, his hands stuffed into the pockets of his long coat, watching the back of Donny's head swill around. There was hardly any conversation between them. The two men had been told to provide Donny with what he wanted and to take him to wherever he wanted to go. The man in the driving seat was a large man with heavy angular bones. He was of mixed race, having light brown skin and the softened features of an Afro-Caribbean heritage. Tattoos were visible on his wrist, one was an inscription of some kind, and as he grinned the gold caps on two of his teeth glinted in the neon light that passed through the windscreen. The man in the back was a large black man with a lethargic nature, but it did not hide his need to exert potent aggression. He regarded Donny in his slow lumbering manner and let his head loll to the side as he looked abstractedly out of the side window at nothing.

They took Donny into the West End, but he was bored by what was shown to him, so they eventually took him to a small club south of the river. Donny was not excited any more while in the club. It was the kind of place where media and business people hang out. Donny was introduced to a young actor who was described as a 'face,' and was told that he should have recognised him from a popular television situation comedy. But he did not.

Donny was then introduced to a semicircle of women who sat near the back of the club next to a small bar. They were smartly dressed, talking and laughing amongst themselves, often lasciviously. The women had come with husbands and boyfriends who were talking elsewhere in the club. Each one of them had tanned skin and smiled a lot, big wide smiles showing copious amount of white teeth, their bodies pampered in expensive settings in a price bracket way above the local health club or corner shop beautician. Donny looked at them, seeing through what had been added to enhance and conceal, finding a foundation of hard vulgarity that no skilled hand of a surgeon or chemical could wish away.

A man was standing to the side of one of the women. She was only showing interest in him because she was not sure of his status and position. He hung around her like a dead weight, leering and whispering close to her ear and then standing back to watch her response with a lewd smile.

He was a pain and a bore to the woman who looked embarrassed by his attention and persistence, but she maintained a wide smile that showed costly dental treatment. At the tail end of her laughter she half closed her eyes and touched her bare knee with her fingertips, careful not to snag the glistening bronzed skin with her talon like nails. The man was Geoffrey Stuart, a lawyer from Northern Ireland. His trip to England had been to do with trimming down details of contracts and overseeing deals for a media group having interests in emerging businesses in Northern Ireland. His face dropped on seeing Donny. Detaching himself from the woman he quickened his pace of movement, sober and concise the easing effect of the drink now gone. He spoke to a man while looking over at Donny. The man sent a message to the person who was taking Donny around the club and introducing him to people. The message said not to introduce Donny to Geoffrey Stuart and for Donny to be moved on elsewhere. Geoffrey Stuart picked up a drink and drank it thirstily as he watched the large frame and head of the man explaining to Donny that they were leaving.

He watched Donny leave the club, and when the departing handshakes and the final waves of farewell were done with, he breathed deeply in relief as he adjusted the waistband of his trousers and straightened his tie. Geoffrey Stuart was relieved because he worked closely and regularly with the legal representatives of government departments and had dealings with councillors and politicians, and Northern Irelandwas a small place. Although not having rubbed shoulders with Donny himself, he had been involved in pieces of work that demanded delicate manipulation on behalf of senior police and military figures that did involve Donny. Geoffrey Stuart showed a clean pair of hands, which spoke volumes for his wiliness when one considered what he had done along the way as he built up his career. He certainly did not want the name of Donny Campbell to be associated with him or the work that he did. He chewed on his thumbnail as he looked at the door that had closed behind Donny, and then his dark eyes surveyed the club, ignoring the woman who a minute or so earlier had entrapped his imagination. His reptilian features gave a sight twinge as he pulled a mobile phone from his pocket and pressed down the numbers he wanted to dial.

Nineteen

During the next few days Donny met up with people having influence over, and a cut of, the fledgling drug industry that was organising itself in Northern Ireland. Duane Bishop was a central figure, but there were those pulling strings behind the scene who had public names and presented a character that was in contrast to the dealing that they actually got up to, and all the while publicly declaring their anathema towards the people involved in organised violence and the growing illegal drugs industry.

Michael Connelly was at one meeting. Donny could not work him out or his role in it all, but like most things in his life he just pursued what was immediate to his interest and desires. He telephoned Richard Piquard who had told him about the party at his friend's flat, and again Piquard stressed that Donny was to come by himself. It was planned to take place on the final evening of Donny's visit to England.

Donny arrived at the swanky flat at the arranged time. Everything about it was expensive. Donny wore a suit with a collarless shirt beneath his jacket and slip-on loafers, all of which he had bought that afternoon. Richard Piquard opened the door, greeted Donny and handed him a drink in a slim necked glass. Donny took a small sip of the drink, looked at it, and then swallowed it as if it was mouthwash and had to be got rid of. Richard Piquard walked Donny into the main living room, a little like an estate agent, watching Donny's response to the room and the people in it. He spoke close to Donny's ear, 'Yes, a lot of the people here are involved in the arts – designers, architects, and some of them have important positions in the world of politics.'

He nodded at a man in his mid-forties with a neatly defined presentation. His hair was layered softly to one side and had a slight tint of blond to mix with the brown at the sides. The man had a youthful affectation although his clothing was traditional. He was wearing a light grey suit, white shirt with understated gold tiepin and cufflinks. Richard Piquard asked Donny if he recognised him, but Donny was not sure and shook his head slowly as he looked at the man.

'Lord Roddy Harding,' Richard Piquard said, 'he takes a special interest in matters that are close to your heart.' Piquard turned and faced Donny. 'He wants to meet you Donny. I told him that you could make it tonight and he is very interested in having a chat.

'Who knows, it could be beneficial for you?'

He nodded at Donny to reassure him of what he had just said. Roddy Harding looked over at Richard Piquard and Donny. He acknowledged Richard Piquard and walked over to them. Roddy Harding smiled as he spoke to Richard Piquard, but his mind was on Donny. 'Hi. Aren't you going to make introductions, Richard?'

Richard Piquard was pleased with himself as he presented Donny to Roddy Harding with an open hand, his manner nearly like a game show compares' assistant.

'Of course, Roddy, of course. Donny, this is Roddy Harding, Lord Roddy Harding, and this is Donny Campbell, just over from Belfast, and I am very pleased to have had his company.'

As Donny shook his hand Roddy Harding smiled, checking the weight in Donny's handshake. His conduct was verging on gushing with excitement at meeting Donny. He had to control himself and not respond over eagerly, and resist the temptation of breaking into rapturous laughter. His eyes were transfixed upon Donny's.

'Very pleased to meet you, Donny.'

Richard Piquard looked on. Noticing the slight flushing that had appeared on Roddy Harding's face. Piquard folded his hands behind his back with an air of having performed a task to a successful requirement.

Roddy Harding continued. 'I've heard many things about you. You are coloured with courage, many people are too gutless for the fight, and too stupid to understand.'

Roddy Harding and Richard Piquard looked at each other, nodding in agreement and they smiled at Donny. Roddy Harding stepped closer to Donny, looking down Donny's body before taking a deep breath and looking into Donny's face. 'I do not intend to be patronising when I tell you that you are an important figure in contemporary politics. In years to come, people will look back and highlight those who had the mettle, the strength and conviction to make change in the face of adversity.'

He moved even closer to Donny, his voice lowering to just being audible.

'Modern day warriors – in a society run by faceless cowards.'

Richard Piquard watched him cautiously as he spoke. Donny felt awkward, Harding was standing too close to him for comfort and he tried to avert eye contact, but found it difficult with the man standing so close to his face. Donny cleared his throat and took a small step backwards. He spoke in a quiet tone that brought a quivering smile to play on Roddy Harding's lips. 'Yes, I have a political duty to do as soon as I get back to Belfast. It's to speak at a sort of rally, to do with political prisoners, to resolve a problem.'

The two men watched Donny, nodding earnestly at what he was saying, swapping sly glances at one another every so often. Richard Piquard looked away having sighted someone across the room. He said, 'Excuse me, I will be back soon, I'm sure that the two of you have things to talk about.'

Donny watched him walk off. Roddy Harding looked at Donny and leant close to him, adopting a manner of deep confidentiality.

'If you don't mind me giving you some advice, Donny, there are people here tonight who you should be aware of – they do not share your, our, feelings.' He checked Donny's response before continuing, but Donny was unaffected by what he had said to him. Roddy Harding flicked his tongue a little between his lips in an action of deliberation at approaching a delicate subject. 'It's okay, it's okay, but, you, more than most, would know that nearly every person who is born lives their life as an also-ran. Feeling safe if they're in the middle of the herd.'

Donny nodded, not sure what he was talking about. Roddy Harding's smile grew salaciously, and feeling more in control he leant closer to Donny.

'I can see that you aren't one of the herd – easily led, given grass...'

He watched Donny, 'When you want meat.'

Donny felt awkward. He looked at Roddy Harding who held back a smile of satisfaction as he said, 'God, Donny, I bet that you could write a book – easily, on your experiences. The men you have known – the scrapes you have been in. You know the kind of thing that I mean? The capers that happen, the types of blokes that you have come across.'

Roddy Harding collected his thoughts and settled himself, waiting a few moments before continuing. 'I'll tell you what, Donny, you and I should have a good session together, recounting our past glories and old tales. God man, it would make most of the people in here run for cover, or hide under their frilly bedcovers more like.'

He grinned as he looked at the people in the room, dismissing them he returned his attention to Donny. 'I've met a lot of chaps like you – and I've admired every bloody one of them. My background is the army. Men have to work together, but I can always recognise the ones that stand out from the others. Having strength in being solitary, an independence that is fiercely defended.'

He looked squarely at Donny, affecting a mock military posture. 'Am I right?'

Donny watched him before nodding. Roddy Harding burst into laughter and slapped Donny on his back. 'Yes, oh fucking yes, I can see that you are a deep river, Donny – a man who defines his desires, the piper has to play to your tune alright. I can see that, I could spot that straight off.'

Donny was puzzled, but nearly smiling he cautiously gave Harding a light, playful cuff on his shoulder. Roddy Harding overreacted to the blow, as if it was hard and knocking him off balance. He laughed loudly.

Richard Piquard heard Harding laughing and looked over at him, the agitation he felt showed in his face. Roddy Harding composed himself before speaking. 'Er, Donny, I'll give you my address before the end of the evening – I think that we have things – not all to do with politics, but we have things about ourselves, to explore and talk over. It could be mutually beneficial.'

Roddy Harding assessed what was going through Donny's mind. Donny looked over Roddy Harding's shoulder and told him that he wanted to go to the toilet. Richard Piquard approached Roddy Harding as he watched Donny walk off. His tone carried a warning as he looked at Donny leaving the room. 'Watch yourself, Roddy. He's a media child – just don't get yourself too excited.'

Roddy Harding turned and faced Piquard. He smiled nervously as Piquard continued in a slightly reprimanding manner. 'It's a nice catch, but when one goes fishing in dangerous waters...' He wagged his finger at him. 'Many men have drowned in the pursuit of the prize, because they got lost in the excitement.'

Piquard stood upright, patted Roddy Harding on his shoulder and added in a more upbeat manner. 'Anyway, only a fool would drop his line by a sewer pipe.'

Piquard smiled. Roddy Harding's glassy eyes stared at him, and the two men smiled slyly at one another at a shared understanding.

Twenty

Donny extended his stay in England so he could fit in a visit to Lord Roddy Harding's place. In that time he met up with Michael Connelly and learned that he was a man who had a large part to play in the setting up and running of the drug industry in Northern Ireland. Duane Bishop was also around, and a couple of other men having a prominent involvement with a publicly vilified marginal nationalist political party. Richard Piquard's name was never mentioned, but it was clear from the allusions to a 'state figure' that it was from Richard Piquard that the means and power came from. It was in the interest of the state to establish the drug industry as it would perform an important function, because its effect would create a socially divisive situation and maintain the existence of fear in the towns of Northern Ireland.

Donny's feelings had not warmed towards the diminutive Michael Connelly. He saw Connelly as having a disrespectful manner, and even his voice caused Donny to want to physically inflict suffering upon the little man, whose accent changed from estuary Essex to inner city London, and then at times sounding like a voice that was contrived and emanating from the Home Counties. Donny knew that he was a fake.

Inroads were made in completing details, putting names in place and what geographical area had what and how much. Donny ran the proceedings on the ground, having the lion's share of Belfast, but there were other areas in the Province that had been drug free and Donny watched Michael Connelly's beady eyes shine at the prospect of this virgin market. Lessons had been learnt from elsewhere in setting up a drugs market in a new territory, having a professional organisation in place maximised the profit to be gained with as few hitches as possible.

People were being assembled to have the operation up and running on time. The fall guys were put in place, areas and sites were identified with even schools highlighted as prospective places for dealing, the petty criminal now had a chance of having a status and being associated with big concerns, a much revered position for some in the run-down wasteland estates scattered across Northern Ireland.

Donny won out over his rivals in the violent competition for control in west Belfast. That was all he needed to know, the rest was words and he was getting bored listening to people he did not like. They did not impress him, but rather got on his nerves. He had arranged to see His Lordship Roddy Harding at his flat the night before he flew back to Ireland. It was that thought which was of major interest in his mind.

Lord Roddy Harding's flat was near Victoria in an area inhabited by influential media people, political figures and their children.

Donny was just going to climb the steps up to the flat when he stopped and looked about himself. He looked at the road he was standing in and considered the address. He had heard of it from the television and in films. Whilst walking down the street he had looked through the windows and into the living rooms of the houses and flats, looking at the large dinner tables, the bookshelves, the type of furnishings, the looks on the people's faces in the rooms. He could not get from his mind the memories and images of when he was a child going to the City Hospital and waiting for his ma to emerge with the other cleaning ladies late at night, waiting for her to give him some biscuits that she had taken from what had been thrown out of the wards. Maybe the patient did not want them, or had died. The surprise he felt when finding out what kind of biscuits his ma had with her left a feeling, and he remembered that feeling as he stood outside Roddy Harding's flat, although it was not tinged with pity or sadness, but with irony, because he now felt that he was more powerful than those that lived in the street where he was standing, and that their kind needed him to do work they could not do themselves.

He felt elated, and he breathed the sweet tasting exhaust fumes with greed, for he was excited, not with happiness, but with a rush of feeling dominant. The pit of his stomach felt hollow and a slight erection made him smile. He turned and climbed the steps two at a time up to the door of the flat.

Twenty-one

Lord Roddy Harding waited for Donny's arrival with excitement and hopes of fulfilling his desires. The visit had been carefully planned, and as with the other activities that Roddy Harding got up to protective covers had to be put in place to shield him from any indiscretion that could result in him being implicated in activities that would damage his reputation. Roddy Harding lived a privileged life and there were those who were employed to beat a path for him to wander safely in the murky jungle where he preyed.

There were some within his inner world that saw Roddy Harding as a liability. His activities and interests, although not out of the ordinary with his type, were dangerous because of his lack of discipline in maintaining the all important secrecy. He had planned how the evening would progress, from the drink to the sort of drugs they would use and how he would steer the proceedings to what he hopefully thought would happen, which was having his fantasies realised. He had learned through the intelligence networks of Donny Campbell's behaviour and of his 'habits,' as they had been referred to. The information was presented in a formal and starchy manner, where details of sex and violence were written in a neutral and clinical way, and that excited Roddy Harding all the more. He wanted details of Donny Campbell's conduct and background, and he meticulously scanned specific parts in the reports, lingering on his activities that were seen as 'excessive and personally indulgent,' but all the same obscured within the cryptic network that was created in the Province. Having such a figure as Donny Campbell visiting his home, or one of them, was seen as folly in the extreme, but it was always a bad wind that Roddy Harding sailed close to. When the doorbell rang his heart jumped and his mouth dried. He carefully checked his features in a mirror before setting in place a smile and opening the door.

The obvious stupidity of Donny Campbell visiting Lord Roddy Harding was felt by both men, but it was all pushed to one side in an unthinking process that drove them both to engage in each other's company. Roddy Harding had considered what to wear for a long time, deliberating on what would be appropriate to greet Donny at the door. He settled for conventional slacks and a shirt, and when he opened the door he examined Donny's dress, seeing that he was wearing jeans and a tight tee shirt. It was bizarre, but it felt natural for both of them to meet up.

Roddy Harding swung from a show of polite diffidence, and a little nervous in ingratiating himself with Donny, to adopting a steady, military-like personality, presenting himself as strong, his voice in control, an octave lower than the defensive dithering of a man inflamed with infatuation, just as a teenager might be. He settled for a facade that was mellow and friendly, but with authority. This was the way he wanted to play it.

He gave Donny a brief tour of his living room, which was elegantly designed and furnished. He spent most of the time explaining two paintings depicting scenes of war. One was of a battle that took place over a hundred years ago, the other a century before that. He told Donny the history of them, giving details of places and dates, the regiments involved, adding that his old regiment was involved in both battles and of how his forefathers had high-ranking positions in that regiment. Donny nodded, matter-of-factly, looking at what he was directed to look at, and moved on to the next exhibit that he was led to. The tour did not last long before they went into the study where Roddy Harding began to relax as he took bottles of gin, whisky, vodka and brandy from an ancient drinks trolley. Within seconds an ornate pouch containing a large amount of white powder was placed on a low, wide table.

Roddy Harding was skirting around what he wanted to get down to while fawning around Donny. He said in a light hearted manner, 'You're a big boy now, pour your own drink, I'm off to get ashtrays and ice for the drinks,' and he shouted over his shoulder as he left the room, 'And cut up a couple of thick lines, will you? There's a good chap.'

Donny looked at the drinks, checking the labels on the bottles before pouring himself some vodka. Music rose in the room from seemingly nowhere, causing Donny to look where it had come from. It was classical music, a slow dirge. He looked around the study, and then standing still, he breathed in the man whose life he had entered.

'Little bit of Wagner – the music – like it?' Roddy Harding asked as he entered the room. Donny shrugged. It meant nothing to him.

'A man who knew our thinking – and of how things really are.' Roddy Harding studied Donny who did not react to what he had just said. 'Think about it, Donny, you've seen the system and how it works – and listened to the sermons from those who know better – judges and the like.'

Donny looked at him and said, 'I thought they were your department, in your pocket, and all that.'

Roddy Harding laughed. He looked at Donny and laughed again to a point of overdoing it.

They sat on opposite sides of the table and loosened up on the drink and powder, all the while Roddy Harding massaging Donny's ego. They snorted one more line and then took their drinks into another room. Roddy Harding had entered into a performance as they spoke about politics. He talked of the futility of it all and the people involved in it. He was preaching, in mock style as he gave his lecture. As he spoke he felt that he had entranced Donny. His scene was set, the music drifting and shifting as he spoke, Donny sitting on a sofa and him standing behind a large armchair, as if it was a pulpit, with him giving judgement, losing himself in his diatribe as he vented his passion, aroused at the words and meaning of what he was saying.

He appealed to Donny. 'Just look around – and see what they've done to us – the real men – they, the weak men have regulated us – the true men of this world are controlled and penned in – the burn marks from the bars of his cage are evident on his skin – and who is the keeper of the true beast? The dishonest – that's who – the worst thing that can be done to a wild animal – taking away its freedom, hating its honesty. It is too much for them, the liberal, homosexual, bureaucrats, because they are scared – because life is danger, real life that is, so they make him a prisoner and enslave that danger – the real man – and they watch as he smashes his skin against the bars of his cage, observing and measuring and judging to further their interests of reaping rewards – and they enslave others to achieve their gains

102

and positions while keeping their hands clean – and they will say, "Who me?"

'Yes, the real men of nature, who are shaped and conquered by those who are resentful – and now they are our leaders – but a time will come when they will be destroyed, and the real men will restore the natural order of nature.'

Harding looked at Donny.

'You're here because you are meant to be – it's just the way it is. People like you rise up because it is natural for them to do so – when the circumstances arise people like you – warriors – will meet the challenge – it will always be the same – but we have now grown and developed into a state of weakness.'

At first Donny thought Harding was joking and that it was all part of his humour, but he realised that he was serious.

Harding settled himself to speak, 'Look at it, how the naturally strong man is regulated by the liberal hierarchy – look how they do it – divulge and destroy – shaped and formed into a malleable substance for use – because they fear the greater strength of natural man and his propensity to attack – so now he is pliant, made safe for them – now that he is twisted out of shape. That is confining nature – potential and potency is now subjugated in those who are the naturally powerful – undermined so that the detestable weak can reign in ascendancy.

'I say, break those shackles – and let an unrestrained man reign – and then see the weaklings flee or stand and be crushed.

'To act appropriately. Why? Who for? For those that benefit – to spread a bad conscience, to imprison oneself and give way to the rule of weaker men who act behind the protection of law and contract – too deceitful to have an honest will of their own – it is the collaborative exercise of policy makers – letting in Jews, blacks, queers and women – and we the natural gladiators – what of us? The people whom they, the weak, rely upon to fight their battles and kill their foes – and so we do go and fight because for us action is all – and then on returning to the place of our making, what do we, the natural men find? A system that outcasts us – us, the people who have given them their kingdoms, whether that be a city hall, the classroom, court of law or place within a government body of representatives. We, are now their product, a tool that has produced for them, we are the beings that have the innate potential to push for change – which makes them resentful hypocrites and cowards.'

He stopped talking, as if acknowledging his own greatness, warming to his speech and nodding at what he was saying. His eyes flitted over Donny who listened attentively, periodically taking large swigs from a bowl-type of glass that could be the comfortable home for a few goldfish. Roddy Harding's eyes fixed upon a spot on the carpet in front of him, and then as if staring at a vision his words started slowly and evenly.

'For they are fools. Who do they think we – meaning humans, are? If you believe in fairy tales, even there you will find that humans are a poison to the balanced nature that exists – humans are an intrusion – a blemish, a bunch of cunts created by the great creator, introduced to an interdependent family in equilibrium and totally functional – and from then on, after the humans have entered the scene, it begins to be destroyed – it is our way – we should revel in it – and not hide from it, from what we really are – it is our true nature.'

He stared down at the carpet, seizing at breath, embittered, his eyes flashed about the room as if looking for something to hang it all on or beat it with.

'They, the powerless, and their thing called intelligence – it is a device to censure and control – they mimic the same habits and behaviour of those that they look up to – but don't ever utter the word respect, no, not to them, for that has no place, it has no meaning in the minds of those that live in superficiality – a fickle water of a mind, where a thing that they call values is upheld – and there are those given charge over others because they demonstrate and show servility towards this intelligence which has polluted all areas of our life and controls what we now call society.

'But what is this intelligence? Who does it benefit? Who does it stigmatise? And why?'

He looked up, breaking from his thoughts, his eyes staring trance-like as he spoke. 'To be an individual, Donny – stand alone – having the courage to do so – an iron will to pursue purpose and action – and it shows in your face – it's not for you to wait for the approval of sycophants and the weak ones, just because they have the power.'

Turning his head to one side he looked at Donny, studying him and said, 'It is the weak – with their fascination of the downtrodden, it is they – the wretched who are the poison who limit with their complaints and whining to be understood and cared for – at the detriment of the race naturally fulfilling its potential, but is held back, by the weak – and now that is the fashion. Their repulsive deformations are a burden on the psyche – their physical weight is an unwanted luggage – and the great parasitic liberals who use these human abominations as their product shout from their civilised self-created worlds, declaring that it is the evil, the spite and unrestrained might of those who have power to do as their will wants are the danger – they, the weak, say it is the strong that are a threat to humanity and a thing they call a future – these weak beings cause us strong willed beings of nature to be self-contemptuous of our very selves because we have to perform the grotesque act of anti-nature – that being self-enslavement – and then they deem that we pine for acceptance at their measly hut entrance, for them to take us into their despicable world of resentment and mediocrity.

'No! It is they who are the threat and hold a danger to nature.

'They want all the material riches – the power of having superiority over culture, and wanting to make wisdom and knowledge theirs – all for them, without fighting for it! But, everything in life is brought about by fighting – they deny the violence that has given them their position.

'They have hijacked a thing called morals and monopolised goodness as their own. Oh, yes, their beliefs and acts are brought about by the use of language and policy – their humanism, and religions have been created to provide a shepherd, or shepherdess, to prompt and divide, and with a staff of authority that dissipates any stirring of dissent within the common herd. And they tell us that the lion will rest with the lamb? Not on this side of the universe it won't, the stupid fuckheads.'

Donny nearly smiled, but he did not really know what he was feeling. As he looked at Roddy Harding he felt that he had to keep blinking in an effort to maintain reality, because he was beginning to see Roddy Harding's head as a balloon, swelling larger in size and rising to the ceiling. Donny tried to concentrate and was conscious that his breathing was laboured and deep. The powder that Roddy Harding gave him was cocaine striped with a shade of heroin, opium, amphetamine and a chemical having hallucinogenic properties, a potion named by Roddy Harding as a 'fun ball.'

Donny felt that his joints were coming apart, easing away from each other. He did not feel queasy, but needed to rest. He leant back into the sofa, his legs relaxing, releasing them to fall wide apart, his mouth dropped open, hanging slack and a warm buzzing purred in the centre of his head as a tingling heat spread from his fingers throughout his body, and he felt that he was moving backwards, into a black hole.

Roddy Harding continued. 'But they need their leader to tell them that they are right or wrong, those in the lofty position of giving judgement – the professed righteous ones – it is they who are the threat – it is they who are the badness that will sully and destroy the rest – when all they are is resentful and wanting revenge on those that have delivered them. They use blame as their leading weapon of attack – never taking responsibility themselves – and whatever clothes they may come in, they always crave for more while telling others to settle for less – and without ever dirtying their own hands – and when looking at that dirt, the blood, the spunk and bone on the hands of others, they will turn their heads with disgust at it being offensive to their civilised ways, when they accept greedily what those sullied hands have provided for them – but, we the strong, will look at the filth and the accompanying pain with no regrets, with no grief, guilt or sorrow – and we will look at our actions and say, I wanted to do it, because I am I.

'And now the I has been sublimated for the we, but that we collective is full of cowardly I's. And they tell us what is good, what is art, emotions, values, while the real good is crushed as these cowards slither in their pathetic way and always pander to the deceitful.'

Stopping for breath he licked his lips, trying to moisten the dry skin, all the while studying Donny, noticing the drugs were taking effect, and as he smiled a greater power showed in his features.

'We need saving from sensitivity and weakness. We need saving from their practices – and it is men like you that we turn to – have always turned to – before it's too late.'

106

Donny watched Roddy Harding move his hands in an act of entreating, noticing his slim fingers and how the soft clean manicured hands folded upon themselves in precise neat movements. His voice boomed in Donny's ears, like an echo from a distance, as if he was talking at the other end of an aircraft hangar. Donny saw Roddy Harding's shoulders as heavily laden with silk and ermine, precious stones tumbled from the glut of luxury around his shoulders and began to pour like a golden stream, glinting a winking flash as a diamond tumbled down the golden flow. And the glinting flashes grew darker and began to crack, sounding like little explosions, like bullets coming from a gun, and the bullets were firing at Donny, firing from the golden stream that ran down Roddy Harding's body.

Donny moved his body from side to side, throwing himself about the sofa in an effort to avoid being hit by the bullets. He saw Roddy Harding laughing, and the cheeks of his face were melting downwards in an lustrous mass, folds of skin bubbled and rose from the bones in his face, and the skin kept falling away, and his face changed, looking like a skeleton of a bird, a hawk, or crow, but it had the teeth of a man, and they were clenched tightly shut, and in the gaps between the teeth gas was escaping, it was green and poisonous. Donny knew it would strip the skin from the inside of his body, and he felt the gas as it slowly drifted towards him and entered his mouth and burned its way down his throat and into his chest and stomach. Donny jumped back trying to escape the gas, but he was trapped on the sofa, and the gas was burning his eyes, and then he felt something, a presence that was close to his face. He thought he saw a long, thin hand. It began forcing itself down his throat. The hand looked weak, but felt that it had great strength as it forced itself further down to his gullet. Donny saw Roddy Harding standing close in front of him, tapping his knee, as if to wake him – and then everything was back in its place with Roddy Harding standing in front of him, smiling and nodding.

Donny breathed deeply and the tight fear dispersed, but only to be replaced by a feeling of sickness, and, as if thrown from an ice bucket, a freezing cold sweat poured down his neck and sprang from his hands. The backs of his hands burned, but were frozen to a point that Donny thought his bones were going to snap because they were so brittle. Bile welled in his mouth as he watched Roddy Harding step back and resume his position behind the large armchair. Donny noticed that the chair had a large crest woven into the fabric, but he could not make out what it was because of the buzzing and whirring that vibrated in his head. Roddy Harding looked down at him and delivered his words.

'These weaklings, thinkers, that's what they are, when what is needed is action – and men of action should be allowed to act and break through the lethargy that's been created. They use all pervading methods to encourage listlessness – they give drugs to subdue, to take away an appetite for life – there is nothing painful, it is made safe, to be dull without desire – to placate and rule, that is their way – and all emotion, real emotion and feelings are stifled – and so with it the notion to pick up weapons and claim back the real source of life's happiness – freedom. Their language is a moral language, free of pain, full of pity – and yet hiding the reality.'

Roddy Harding looked down at the carpet. He was sweating and his mouth stretched so far open it looked like something was forcing his jaws apart. He started to shake, as if losing control and his teeth gnashed at an invisible object just outside his reach. He let out a low howl of pain before continuing with his speech.

'And they work towards what they say is the, improvement of man – a tamed man. Ah, that's fine in a world of mediocrity, but when their potion is applied to the likes of you, Donny, to real men such as you – well, can't the fools see that it doesn't, that it can't work – for it fuels the frustration you feel because of the shackles that have been employed to restrain your true self – and I will say shackles, because that is what they are – literally – and I won't say that it's an injustice in the way that you have been treated, because I will not use their words, because words like justice is a concept that is their invention – they talk of justice – conscience, guilt, and have even invented rubbish that they call a contract – where there is meant to be a negotiation between what they call the state and the individual for fuck's sake – what deceit! The hypocrisy – what have they of worth to negotiate with? And what of yours will they accept for negotiation?

'They utilise their created language and religions – and through the use of their ethics which they relate to their professions – they have combined a conglomeration of weapons – soft weapons – used for the purposes to control.'

Donny gave up listening to what Roddy Harding was saying, but felt the meaning of the words and drew them into himself, and as he did so he realised, although it did not make him jump, that his uncle was sitting next to him, listening to Roddy Harding. Donny looked down at himself, he was not a child, it was now, his uncle was actually there in the room, but unlike the flashbacks he was now a man, not a child, and he looked at his uncle, seeing that he was dressed as he nearly always was in a white shirt with a heavily stained collar and frayed cuffs. The smell of tobacco and cough linctus pastels on his breath was the same as it always was, and Donny looked at the dirt under his uncle's nails, but he seemed to be in black and white, as if coming from an old film. Donny looked at the cheapness and crudeness in the cut of his clothing, his hygiene, the squeak of his polished leather boots, all completely out of place from where Donny was sitting in Roddy Harding's room with its luxuriant trappings and the air of confidence and power that Roddy Harding and his ilk have. His uncle's veiny forearms tensed and his mean mouth tightened as his dark, sharp eyes pierced into Roddy Harding, and Donny wanted to show his uncle the size of his arms, the physical strength he now had, built up over the years, and to let him know that someone like his uncle could never physically harm him again, because he was now a man, not that skinny little weak boy that was told by his ma to run errands for 'uncle Alan,' even though she sensed that the young Donny did not like going round there. But she was tired, poor, lacking insight and in need of the little bit of money her brother-in-law gave Donny for the errands.

Donny's uncle took no notice of Donny being a man. He looked down at Donny the same way he always did, and Donny wanted to tell him that it was different from before, he wanted to stand up, puff out his chest and let him know that he had money, that everything had changed and that it was now he, Donny the man, that would do any beating if there was any to do. But words would not come, and he could not lift his arms, not even the tips of his fingers, and his lips were like iron shutters ground firmly in place as if rusted from years of disuse, and a feeling he had not felt for years rushed into his chest, growing from a petty fluttering to an extreme beating, and blood pounded in his head so violently it deafened him. It was the crashing rush of fear. His uncle looked down at him, agreeing with the words that Roddy Harding was reeling out, and the bitter sneer showed on his uncle's face. His eyes ripped into Donny, and Donny flinched as he knew his uncle was going to strike at any moment. Donny's breath froze as he looked at the back of his uncle's hand, hard and large, and it flew into Donny's face, and his uncle mouthed words that had no sound. Donny watched the soundless words spilling from his uncle's mouth, churning in the spit that spewed through his stained teeth. Donny could not move, and the buzzing in his head grew as he watched his uncle stand, his eyes fixed on Roddy Harding as he walked towards him, but Roddy Harding also looked like his uncle, and he pointed at Donny.

Donny could not hear what Harding was saying, but was frightened because Harding had turned into his uncle and he thought that Harding, or his uncle, was going to punish him. Donny pushed his head into his chest and tried to scream, but nothing would come. He tried again and again until at last a sound did come. It came from deep inside his body, and it wailed, becoming higher in pitch and sound, and Donny saw the sound as an image, the wailing and screaming came from a body, a person lying on the ground. Donny tried to recognise who it was, but it was a faceless body, and Donny was standing above this person who was screaming. The man on the ground was pleading to be left alone, begging for mercy, but Donny stamped down on him, and jabbed at the twisting body with a long metal spike, aiming at the head, especially the eyes. The screaming intensified, growing louder and louder. And Donny threw his head back, gasping for air, and as Donny started to breathe he saw Roddy Harding standing behind the large armchair, just as it was before, and his uncle was nowhere to be seen. Donny drank down air as if he had just been pulled out of water after fighting for his life.

Donny became conscious of tension leaving his chest, the muscles and tendons relaxed, and as they did so they made sounds of something snapping, and the sounds became like lightning flashes across his chest as if it was ablaze in an electric storm. The tension in his chest subsided and his breathing grew deeper and regular, his mouth slack and open, his teeth parched dry and his tongue stuck to the roof of his mouth that bled poison from stalactite-like formations encrusted in the skin. He felt his eyes were set in hot liquid and the skin of his face fell in layers, ready to shed and reveal something that he could not imagine. He breathed deeply as Roddy Harding drew back a thin smile into his mouth and then digested it bitterly. He was exultant as he spoke.

'Oh these weaklings – peasants, and sons of peasants now having a status and they are eyeing greater pedestals, feeling it their right to touch the throne – and having intentions of occupying it.

'And what of this God? Their God – made so simple that their simple little minds can understand – it is a mutated essence that alters and adapts so that they can interpret it and relate it to their petty little lives and all their fears – so that they have a divine entity within their little lives with ethics and morals, and they go about their little lives, depositing their little shit filled arses on the plush leather seats that cover the treasured items that they crave – luxuries – but where the leather comes from they do not know or care – they do not think about how their little luxuries have come about – how they have been produced, for their hankering wants – for they want what they can see, and they see it as theirs – and they want divine support to enable and justify their wanton cravings – and when tragedy befalls them in their little lives, they have their oh so placating God to sympathise and justify – their personal little helper – a God – for them – because above all and everything they see it as only them that matter!

'How childish it is – a prying and judging God – intrusive, to fit their own intrusive little lives – they are glad, if conscious of the fact, to be a product, a thing that is the result of a moralising movement in search of power and control.'

Harding stood erect, straightening his back and considered what he had just said. His eyes passed over Donny and focused down at the carpet for a few seconds before looking at Donny. His glare intensified and his breathing became irregular, sweat formed on his forehead and his gaze glazed as a look of delirium passed over him. He became distant, as his brain responded to the drugs and alcohol. Music played in the background, drifting its lamenting, flat depressing tone. He glowered at Donny, whose bloodless face was fixed rigid as he stared at Harding as he said,

111

'Men of action – for it is in the act that one will find life – that is the essence of what we call life and all its meaning – in action – and action for us, the Homo sapiens, is violence – violent acts in order to live – to fight for life during birth – to eat and die – and those who resent that reality, will surely resent those who act – and they, those who resent, they feign lameness and justify a world for lameness and the inadequate – and it is a world that is created at the expense of those beings and actions that have created the world that they live off.'

He became increasingly intense and manic as he toppled forward and gripped the armchair.

'Do they think the planet on which they live was formed by peaceful means? Have they never seen electric storms, earthquakes, tornadoes, volcanoes and hurricanes? This moving rock has a tempestuous history, as does its origins of it coming into existence, and so have the fragments, the bits and pieces that have become the Homo sapiens.'

He suddenly stopped talking, turned to a bureau and took out a dagger from a drawer, its handle encrusted with diamonds. He looked down, gloating at the dagger, his breathing became calmer and he looked up at Donny, pointing the dagger at him.

'Uninhibited – that's your strength – and beauty – unfettered by the contemplative bum lickers of intellect and fuck knows what. Action – in bravery – to be – unimpeded by the neurosis of the modern mind – that fearful, neutral, acquiescing substitute for a natural mind.'

The words drifted in Donny's ears, coming and going out of his hearing until they had gone – and then there was nothing.

A couple of hours passed before Donny woke from a sleep in which he saw a creature of no earthly description tethered to the ground by hundreds of what could have been fishing lines, and attached to the creature's eyelids were barbed hooks. It seemed that the creature had the ability to fly, but had been subdued and tortured by a physically weaker species that Donny could not see. But he knew it was them that had done this to the restrained creature. The sleep had refreshed Donny, taking away the draining nausea and weakness. He looked around and saw that Roddy Harding was not in the room. Donny stood up, stretched himself, flexing the muscles in his arms, amused and excited about the situation he was in. He looked around the room, idly, without much interest and then opened a door to an adjoining room and entered.

Roddy Harding was lying on a couch behind a low table. He watched Donny enter the room and smiled. 'Welcome back, I've got something for you.' He nodded at the tabletop where some lines of powder were cut, and next to them a short straw that had advertising on it for a burger chain, the words written in primary colours with a cartoon character aiming to attract the attention of young minds.

'An upper, take away the mind swerve of the other stuff,' Roddy Harding said. Donny knelt down, picked up the straw and looked at the advertising on the side of it. It made no impression on him. He snorted a couple of lines. Roddy Harding smiled contentedly as he watched Donny closely. He was satisfied. Donny stood up and cleared his nose. Roddy Harding's eyes followed Donny's movements carefully as he sat in a chair the opposite side of the table. He began to speak without taking his eyes from Donny's legs and arms. 'I really want to know more about the things that you've done, things you've had to do – I find it important, in getting to know who you really are.'

Donny breathed in deeply and looked down at his body, tensing the muscles in his arms. He looked at his arm, flexing the muscles a little, watching the play beneath the skin and tattoos, and then he looked at Roddy Harding with a smirk rather than a smile.

Roddy Harding smiled. He was excited. His eyes widened as Donny said, 'What do you want to know?'

Donny checked his arms, flexing them in a lazy manner. Donny considered how much physically stronger he was than Roddy Harding. He looked at Roddy Harding reclining in front of him, looking at his body, his build, how weak he was, comparing his own strength to his. Breathing in deeply his mind raced through a few scenarios of ramming Roddy Harding into the wall, lifting him on his shoulders as he ran across the room, finding a sharp edge to crunch his back into. He thought of the dagger with the handle encrusted with diamonds, it seemed that years had passed since he saw it rather than a couple of hours. He imagined holding Roddy Harding's head in place as he screamed and attempted to struggle free, and then digging the blade into his

113

throat, feeling the hot blood gush onto his hand, pulling the blade across his throat, cutting backwards and forwards, ripping and grinding through the bone, then throwing the head on the ground and stamping on it, again and again. This fantasy had given Donny the start of an erection. Breathing heavily he gritted his teeth and tensed his stomach. Roddy Harding's excitement was growing as he watched Donny.

'I've done so many things, I don't know where to start,' Donny said, looking down at himself. Roddy Harding moistened his lips. His voice had a slight weakness as he spoke. 'I bet that you never let anyone off the hook?

'When you're grinding information out of them.'

He watched Donny for a reaction. Donny looked straight at him.

'Never,' he said, 'I let the bastards think they're going to get through it, then bam! I fuck them into heaven – or wherever the fuck it is they go.'

Roddy Harding bit his tongue, shifting a little on the couch he attempted to control his speech as he tried to appear objective, as if it was a professional inquiry. 'No regrets? Any mercy? When you have someone on the floor at your feet, helpless – and you just grind them out?'

'Always.' Donny replied, noticing that the music was not playing any more in the background.

Roddy Harding breathed deeply and placing his hands behind the back of his head he leant back.

'What do you use? What's your favourite tool, or appliance when you are extracting information – punishing, or despatching? Whatever it is, I know that you are efficient.'

Donny just offered an inane grin and gave a small shrug of his shoulders.

Roddy Harding started to speak, his voice sounding like a small, spoiled child. 'Tell me – tell me about them, and what you have done,' he said in a squeaky little girl's voice

Donny looked at him. He was confused by the weird little girl's voice and an edgy feel ran through him. Roddy Harding continued, dropping the small whining voice he replaced it with a tone he felt befitting a man of authority and responsibility.

'I want all the details. What all those squirming pieces of cunt shit said and did.'

Donny relaxed and dropping to one knee he took the child's straw and snorted a thick line off the tabletop.

Roddy Harding's mouth opened a little in stimulation. 'Come on, it's all safe – I'll tell you stories of our little secrets – places that we have for worship – who knows, if it's your fancy, maybe one day you will participate – if that cold old heart of yours desires.'

Roddy Harding was sweating heavily as he watched Donny stand up in a lethargic manner. Harding spoke in a voice that was low and thick with anticipation and excitement. 'I'll show you some videos – of our – privileged activities.'

Donny looked at him, he was puzzled by what Harding had said. Roddy Harding was savouring the situation. He said, 'It has always been the same, Donny, the king of the jungle selects his prey – and his pleasures.'

He broke into laughter, loud and hard, and it stopped as suddenly as it started.

'To seek pleasures, it's only the powerful doing as they please with the subservient little people, after all, they are conditioned to what they are allowed, their expression and enjoyment is limited. God bless the poor, ignorant, loyal, unenlightened, stupefied – vessels of useless shit.'

He fell back, laughing hysterically and clutching his sides. Donny watched him. Roddy Harding recovered enough to stand, although he was unsteady on his feet and suddenly appeared drained. His eyes were heavy and hooded as he spoke thickly, 'Come on, Donny, I want to show you some of my toys – let's stop fucking around, we both understand the picture by now.'

Roddy Harding walked from the room, staggering slightly as he looked over his shoulder and with a crooked finger beckoned Donny to follow him.

Donny followed him upstairs to his bedroom. Roddy Harding dropped on the bed, lying flat out, his voice distant and dreamy, as if falling asleep. 'I have lots of goodies, and objects of interest in my little sleepy, byesie byes room.'

He told Donny to look through a large wardrobe and then he lay back expectantly. Donny opened the wardrobe and almost disappeared into it. Roddy Harding raised his head, watching Donny step back holding a chain mail hood.

'Appliances of pleasure, Donny, their functional duty now gone, unfortunately.' Roddy Harding said this as he settled himself into a more comfortable position, his eyes bright with expectancy. 'Armour to adorn men, real men, who gave their lives, proudly, in battle with other brave men.'

Donny inspected the hood, fingering it carefully and then put it back in the wardrobe. Roddy Harding studied his movements. 'Anything take your fancy? To give you pleasure?'

Donny turned and looked at him. Roddy Harding fixed him a stare and said, 'Toys for the doomed.'

Roddy Harding squirmed in delight as Donny emerged from the wardrobe wearing studded wristbands and holding a large knuckleduster.

'They suit you, Donny. I can see you wearing them – and using them. Years ago men like you had their place, a position that was feared, revered and honoured. When the real work had to be done, it was to men like you that the kings and leaders turned to.

'Any dissension, enemies, traitors – they were pulled into line. Torture was a healthy practice. It was healthy and honest – an age of real men.'

Donny put his fingers through the loops of the knuckleduster. He inspected it, clenching and unclenching his fist, finding a point of comfort.

Roddy Harding took a sharp intake of breath before speaking. 'Natural instincts of persecuting – show of strength – physical power, torture and cruelty – to see a person suffer for what they have personally done against another – these instincts aren't allowed to be exhibited anymore – they are seen as wrong and offensive to progression. The fools! Because when these natural practices and venting of feelings aren't practised externally, they turn inwards – becoming internalised – and because of this men are now neurotic, rather than free.'

He pushed himself up and sat on the side of the bed. He pointed at Donny. 'But now we have legions of state workers, and lawyers, profiteering and weakening the race, and disrupting nature with their hypocritical meddling – a created industry that shields the truth.

'Punishment tames man, but it doesn't make him better.'

He gestured for Donny to come over to him.

'Donny, here – look at this.'

Donny ambled towards him, checking the knuckleduster on his fist. Roddy Harding took a book from a bedside drawer and directed Donny to sit next to him, but Donny remained standing, looking down at him. The book was a collection of drawings of torture rituals and instruments of torture. There were drawings of torture implements from years ago and photographs of modern ones. He showed Donny the book and as he read out loud he pointed to the screaming faces on the pages and commented on the merit of a certain implement and practice of torture.

'It was healthy,' he almost pined, 'we're repressing what is natural.'

Donny grinned, pointing to a drawing of a man being torn apart. 'That's what some bastards need – a bit of that.'

Roddy Harding's eyes moved down Donny's body as he slowly turned the pages of the book. Donny carried on. 'Weak men didn't rule once,' he nods at the book, 'when you could use a bit of that on some useless fucker – you had to be strong to hold a double handed sword in battle – and the weight of the armour – you had to be strong'

Roddy Harding nodded, his excitement growing. Donny became more aggressive as his face twisted with viciousness.

'It was the toughest who ruled.'

'And quite right,' Roddy Harding said. 'Unfortunately, those days are gone.'

He stared admiringly at Donny. 'It would be good to feel what it was like. Maybe you could show me?'

Roddy Harding stood up, dropping the book onto the bed and went over to a table. He spread some powder on the surface of the table and gestured for Donny to join him, 'Here, get involved.' He snorted some powder and watched as Donny hungrily inhaled powder up a children's drinking straw, although it was a different straw from the one used downstairs.

Roddy Harding noisily cleared his nose and throat, and sucking in air he began talking at a faster pace.

'You and me – we understand each other. We're about the same age. We remember the...' He stopped talking as he considered the word he was about to use, 'The – invasion!'

His eyes widened. A maniacal grin could barely hold laughter from spilling out of his mouth. He threw a playful punch at Donny's shoulder. 'You – me – we remember the invasion. The dismantling of a man's world – sullied and perverted – and rubbished forever, by the lefto, Trotsky, pink bollocksed – parasitical – fakes.

'An invasion of weakness. For fuck's sake, Donny – music was played by men – but they weren't really men – it was played by men who looked like women.'

Roddy Harding's breathing was laboured. Donny watched him with a simple grin forming on his face. White powder dusted his mouth and nose. Roddy Harding ranted at Donny. 'Yes – oh fucking yes – pop groups, bands – or whatever the fucking fuck they're called – men dressed in long boots with long hair.'

His intensity increased. 'Sprayed and fucking glittered! Fuck me, Donny – they were girlie boys – fucking bastard girlie fucking boys – and men like you were shunted into the background. Natural men, like you – attacked – challenged – by girlie men weirdos.

'Look at it now, for fuck's sake – they run everything – telling us how to live our lives – telling us to do this and do that – I'm fucking sick of it.'

Donny stepped over quickly to Roddy Harding and knocked him off balance. He fell onto the bed, Donny stood over him and growled violently as he raged.

'I hate every cunting one of the fuckers – weakling cunts. We're being destroyed – the fucking cunting fuckers get in my head and...'

He struggled to find words. Roddy Harding watched him in amazement. He urged Donny on. 'I know, Donny, I know – all the men on the television, they are girlie, weakling men.'

He nodded to another doorway from the one they entered earlier and said, 'I have a room where I keep lots of their stuff – the girlie men stuff – keeping a check on them – knowing what they're up to.'

He watched Donny turn towards the doorway. Roddy Harding's face was twisted in grim pleasure. He smiled, licking his dry lips, his eyes heavy, the drink and drugs shaping them into slits. 'In that room – I think we can come to a satisfying and mutual arrangement, Donny – you do what you do best.'

He jumped up from the bed and stood next to Donny. His mouth loosened and formed into a sneer as he said, 'Mix that girlie man to fuck this ball of shit.'

Twenty-two

The light from two candles on the wall offered the only light that there was in the room. A large bulky shadow was thrown against one wall. It was the crude shadowy form of Roddy Harding strapped to a large leather bench. He was lying on his back wearing only a thong. The bench had lots of sharp studs on its surface and he squirmed against them to increase his pleasure. His voice was parched as he spoke in a low tone. 'You better hurt me good – I don't want to think that you and your type where you come from are becoming girlie men. I bet you haven't the know-how or guts to crunch my bollocks – and put the fucking music on now, for fucking Christ's sake – get it right – yeah, let's get it right.'

Donny turned from a music system and faced the bench, looking down at him. He was stripped to the waist, wearing a long blond wig with glitter sprayed across his face and chest. He had covered himself in talcum powder and was wearing studded leather mittens. His fingernails were painted in bright varnish, make up had been crudely applied around his eyes and lipstick gave his mouth a torn appearance. Donny was holding a leather strap in his right hand. He glared down at Roddy Harding and a demented grin formed on his face as he watched him fumbling with a small funnel, struggling to push it under his thong. Roddy Harding shouted out, 'Fuck my dick you fucking scum – come on – get up here and fuck my dick.'

Donny grabbed Roddy Harding's bollocks and twisted them, and as he winced Donny hit him with the heel of the strap on his stomach and then brought the strap down on his face. Roddy Harding screamed at him. 'Not my face – not my face – you useless scum fucker.'

He spat at Donny. 'Do better than that, you girlie scum fucker – show me how you dish out the goodies.'

The music suddenly blasted out. It was 'Wig Wam Bam' by The Sweet. Donny hit him with the strap, leaving the bench only to change the music. Donny gyrated in front of the bench as 'Mystery Girls' by The New York Dolls was playing.

'You hit like a girl,' Roddy Harding whined in a nasally, strangled tone, 'because you are a girl.' Donny climbed onto the bench and straddled him.

Their session broke for periods of rest and more powder. At one point as Roddy Harding tried to break free from the straps Donny looked down at him struggling, 'Vietnamese Baby,' by The New York Dolls was playing and Donny's senses blurred as he became as one with the music, feelings and darkness in the room.

A few hours later Donny examined himself in a full-length mirror. Roddy Harding was lying on the bench moaning, gurgling and letting out sporadic bursts of talking like a young child, burbling and babbling baby talk and then switched to the heated raging of what he had become as a man, as if in defiance and feeling reluctance to that fact. Donny walked over to the bench, punched Roddy Harding in his stomach and watched his face as he let out a squeal. Donny picked up the strap, spat in Roddy Harding's face and returned to the mirror.

Striking a pose, holding the strap above his head, he looked at his reflection, at the make-up that had mixed with the talcum powder, noticing how it had congealed with the eyeliner, foundation, blusher and lipstick. Watching it run down his face he growled at what he saw.

'Twentieth Century Boy' by Marc Bolan was playing loudly.

Twenty-three

The opening of a new civic centre in Belfast had coincided with signings in the peace process. The new hi-tech building was heralded as a monument to a new progressive democracy encompassing shared interests of different factions working towards an agreed goal of peace, justice and prosperity for all. There was a large industry emerging in Northern Ireland that was often referred to as Peace and Reconciliation, many of the people involved in that industry had descended upon the civic centre that day for a large conference.

There were delegates, professional and otherwise, coming from support groups, government agencies, charities and the private sector, an array of pressure groups and those with the power to give out state funding. It was a variety of people, groups and organisations with interests in the Province, with most having motives of self-interests. The place was buzzing with what was on offer. There were mission statements, holistic therapies, courses that taught skills in 'understanding and empathy,' and the words, 'resolution,' 'truth,' 'peace' and 'healing,' rung out in the new hall as a profusion of 'post-conflict' goodies was on offer at the vibrant market place that had stalls set up on the broken ground of human suffering.

High rates were charged for high profile speakers, and on that day the representatives of these different groups, trusts, charities and departments had descended to peddle their wares and vie for a piece of the cake.

Young women flew in from other countries, just out of university, beaming their shiny faces, furrowed their brows in understanding and sympathy while clutching firmly in one small fist the glossy prospectus outlining the 'values' of the organisation they were representing and holding a computer in the other hand, its style matching the dark business suit they were wearing, sharp, just like their presentation.

Donny Campbell had found a place within this new order as a person representing the community from where he comes.

Although he was not called to speak, there are those that do that for him.

Donny Campbell had returned from his trip to England to attend the conference, he was present for speeches that were made concerning the rehabilitation of political prisoners into the community. He was standing in the main hall of the new civic centre dressed in a suit and holding a glass of wine. There had been speeches by people representing businesses, companies and consultancies. A large banner hung on the wall proclaiming Belfast's intentions of, Building A Positive Future. Some people had remained seated at their tables, but most stood in small groups talking and introducing themselves to the other people in the hall.

A man in his mid-thirties approached Donny and said, 'Good to see you Donny, I'm just out a couple of weeks ago.' He held out his hand, grinning from ear to ear. Donny nodded, and as he shook his hand Edward Scriver came up to him with Sue Black, a woman in her late twenties, dressed in a business suit, a style that was once the preserve of the corporate image, but had become fashionable attire in social service presentation.

Edward gestured for Donny to move away, 'Could I have just a word, Donny?'

Donny nodded at the man whose hand he was shaking and followed Edward Scriver and Sue Black.

Edward stopped walking after a few steps and said, 'Donny – this is Sue Black, senior social worker.'

Donny looked from Sue Black to Edward Scriver, waiting for him to continue.

'Sue is our repatriation and development worker.'

Edward continued to try and sell her to Donny.

'Sue is a very experienced community social worker; she has been living in Belfast about two weeks now.'

Donny was unmoved. It was apparent that he was not impressed. He stared at Edward Scriver. Sue Black decided to introduce herself and held out her hand, but Donny's expression did not change. Sue Black let her hand drop to her side and broke the silence as she spoke in a jolly manner.

'Well, Mr Campbell, these certainly are positive times.'

Donny turned slowly and faced her. She continued unabated. 'I have confidence in breaking initiatives in regeneration work. Let us not lose our chances, but to take the initiative in building bridges, paving a solid base and erecting towers from which to fly a new flag of confidence.'

She stopped, feeling that she had made no impression on Donny who studied her with a cold stare. Donny turned to leave, but Edward Scriver stopped him by gently tapping his forearm and calling over a man in his early thirties who was dressed in an expensive suit. 'Someone I would like to introduce you to, Donny,' Edward Scriver said as the man joined them. 'This is, er...' The man interjected, his voice concise and having a distinct Scottish accent that he liked to play upon, although its edge has been softened by his time spent at university in England and the years that he had lived in an expensive part of London. A smile was breaking on his thin face, but his eyes were sharp and searching.

'Robbie Cheshire,' he said, holding his hand out to Donny, who after looking into the man's face eventually gave it a brief shake.

Robbie Cheshire continued. 'I'm heading a new innovation, the Belfast Vanguard Initiative. The needs and aspirations of diverse community members are of salient value, and it is in our mission statement to provide a holistic package that embraces multi-disciplinary professions to address in partnership with other agencies and community groups – and of course individual...' Edward Scriver cut him off as he attracted the attention of a passing man. The man was Danny Ward. He had recently been freed from prison under conditions in the Good Friday Agreement after serving time for his involvement in nationalistic activities. Danny Ward was pensive, casually dressed and generally out of place with the corporate image that dominated the function. His clothing, demeanour and soft tone of voice reflected a man who had been wearied and troubled, but whowas driven to see through what he believed to be fair. His reason for attending the function was because he wanted an acknowledgement from the state that it had wrongfully imprisoned innocent people, and an apology for the physical violence that was used against those people.

Edward Scriver introduced him to Donny and Robbie Cheshire and a synopsis of his background and intentions were explained. Sue Black and Edward Scriver had been in his company earlier. Donny and Danny Ward did not shake hands. Their eyes never left each other's as they both offered a short nod. Sue Black smiled breezily and Edward Scriver placed his hand on the shoulder of Robbie Cheshire's finely cut suit as he looked at Danny Ward and Donny.

He said, 'Robbie is representing the Community Cohesion steering committee that has been given central Government support and funding.'

Robbie Cheshire held his out his hand to Danny Ward. The two men shook hands and Robbie Cheshire spoke with a slippery ease. 'Very pleased to make your acquaintance, and may I say it will hopefully be a friendship in working in partnership towards ongoing projects in a community that is under reconstruction. I was just saying to your colleague here – ' and he held out the flat of his hand towards Donny. This caused Edward Scriver to take a sharp intake of breath. Both Donny Campbell and Danny Ward watched Robbie Cheshire as he spoke. ' – we are working towards delivering real meaningful improvements in raising life-chances and the quality of life for community members by ordinary citizen involvement projects. We are going to engage residents and support them in making informed choices about their future in their city.'

Robbie Cheshire looked at Sue Black, and she nodded with enthusiasm and at the profundity of what he was saying. He went on, 'The complexities of local government policy are to be relevant and understandable for residents as their needs and aspirations are considered.'

He stopped talking and looked at Danny Ward, as if for a response. Danny Ward nodded and said in a flat tone, 'Fine.'

Robbie Cheshire continued to speak while looking at Danny Ward. 'A priority is to promote the cultural diversity within the population.'

Danny Ward looked at Donny Campbell and then back to Robbie Cheshire before saying in the same flat, uninspired tone. 'Well, good luck.'

There was a pause, but just before it became uncomfortable Sue Black spoke to Robbie Cheshire. 'Well, Robbie, you know where we are coming from, our agenda is clear and pragmatic.' She tapped one finger into the palm of her other hand as she marked off her points, 'Policies of inclusion – of ancestral respect – of repatriationary methods – rehabilitative work – conflict resolution – respect for diversity and heritage.'

Robbie Cheshire nodded and fired back at her. 'With a rugged insistence to equal opportunities – challenging race and homophobic incidents of discrimination.'

Sue Black nodded, but as she was thinking what her reply might be Robbie Cheshire beat her to it. 'To further aims of pro-active strategies for promotion of cognition in one's healthier lifestyle. It's very exciting times for bringing new thinking to the table,' he said with a smile spreading across his face. He was winning the duel and he knew it as he continued, 'The natural beauty of the surrounding countryside is an area needing advantaging and also requiring a raised profile in its effects of contributing to a good quality of life. Relevant and appropriate policy-making is called for to engage all members of the community with an over-riding mission for inclusion that runs through our regenerative work.'

He stopped. Nobody in the group spoke.

'Who is it you said that you work for?' Danny Ward asked Robbie Cheshire in a tired voice. Edward Scriver answered his question. 'Robbie works for a private consultancy – they have a brilliant record for their community work in the States, and are at present drawing up directives in South London and Birmingham...'

'Birmingham, England.' Robbie Cheshire quipped. His remark was met with silence from Danny Ward and Donny Campbell.

'So, there's plenty of work out there for you to do – in these very exciting times, Robbie,' Danny Ward said derisively.

Robbie Cheshire regarded him thoughtfully. 'Believe me, I feel, personally, privileged to be given the opportunity to be involved in work that makes positive contributions to improve the quality of people's lives, and work that has aims to educate and eliminate inequity, giving opportunities for all to compete...'

Danny Ward cut in. 'And just how much, if you don't mind me asking, is it costing the taxpayer for your metaphorical bulldozer to level the playing field?'

'I believe equality for all is a prerequisite for...' Robbie Cheshire said, but this time he was cut off by Donny who said, 'It's not natural.'

Robbie Cheshire looked at him. Donny said, 'You can't have everyone being or wanting to be the same, because they're not – you can try, but you'll fail, it's nature, everyone wants for themselves – and yours is the same as everybody else's – it's inborn, it's natural.'

Robbie Cheshire chose his words carefully, and all the while Danny Ward was watching him closely. 'Yes, I see your point, Mr Campbell, but we have to move away from the primeval basics in our understanding of natural instinct. Maybe within the community in which you were brought up in, impressions were made, and may I add, a false impression of what I call blind evil...'

Danny Ward stopped him as he said, 'I'm hearing words used as a magician uses tricks to pass off his illusion. You use language – that's your tools – I've spent most of my life listening and being told what's right and what's wrong – by people who use language then use other people to do their dirty work for them...'

Sue Black tutted, she intended to speak but Danny turned to her and carried on. 'Yes you do – while you stand to the side – you wouldn't break one of your polished nails.'

Robbie Cheshire said, 'May I please redirect this line of...'

But Danny Ward continued,, 'People have been battling for years to have their voices heard, and now they see people flown in on first class seats to stay in five star hotels while they continue to ask for information about their relatives and friends. They have discovered that the state evades its responsibility and hides behind a smokescreen made up of social and therapeutic professionals with proposals of good intentions. Many people are disillusioned and dissatisfied when seeing known criminals becoming spokespeople. Their frustration grows when confronted by a modern state agent using crafty linguistic weaponry with talk of justice, positive visions, forgiveness and reconciliation.

'You'll find people over here suspicious of fast talking suits – you'll have to earn your respect by proving what you're saying, because people have heard it before, in all its many guises – and even in this contemporary age of enlightenment, that still stands.'

Robbie Cheshire raised himself to his full height, his manner supercilious and that caused Danny Ward to react. 'It is imperative for what you call an "evil" to exist in order for the rich and powerful to get what they want – it's an age of falsehoods – as ever – with people like you steering the course.'

Robbie Cheshire looked at him, his mind in full calculation as he made a point of remembering his name. Edward Scriver looked on nervously.

Danny Ward stepped closer to Robbie Cheshire and said, 'I've seen what's behind what you call civilisation – it's bloodier and more cruel than an honest desire shown in the action of natural instinct – but you've got the key to lock that up.'

Robbie Cheshire and Sue Black looked at one another.

Donny gestured for Edward Scriver to move away from Robbie Cheshire and Sue Black. They walked a few steps away from the others and Donny turned and faced Edward Scriver. 'I knew you years ago, Scriver. It was the same thing then – organising other people's affairs, and never minding your own. But you've done well for yourself.'

Donny sneered contemptuously, moving his head close to Edward Scriver's face he spoke through gritted teeth. 'You always were a cunt – fraternising with Taig scum.'

Donny looked over at Robbie Cheshire and Sue Black as they were walking away, both talking at once to each other.

Donny said, 'You better scamper after your meal ticket – like the little lapdog that you are.'

Edward Scriver held Donny's stare, but only for a few seconds before turning and walking after Sue Black and Robbie Cheshire. Donny watched him follow behind them, and then he noticed that Danny Ward was watching him. The two men looked at each other, their gazes fixed, and they remained like that for a while. Eventually, they both turned at the same time and walked in opposite directions like two men who knew they would never speak to each other, even if they were the last two people left living on earth.

A small, sinewy man in his mid-fifties approached Donny. His name was Norman. He was a nervous, intense man with eyes the colour of coal that glinted a foreboding that was bedded on an inner conflict of fear and guilt. His clothing old and battered, he wore a threadbare suit showing a Minister's collar that was also frayed. Donny had known him all his life, since childhood. Norman was a figure of fun, condemned for being different when a young man, he later entered the ministry. His ministry was a local Protestant one that was small in size. Norman evangelised in an urban area that seemed to be the actual manifestation of what he was, a broken place dominated by corruption and fear.

Norman's eyes bored through Donny and straining his veiny neck he looked upward, showing a set of capped teeth that were broken and dirty.

'Having a good day, Donny – with your new found business friends?'

Donny regarded him with impatience.

Norman continued, bitterly. 'Isn't it nice of these young people to visit our humble little town, Donny?

'Struck up any deals with these well intentioned smart young things?'

Donny shrugged and said flippantly, 'It's progress.'

'Progress!' Norman spat the word out as if it was poison. He gestured around the hall. 'They will go anywhere for profit, wearing the clothes and saying the words, it has always been the same – look at them! Look at all this! A stage for false prophecies with intentions of self-interest.'

He looked closely at Donny, noting his disinterest in what he was saying. 'Just to remind you, that there are those who can't be bought – because what they are, and what they represent is not for sale.'

Donny sneered at him. 'Because you're the only one who knows the truth – isn't that right, Norman?'

Norman did not attempt to answer. He just looked at Donny, and then moving closer to him he started to speak with a growing conviction in what he was about to say. 'Whoever, whatever, pulls the strings and gives credence to you and your actions, is the enemy, and they are to be defeated in the pursuit for a righteous truth and justice.'

129

Donny was bored with Norman, but that only caused Norman to speak with more intensity. 'What are you? You, the modern hero, exemplifying greed and evil – your being is to do with the work of gangsters,' he waved his hand at the banner on the wall, 'rather than the politics of resolution.'

His acrimony was growing as he went on. 'All this – and you, being part of it all – having a – duty to country and history...'

He pointed into Donny's face. 'I'll tell you what all this does' for you. It allows you to practice a life that is the fear of decent people.'

Donny remained detached, watching Norman's face twist in disgust as he spoke to him.

'This allows you to be seen as the hard man – whilst fornicating wee boys up the arse – and all the while keeping that front of the hard man – and people will respect you – but only because of fear. In your world, the weak, the vulnerable – they get beaten and crushed under – and you're scared of that, Donny boy – scared to be seen as inadequate – it's a good shield to hide yourself behind – with all your depravity and sick wanting – the shield of King Billy – and in its shadow lurk the sexual deviants, paedophiles, rapists, perverts, drug runners and murderers – God, Donny, lucky for you it's a big shield, because you fit every bill there son – on God's name you do.'

Norman paused to wet his lips. He looked as if he was going to spit on the floor before he carried on speaking. 'And on God's name, someone has to be witness to your actions – it is right and proper.'

Norman looked about the hall, his eyes darting in all directions. Donny watched him and then he began to speak, his voice low, and as he spoke his face did not change in expression.

'I hope that I am not hearing what you are saying, Norman – not to stand in a court of law and point your finger, at me?'

Norman's expression sobered. He studied Donny, trying to meet his gaze, but his resolve was not strong enough. He looked down, becoming scared and breathing heavily. Donny sensed Norman's fear. Moving his head close to Norman's he spoke into the side of his face. 'You remember that old fish market, Norman?'

He waited for Norman to respond, which he did by nodding his head bitterly.

'As a wee boy I would watch them cut the head off the fish – slice up its body, taking out the guts, and just throwing them into an old bucket – scraping clean what's needed – the body to eat – the flesh – the rest is shit – and I would look at the head of the fish – at the eyes – they were dead, but still alive – watching – but helpless.'

He looked closely into Norman's face. 'You know, Norman, I've seen that look in the face of a man – lying on the ground – all life completely fucked out of him – and all that is left is a question in the eyes – saying why?

'A nothingness – just helpless – and I would put my heel on the face, and crunch down – trying to make the eyes pop out – just like I did when I was a kid – after knocking the fish head on the ground, and squash it down – till the eyes bugged out and it spluttered shit all over my shoe.'

He grinned into the side of Norman's face.

'Wee bastard – the fish was.'

Donny stopped speaking, but he continued to watch Norman, enjoying his discomfort and fear. Norman tried to meet his eyes, but could not. Donny continued in the same tone of voice. 'You're an outsider, Norman – you're not invited to the regular church – you're as mad, and as loose as the rest of us.'

A nervous tick started up in the side of Norman's face. He went to turn away, but Donny stopped him by placing two fingers on his chest. Donny stared at Norman, a harmful intent broadened his merciless grin. 'You better start praying some shit from that big book of yours, Norman – look at you – waltzing around here, thinking they'll be some crumbs dropping from the table that you'll be able to have – giving it all the talk of hypocrites and arrogant men – you dumb fuck up – do you think this new breed of suits and smiles are gonna want anything to do with fuck ups like you? Eh? It's known, Norman, that you like your children – so much so that you stick it up their wee holes for Jesus – with all the other cunts, except you're small fry, Norman – and stupid – and you're so sick and fucked up, even the fuck ups that run the show can't have a sicko, wanking Jesus fuckhead like you spunking all over the fucking place.'

Becoming heated he pushed his face into Norman's 'You're gonna be fucked to fuck – I've got witnesses who can point at your face, when as wee boys you made them hold your cock and then you stuck it in them with warnings of God killing their families if they said anything – you lapped up the bum gravy of boys...'

Norman cut in, but not forceful, he was trembling as he uttered a weak protest. 'I'm no fornicator.'

Donny watched the twitch play its way around the side of Norman's face, thinking it looked like lightning, striking at points on the blotchy skin. Donny looked over at Sue Black. She was in conversation with another woman who was dressed almost identically to her. Their glossy smiles appeared to be in competition with each other. Donny nodded over at Sue Black before speaking, and Norman looked at her, his eyes weak and desperate. 'If I had a word with Princess Bullshit over there, she'll stop you attending bollocks like this – sliming yourself around with your God suit on, making out you're working for some other great power – and she, and her like won't want you around, Norman, once she learns the score about you – and then you'll be getting a visit, and your big boss up there better know a good lawyer to spring you out of that one.'

Norman looked from Sue Black to down at the floor. Donny watched him. Norman turned, and without saying anything walked away, one shoulder hunched, his head bowed. Donny continued to watch him, his expression not changing as he began to stare into nothingness, reflecting, thinking back, not seeing what was going on in the hall or hearing the clamour of voices. His mind was holding a vivid image of the bedroom in his uncle's house, as it was when he visited there as a child. He could smell the room. A record was playing. It was 'Cool Water' by Marty Robbins. He saw himself as a young boy sitting on a chair by the table. His uncle was staring down at him and the film projector was set up, but now turned off after having been playing footage of scenes from the Second World War. His uncle was speaking and Donny felt the anxiety in his stomach as he spoke.

'Can you imagine the loneliness, of spending months in the prairie, the only company being that of men – tough men?

'There were no women out there. Those men also had a mental prairie – isolated, they are different from other men, who succumb to the softness of a woman. They aren't like people who need to live to a plan that is designed by others.

'They confront the world – real men shape the world – they will not – cannot, kowtow to those in authority who have no personal strength.'

He was working himself up, his breathing was heavy and Donny knew he would shortly lose his temper.

'The physically weak, and inferior hold judgement – having power over real men – they create laws – but in an arm wrestle, or a fight in the street, they would lose – every time – can't you see it? Eh? They are cowards – weak men and women holding sway over real men – the hearts of real men are being destroyed by the deceit of perverts.'

He stopped talking and stared at Donny. Placing his hands either side of Donny's head he drew him close to his chest. Donny was scared, his mouth dry and a feeling of numbness filled his head. His uncle looked up at the ceiling, his words just audible as he spoke through gritted teeth.

'What do I do? What do I do with this bad, bad boy?'

He released Donny, stepped over to the bed and picked up a set of chest expanders and a body building magazine, his voice low and quiet.

'See the men in this? Do you?'

Donny nodded, but only slightly, he was confused. His uncle dropped the magazine on the bed and pointed the chest expanders at Donny.

'That is what you have to work towards – build arms that can crush a man – shoulders like Jack Dempsey – a strong body – a beautiful body.'

He dropped the chest expanders onto the bed and fussed over the projector until the reels of film began to whirr. He stepped back as the crackling black and white images trembled against the white sheet that was pinned to the wall. The film was of a Nazi rally. He raised his voice over the sound of the marching music.

'Don't waste your time with women and silly girls – they will make you weak – physically weak and mentally weak – there is no place for women on the battle line – catch germs and all

133

manner of diseases off them. Think of a world where woman kept their noses out of it – stupid – stupid...'

'But my ma's not stupid,' Donny said.

His uncle looked down at him. At first Donny thought he was going to be aggressive and strike him, but he nodded, and Donny felt it was in a kindly way, for his uncle.

'Of course not, Donny, your ma's special – that's why you're not to tell her about the things we do round here – this is a place for men – men to get to talk and think. Look at the men in the film – hear the drum? It has the soul of a man, not an ordinary man, but a strong man – of a man suffering – but superior. You see?'

Donny watched his uncle stare at the images, at the flickering lights as they played their shadows on his uncle's face, his mouth set in a tight line, speaking all the time. 'And some of the things that I have to do, Donny, well, you know that they are for your own good – and will act as a firm foundation – for what I do pains me – but it will be your salvation.'

The sound of the marching grew louder and the words his uncle was saying disappeared under the relentless ranting voice on the soundtrack that spoke a language he did not understand. The sound in the bedroom grew louder and louder, and then suddenly, Donny emitted a gasp for air. He found himself standing in the Civic Hall, not hearing anything for a few seconds, as if in a vacuum. Gradually the sounds in the hall broke into his hearing.

Donny looked around at the different groups of people, breathing deeply his eyes focused on a thin man. Donny watched his Adam's apple oscillate in his throat as he spoke to a man and woman. The two people he was speaking to also had thin faces. Donny felt nauseous. He could not stop looking at the man's weak throat, with the Adam's apple bobbing around, reminding him of a cockerel. An adrenalin rush surged through his body and he imagined holding a blade in his hand and slicing it across the man's throat. He felt the hot blood spilling over his hand and saw the weak man fall to the ground, surprised, fear shining in his eyes as he looked at Donny, twitching and writhing as he struggled to gulp at air that would give him life.

Twenty-four

Later that night Donny had a meeting with Duane Bishop and Michael Connelly who had arrived in Belfast. Donny was not pleased with the way he felt that things were happening. He knew that there were always other motives and hidden plans at work. On this one, the big one, he felt that promises were broken as people were put in place above him in the order of power that dominated the emerging narcotic market.

During the next few weeks that followed Donny Campbell brooded as he thought about the involvement of the English contingent, and of how he felt that he was being pushed aside. Things did not seem as simple as they were before when he knew where everybody stood. He was also troubled about existing arrangements. He could sense a mood change. Certain people were acting differently towards him, he felt that he was losing respect and things were beginning to slip from his grasp. His insecurity and suspicion was rising out of all proportion in the smallest of interactions, the symptoms of psychotic paranoia with all its delusions, a mental condition that had limited, fuelled and protected him throughout his adult life.

One evening, Donny went back to his uncle's old house and drank a bottle of vodka, icing the glass with cocaine and an opiate-based powder. He was revved and yet calmed. He had a masturbation session, wanking as he watched the television screen play the recording of him torturing the teacher whose fingers he had cut off. Dusty Springfield singing 'You Don't Have To Say You Love Me' opened his choice of songs.

As well his uncle's place, Donny owned a small terraced house in west Belfast, but in the last two weeks he had only slept in his uncle's old house, and although it had only been a short while since he slept overnight in his own house it felt to him as if he had never slept there. It seemed so distant, and he had to remind himself what the furnishing and the house looked like.

He bought his uncle's house because he felt it would give him some kind of ownership of the past. No work to update the place had been done, it was kept as it was, its main use to interrogate, torture and murder people in the bedroom. At first he did not want to sleep in the bed, it being his uncle's, the one he used to lie on when he was a child, full of fear, scrunched against the wall as his uncle moved about him. But now he felt it to be like home, maybe an attachment to his past, the only thing he had. Donny did not believe in a future, not for anyone, he trusted in nothing and no one. There was Dougie, a person he relied on, having known him for years. Dougie was one of the boys with him when he hit Philip Alexander with the bottle of cider all those years ago in the youth club. Donny felt that Dougie was loyal because of his own reasons. He wanted to be, and maybe it was in his interest to be so, but that was it. He and Dougie never spent time together for what would commonly be called socialising. It was always to accompany Donny to sort something out, to clean up for him afterwards, physically, or to make arrangements for cover ups, inform who needs to be informed and of course to drive Donny around. It was seen as a joke in some quarters, sly remarks were made such as, 'Dougie's out with his wife.' Donny had never learned to drive, even as youngsters when cars were stolen for fun he did not indulge. He did not like the idea of driving. It did not excite him, in fact it disturbed him, he got his excitement from dealing with people. Dougie was married, he had children, but Donny had lost count of how many. He never asked and Dougie did not talk about it, other than making a passing comment about a birthday, but Donny did not respond to such talk. It was not that he was consciously uninterested for a specific reason, he just could not understand it all. And it made him physically sick if he gave it too much thought.

As a youngster Donny had been put in front of psychiatrists and psychologists, but had gained nothing from the experience. He viewed them, as do many others, as just another arm of the state used to condition and control. Although there was a person who Donny did have a feeling of being close to. He could not describe the feeling, but he felt that he connected with this one person, even daring to believe that they understood each other. Donny would talk to this man. The feeling he had was strange, but it was a feeling of being safe with another person, just this one person in the world that he lived in. Donny referred to the man as Little Willie, his real name being William Whitman. He was an extremely short man, four feet four inches in height and very small in build. He was lame from physical difficulties occurring during his problematic birth that had also left his face severely disfigured. William Whitman was an albino.

Donny met him while serving a short prison sentence when he was in his early twenties. William Whitman was in prison for the crime of forgery, at that time having an office job in a company, he loathed the company and the people that worked there. Even though his mother told him that he should be grateful to the company and the people that gave him a job, when considering his physical defects and the stigma that goes with it, but he felt isolated, his distrust of others born from experience, and he travelled into himself trying to resolve emotional wounds in a solitary state where he used alcohol and drugs. He evolved into being a recluse by his late twenties, living off incapacity and disability welfare benefits for the great part. Donny was not able to explain why he connected with this physically weak person, but there was a closeness, a feeling of intimacy, and if there ever was something of a guru in a person's life, he was that for Donny. He felt that he could interpret his feelings through this ostracised man who had no place within the society into which he was born.

William Whitman read books in prison, and always had one on him. Donny was drawn into standing close to William Whitman in the recreation area, although not because he wanted to protect the weak man, who was surviving in a hostile environment. Why he wanted to speak to him was unknown to Donny, other than an obsessive interest in his physical difference. William Whitman spoke to Donny as if he was not present, and this objectivity made Donny feel safe with him as he did not feel pressure. And Donny spoke to him, but only in short, confused cryptic sentences, and William Whitman would respond with his objectivity, often speaking in riddles, and when they disengaged from their unusual form of communication Donny felt satisfied that he had exposed himself without feeling anxious in doing so. If anyone had listened in to their clandestine talks, which would have been difficult as they took place out of earshot, and if possible out of sight of others, they would not be able to make sense of the verbal conundrum that had taken place anyway.

Donny had stayed in contact with William Whitman and on occasion would have Dougie drive him to the desolate place that he had set up home in, as if having a need to engage in their enigmatic interaction.

Donny was not thinking about Little Willie during those weeks when he had meetings with the English contingent, his thoughts were consumed with a man that had become a constant in Donny Campbell's mind. The man was Geoffrey Stuart, the high placed lawyer. His presence loomed large and was burning into Donny's mind. It had become obsessive. All day, every day he imagined what he was going to say to him and how he was going to shove him to the ground and torture him. Scenarios filled his waking day and plagued him during the thin sleep that he had. Chaotic dreams tormented him with scenes of Geoffrey Stuart setting him up, siding with the English contingent, manipulating people around Donny, doing deals and changing the minds of high ranking police who had given Donny his place of power over the years. He would wake up in a panic.

Donny had never spoken to Geoffrey Stuart, a man who was widely known to all involved in crime and state politics. He represented the staunch tradition of Protestantism and loyalist interests, along with pushing the virtues of family ethics, hard work and praising a society that rewards honesty and merit, although Donny knew full well his real intentions, interests and activities.

Donny had seen Geoffrey Stuart on the television being interviewed about his concern for the high profile, and even the credence, that was given to paramilitary groups in the media, and of how he embraced and supported a free press and was against censorship. Stuart told of the misgivings he had when considering the intentions of people coming from a background of violence and corruption and who were now participating in the mainstream political arena.

Donny knew that Geoffrey Stuart had become a big player in the evolving structure within the Province, and his influence was being felt in the area of activities that had become Donny's domain.

Donny decided that there was some clearing up to do as his suspicions were becoming realised amongst some people in his own camp. He knew that if he did not keep a tight grip there were those who would scheme with others to bring him down. He had Dougie drive him over to where Geoffrey Stuart's family home was. He lived in a place on the coast not that far from Belfast called Hollywood, people having money live there. Itwas referred to as the Gold Coast in Northern Ireland. Donny would sit in the passenger seat of one of his Range Rovers, studying the house at all times of day and night. Donny found out where Geoffrey Stuart bought his Mercedes car, checking the number plate, just to see if it was significant in any way.

He found out the names of his three children, visited the schools the younger ones went to and the flat in Belfast where the oldest one, his daughter, was living while studying at Queens University. The eldest daughter became an object of compulsive preoccupation for Donny. He found out that she went to a club that his group was running. He checked membership slips, becoming excited when her name turned up. He asked Dougie to get a trusted youngster to give some feedback about what she drank, if she did drugs and what the names of her friends were. Donny spent hours looking at her car, and even went to the garage where it was serviced.

Geoffrey Stuart's wife was also a lawyer, both of them coming from similar upper middle class backgrounds in Northern Ireland. Donny learned that she was a good sportswoman when younger, and that she was a bright fledgling lawyer, sharper than her young husband, but childbirth retarded her career while her husband made a name for himself working on big name cases with the support of the state that condemned and pursued its victims with all the might of the law that it had created itself.

Geoffrey Stuart's face had been on regional television news programmes a number of times. He enjoyed the power, and demanded the protection that he was assured went with the function that he performed. So Donny had to be very careful in his tailing and monitoring of Geoffrey Stuart and his family.

In the past, names of nationalists, although innocent of committing crimes, had been passed to Donny who duly 'despatched' those men, and boys, and somewhere down the line

Stuart had been involved. Donny was preoccupied by Stuart and his family and was getting to know everything about them. He ran imaginary scenes of Stuart's family life in his mind, of the interaction that might take place between family members while at home. He then included himself in the family dynamics, as if he was a family friend, even as a paternal uncle figure, close to the bosom of the family, sharing family reunions and celebrations. Donny carefully constructed one fantasy of it being Christmas time and the family opening presents together, the teenager daughter giving him a hug because 'uncle Donny' was there to share Christmas with the family. And he would roll on the floor, allowing the young children to climb all over him – and then he would turn the situation, enjoying the horror in the face of Geoffrey Stuart's wife as he tears a knife through the pit of the teenage daughter's stomach, then picking her off the ground and shaking her blood over the Christmas tree. Elderly relatives are on the sofa, tied up with tinsel, with brown paper bags over their heads, the bags are splattered with blood because Donny had shot them in the head, and the two young children, also trussed, laying naked and dead with a piece of cardboard on top of them, the word 'turkeys' written on it. Geoffrey Stuart was in the garage, his head severed, in the boot of his Mercedes car, his waxy features still and his eyes staring in the darkness.

Donny exhausted himself thinking about scenarios of how he had entered their family life, something he had gone through with past people he had stalked, before his mind turned to ways of destroying them. The childminder's car was watched with interest. Donny had a plan of planting an explosive device in it, killing the young female childminder and Geoffrey Stuart's youngest child. This excited Donny. He had watched the childminder leave her house. She was an unmarried single mother from a middle class family doing a distance learning course that had some of the modules at Queen's University in Belfast city centre. It was a long drive for her, and when she hit the busy streets of Belfast, she also entered an area where Donny Campbell could exercise his malevolent intent with impunity.

Donny wanted to enter Stuart's house to smash and kill everything and everybody in it, but he knew it would be stupid to do so. He enjoyed the aching feeling of wanting to wreak pain on this man and ruin everything that he had. Donny's emotions blazed at the thought of Stuart and his family, his rage growing all day and every day. Donny thought of a plan, it was to do with Roddy Harding. Donny wondered if, with Harding's influence, Geoffrey Stuart could be got rid of. The Troubles had been used to pay generous dividends for the opportunistic lawyer, who publicly presented his loyalty to Crown and his countrymen, as many others had before him. The Troubles could also be used to discredit a person, and that reason was often an accepted basis for a sudden violent end to a person's life. Donny Campbell knew more than most, from the 'contracts' handed out to him to carry out 'executions' in the interests of the 'system,' that it was indiscriminate as long as the desired result was accomplished.

Sleep was something that never came easy to Donny Campbell, and in the recent weeks when it did come it was plagued with haunted images that played to a chaotic soundtrack. He would fall into lapses of restless unconsciousness, seeing the faces and hearing the voices of people that were plaguing him, and delirious images were repeatedly run at a great speed onto a flashing screen that played constantly in his mind.

The face and presence of Michael Connelly disturbed him. His voice ever present in a continual abstracted dialogue. He did not trust or like him from the first meeting they had above the pub in London, and trusted him less after meeting him in a 'safe house' in the Province. This had convinced him that Connelly was sent to Belfast under directions of those who had previously dealt directly with him, but now Connelly and other names were involved. It was to Connelly that he was to make contact with ever evolving dealings in the newly established drug networks operating throughout the Province.

The lawyer, Geoffrey Stuart, had been cut into the new dealings handsomely. Donny had learned this from whispers in the grass, touts who were usually low ranking police officers, one of them, a man called Stevens, was an occasional accomplice of Donny's. Michael Connelly was to be the new baron's main operative.

Donny sat up in bed, his back against the wall, and without consciously thinking of what he was doing he turned his head and looked at the wallpaper. Time and accumulated stains had dulled the print. Donny looked at one of the little islands, a part of it now worn from where he had leant his head against it over the years. He examined the palm tree, looking from the crudely drawn trunk to its base in the sand. The little island was surrounded in its own dab of sea, the water an impossible blue, carelessly drawn around the island in not more than a smudge. It represented an idyllic place in isolation, probably intended to comfort a person who had emerged from sleep or aid a tired head to slip into restful slumbers. Donny sat there with his neck strained, looking at the island for a long while. He climbed out of the uncomfortable bed, its bowed springs now useless to support a person to have relaxing sleep, but then its occupants had never known peaceful sleep. His jaw ached from being tensed, his mouth was dry from the constant rush of adrenaline excreting into his system, and through all this an excitement purred warmly in his stomach, giving a feeling of strength in his arms. He gripped his hands, making fists. He expelled air from his stomach and lungs. He knew what he was going to do.

Twenty-five

Donny tried to make arrangements to meet up with Connelly and Bishop, but every time a place and time was settled upon it was put off with an excuse of other commitments. Donny knew where the English were staying, and he learned through the grapevine that there were more people coming over from England. He was informed that Geoffrey Stuart had hit deals, was shaking the place down with his growing power and had been pointing his finger at those who were stubborn in yielding to the new order and its arrangements. Stuart had pointed his finger at men that Donny had known, and known of, for years, men from other factions that Donny's group had been having violent disputes with. There had been constant tit for tat killings and the turfs had been clearly demarcated as to who operates where, with Donny's group having the lion's share.

The network surrounding Donny's group brought in people from various positions in society, and because Belfast was a small place information was relayed quickly around and through the sectarian groups from all sides, and then winging its way across the countryside of the Province, where in even the most barren of places all voices and words were within the hearing of those that rule in their characteristic bludgeoning manner.

Donny Campbell's rage was growing. He knew that the state was evaluating the situation in Northern Ireland and putting in place new people to operate a much larger racket in drug pushing. The new people were seen to be more sophisticated. Organised crime was to be better protected, camouflaged by a more educated elite who were going to enjoy the benefits provided from the highly profitable market of the drug industry. Donny knew he was to be cut out, and the first man he wanted to get hold of was Geoffrey Stuart. His original intention was to contact him by phone and play it cool, but his anger boiled over and he ended up threatening the cunning lawyer. He contacted Stuart in his office. It was late afternoon. Donny looked through the glass sides of the public phone box at fine rain blown into wild swirling shapes by a thunderous wind that shrugged in bad temper under a low, heavy lead sky.

Geoffrey Stuart's face grew pale when he heard Donny's voice, and he looked around his office as if Donny was physically present in the room. Stuart looked over at his secretary who was sitting behind a desk tapping at a computer keyboard, and gestured for her to leave the office with the back of his podgy, pallid hand. When the door to his office closed behind his secretary Stuart breathed deeply, letting himself sink into his large leather armchair

'What is it, Mr Campbell?' he nearly spat the words into the telephone.

Donny started off slowly, trying to control himself as he explained in clumsy broken sentences his feelings towards the involvement of the English people and how he intended to maintain his grasp on the established order of things in the territory that he saw as his. But his restraint did not last long before he became aggressive. Geoffrey Stuart plotted as Donny spoke, looking at the cut of his trouser and how it hung on his expensive leather brogue shoe. As he listened and schemed, Stuart's eyes lowered and settled on a loose piece of thread that hung from the side of his sock. His eyes were heavy and hooded and his waxy complexion creased as the skin on his face folded and hid his eyes in the deep folds of flesh. He became like a predatory creature immersed just beneath the surface of the water, eyeing its quarry.

Donny told Stuart that he knew where his children went to school, where his eldest daughter lived in Belfast and the times that the childminder came to his house. Stuart gave no physical reaction. It just caused him to nod more slowly. He sat still, gazing at his shoe. Donny heard the words tumble out of his mouth, knowing that he did not want, or intend, to say them, but his threats of violence against Geoffrey Stuart and his family continued as he said, 'You listen to me, Stuart – and don't speak while I'm talking – fuck you! And fuck all you cunts – I know what you're up to – I can't get hold of that little sneak Connelly or the other English cunts, and I'm meant to be a player in all of this.

'I've been keeping the different groups from biting each other's fucking heads off, and I'm being pushed out of the big deal that's going on.

'They might be bringing in slick cunts like you – but you know what?

'You'll squeal like a baby having its leg torn off.

'And you listen to me Stuart – your daughter, the one at Queens University – some of my men have been watching that piece of slag meat for a while now – like where she goes for a fuck with her student friends – who knows, if she's fucking unlucky she might have a date with Donny boy – fuck you, and watch your back you cunt.'

Donny had now finished with plans and bluffs. His way was of action against all who opposed him and planned against him. Donny slammed the telephone down, stood glaring at it for a few seconds, and then smashed his fist into it.

Stuart sat in his chair, unmoving and contemplative. Sighing deeply, he leant forward and replaced the telephone on its receiver. His hand remained hovering over the telephone for a few seconds as he gained his thoughts before picking up the telephone and dialling a number. His expression did not change as he breathed in and rehearsed in his mind what he was going to say. As the other person answered his physical presentation moulded into what he saw as being appropriate for whom he was talking to.

The person who answered the telephone was Chief Constable Murray, the man who had been sitting with Philip Alexander and Edward Scriver in the Conference Room in the city hall. He was sitting behind a large desk, on which, besides having a folder, pen and the usual administrative matter, there were many photographs. Some were of his family, but most were of the police force, some going back many years. There were also photographs of Philip Alexander shaking hands with past Prime Ministers, but in prime position was a photograph of him shaking hands with a leading member of the British Royal family.

The walls of his office were festooned with flags, photographs and a large oil painted portrait of an initial forefather of his regiment. This was mirrored on the opposite wall by a large photograph of him in full regimental uniform.

145

Murray pressed his lips together as Stuart sprang immediately into his speech, telling of how Donny Campbell had threatened him and his family, and of how Campbell had details of his children's coming and going. He gave his plans to Murray for getting rid of Donny Campbell. Murray felt that his tone all the while was consciously posturing a courtroom patter in its style, and he gave a faint frown at what he detected was a veiled patronising edge to the lawyer's tone.

Stuart relaxed into his dialogue, feeling that he was in control. 'He has been useful, but it has been decided to move on and expand.'

He spoke of the involvement of the English who had arrived in the Province. 'These people are more professional about their work – we have to take it away from the home-grown buffoons – give them cheap beer and meat, and the little rewards for good behaviour, but don't let them have responsibility – they don't know what it is – they're not capable. These people from the mainland have links and sources, a wider experience and aren't bogged down in provinciality – they're more accomplished, everyone knows their boundaries, and keeps to them – they see the bigger picture – the big fish small pond scenario is finished here – it's bigger business and better times.'

He paused, considered what he was going to say and then spoke in a way as if he was standing next to Murray and had leant close to him in a confidential manner, indulging the older man to the scheme of things, as if tapping him on his shoulder. 'Better times indeed – for you – you'll not be forgotten.'

He smiled a slippery smile into the receiver, feeling pleased with himself in the way he was handling things. But he did not see the expression on Chief Constable Murray's face, or the way his eyes narrowed and the bones tightening in his jaw.

Twenty-six

Donny Campbell was working on plans of his own as Stuart and Murray put down their telephones. Donny had contacted Dougie, telling him that there was a lot of 'work' to be done. Dougie knew that Donny Campbell was on a mission with amplified emotions, and in turn this raised the adrenaline rush in his own body.

What he actually thought was never open to question, but his wife also shared his dedicated loyalty to the paramilitary group and Donny Campbell. He was a family man and did family things. On Saturdays they would visit, along with thousands of other families in a trail of traffic, the emerging retail parks on the edge of Belfast, participating in the joys of consumerism as they shopped with their young children for the latest fads, and completed the family outing with a pizza. It was the way of things, and he played his role.

Donny directed Dougie to drive to an area of town that was well known for those who had fallen to the side of society, propelled to their wretched position by alcohol, drugs and the situation in which they lived. Dougie parked by the side of a block of flats that were mainly derelict. Donny got out of the Range Rover and walked into the entrance of the block, purposefully, knowing exactly where he was going and what he was going to do. He climbed the two flights of stairs, holding his breath to block out the stench of urine, excrement, blood and the other bodily fluids that contributed to the thick, acrid fetor that humans leave in their wake. The walls of the stairwell were sprayed and scored with images, symbols and names, all of which belonged in the shadows of a society. Donny's eyes were drawn to an old jacket that lay on one of the stairs. It was crumpled and battered and was about the size for an eleven-year-old, but it did not take his attention longer than a second.

The small front doors of the flats faced each other along a narrow passage, every one of them had marks left from kicks and sharp implements, and some also had graffiti sprayed on them.

Donny knocked on one of the doors and waited no longer than three seconds before barging the door from its hinges with his shoulder. A rat, the size of a small cat, darted away from the doorway as Donny entered and scurried along the floor, which looked like it had never been cleaned, into the kitchen. Donny took the few steps needed to reach a room on his left and pushed the door open.

There were two men in there, one in his late teens the other in his early thirties. The older man lay on a couch covered with a heavily soiled blanket. The younger man sat on a kitchen chair, his eyes nearly closed. He too had a blanket over him, from which his thin wrists and hands emerged. Deep cuts, scabs, and Indian ink tattoos covered the bleached skin. The other man was barely conscious, his eyes buried somewhere in the painful looking slits that Donny looked into. Donny dropped a bag of heroin onto the floor. Both men looked slowly down at it, Donny knew they would take it in one go, and there was more than enough to kill the pair of them. Donny pulled a packet from his pocket, and from the packet he took out a syringe and fixed a needle into it. Nothing was said as he pulled back the blanket from the man on the couch. Donny quickly checked his thin, scabby arms and then decided to pull the blanket back further, exposing the man's wasted legs. He stuck the needle into the top of the man's leg, near his groin, and filled the syringe with blood that Donny knew was infected with HIV. The man did not flinch. His dull eyes lingered on the bag that lay on the floor.

Donny turned, walked out of the room and left the door of the flat open behind him.

Twenty-seven

Donny spent the remainder of the day chasing up people for information, some whom he was close to and others he was not. The word got round that Donny Campbell was on the warpath and that he was spiralling into a paranoiac frenzy. So the warning was out to be ready and armed, prepared if he suddenly turned against you.

In the early evening Donny asked Dougie to drop him off at his uncle's old house and to pick him up later on that night. Dougie was pleased because it was his youngest child's birthday and he wanted to spend some time at home. He did not mention it to Donny because he knew that Donny was not in the right frame of mind to talk to about such things.

Donny wanted to rest. Too pumped up to eat he mixed himself a protein drink, injected steroids into his buttock, pulled the curtains together and lay on the bed. He looked about the room, his eyes flitting around objects as he thought about doing something that might satisfy him. He decided against watching one of the video recordings that he had made. Pulling a blanket over himself he started to masturbate, his mind like a skidpan with heated ideas, images and voices from broken conversations sliding across it. He started to ejaculate as a vivid scenario of him crushing a man's head in various ways fixed in his brain. He relaxed, his muscles easing. Breathing deeply, he turned onto his side, and just as he lost consciousness his eyes lingered on one of the little islands set in its own bit of blue water on the wallpaper. But he was asleep before any other thoughts came to his mind.

Twenty-eight

Earlier that day it was a pleasant scene in the city centre as sunlight reflected from the new glass buildings. There was a bright airiness in the shopping area as the bustling shoppers swarmed around the pedestrianised streets. Katie Preston sat behind her desk looking at the sun ricocheting from the shop windows opposite and catching the silver balls juggled by a street entertainer, whose audience stood around him in a semicircle.

Katie was glad when the building society emptied, it gave her some breathing space, but just as she looked down at her desk to get on with her work a loud tapping on the window caused her to look up. It was David, standing outside with one of his workmates. The two young men fell about laughing at seeing the surprised look on Katie's face. She was a little embarrassed by the attention drawn to her. Standing up and walking to the door she looked at the other staff in the building society, one of them smiled warmly at her. Katie was pleased to see David, and excited as she had news of the mortgage that they were going for and the house that they were intending to buy. They arranged to meet later when she had finished work for a coffee in the newly opened Starbucks. Katie went back into the shop and got behind her desk, smiling at the woman who smiled at her earlier. A feeling of butterflies that unsettled her stomach gave way to a warm, pleasant feeling. She smiled, at nothing and everything, feeling snug behind her desk.

Later on, Katie and David held hands across the table as they had a cup of coffee, talking of the mortgage and the house, their hands squeezed together as they looked at each other. The feeling of sharing a life and building a future brought them closer, together as one. Katie was going to her health club later that night and they agreed to meet at her house afterwards. David spoke of his brothers, and especially of his concern for Ian, his older brother. Katie let him talk, knowing that he needed to get it off his chest. David had heard that Ian was getting himself involved at a high level in the criminal world, and though it was good for his street credibility among those that he hung around with, he was only ever going to be used as a boy to run errands and carry drugs, and then after being used, to be extinguished in the routinely horrible way.

Having finished what he wanted to say, David looked down at the table. Katie leaned forward and gently kissed the worried lines on his forehead, the worry bonding them closer together. She loved him so much and she knew things were going to work out for them, and who knows she would tell herself, maybe their future might be elsewhere, in England, even the United States. They were both hard working and wanted the good things in life, enjoying a culture that involved activities in the sun, something rarely experienced in Belfast. But the, seemingly, omnipresent clouds that shrouded the city where they lived could not darken or dampen the love they had for one another or the optimism they shared at their future possibilities.

They kissed and parted after agreeing where to meet up with some of their friends at the weekend. It was somewhere in Belfast's Golden Mile, an area of vibrancy emerging from the times of the Troubles when the city centre was vacated of tourists, but now a welcome intrusion making its presence felt in the city. It was corporate, young and diverse in ethnicity, a blaze of neon offered the usual design houses, theme bars, night clubs, pizza parlours and burger bars. Student life had come into its own and a sense of joining the wider consumer community had been ignited by brightly lit, late night businesses of entertainment, where the offerings are devoured greedily and thankfully as if the city had woken from a long dark age and come alive.

Twenty-nine

Later that night Donny was sitting on the side of the bed looking at his reflection in the full length mirror when Dougie's dutiful knock sounded on the front door of the house. Donny was dressed in a tight black tee shirt, jeans and trainers. He picked up a black flying jacket from the back of a chair and left the room in a sober, determined mood.

They arrived at a large warehouse where a rave was taking place and entered the building through a side door. Two men working as 'security' nodded at Donny as he and Dougie approached the door. Music pumped and reverberated in the main area of the warehouse, but in the back of the building the sound was dampened. A dingy corridor in the back of the warehouse led to a room that was used as an office. It had not been decorated for years and had a derelict feel about it, the only furniture being a few chairs and two small sofas.

The room was crowded with a group of men and two women, most of them were holding bottles. Johnny Ferguson was standing next to a man called Hudson, who carried an attitude of being the principal character in the room. A young man in his early twenties entered the room, this was Ian McClelland, the brother of Katie Preston's fiancé David McClelland. Ian was thin with a pock marked face and an unhealthy washed-out complexion. He snatched at the door handle in haste, his furtive face contorted in several directions as he sidled up to Hudson. He said, 'Donny Campbell's just turned up – he's coming through now.' He then added with a sly grin, 'I saw him in the passenger seat of his Range Rover.' Nerves quivered all over Ian McClelland's face as he licked his lips. Hudson squared his shoulders, fixed his jaw and twisted his mouth as he looked over at the doorway. He then looked quickly around the room and asked, 'What the fuck does he want?'

Donny entered the room before anyone could answer. Dougie toyed nonchalantly with a set of keys as he followed behind Donny. Donny positioned himself in the centre of the room and looked around at the people in there. His eyes settled briefly on the sly young man who informed Hudson of his arrival before focusing on Hudson. One of the men in the room offered Donny a bottle of beer, but he refused it with the faintest movement of his head. Hudson was wary, baring his teeth in that primordial grin of false peace. The atmosphere in the room turned cold and still.

Donny's voice was flat, looking at Hudson he asked, 'How's things here?'

'Fine, just fine.' Hudson replied, watching Donny carefully. 'A good night's work.'

Donny looked around at the others in the room. He returned to Hudson and said, 'I'll say this in front of everyone here – I've been hearing a lot of things about what's going on, and just one thing is about the filth Stevens. He's working for a cut of his own now. He's a copper going out on a limb, becoming greedy and he's moving some of our boys against each other. He's doing a snidey behind everyone's backs with his other people.'

Donny looked at Hudson and tension grew in the room. Donny went on, 'But then there are others around here who are being snidey.'

Hudson watched Donny, meeting his gaze for a few seconds until deciding to confront him. He opened with a grin. 'No worries here, Donny boy.'

Donny was not convinced. He stared at Hudson who continued to grin as he said, 'Smooth as silk – like clockwork – everybody's happy.'

Hudson nodded, it became apparent that he had finished speaking. Donny's stare intensified as he looked at Hudson. He snapped, 'I'm not happy.'

Hudson's grin widened. Shrugging his shoulders he looked around the room and said, 'Well – some people never are.'

'Oh, explain that one to me.' Donny said, his eyes following Hudson's every movement, 'You see, because I don't understand.'

Hudson looked down at the floor, and taking a deep breath he stepped forward having made a decision.

'Well, you tell me, Donny – when are you happy?'

He nodded at what he had just said and looked around the room, as if for support. He turned to Donny. 'For fuck's sake, you ought to chill a little – if you knew fucking how.'

Donny did not respond. Hudson's grin returned, gaining confidence he was set to challenge Donny. One of the two women, Pauline, smiled at the situation, anticipating what might happen. Hudson waved his hand at Donny. 'Come on man, everyone knows – well – you know.'

He lifted his head, revealing a devious smirk.

Donny's tone had heated, but his expression had not changed. 'I'll tell you what I do fucking know – there's a snake in the grass.'

His eyes narrowed as he looked at Hudson. 'And I don't want him to creep under the door and do a little deal with the copper and the others.'

An uneasy silence came upon the room. Hudson and Donny stood just a few feet apart. They were given greater presence in the room by a naked light bulb that hung above them. Hudson broke the mood as he started to speak, his tone started defensively but grew in disdain. 'Come on, Donny, we go back a long way.'

But Donny was not swayed. He stared at Hudson, blood draining from his face and Hudson realised that there was going to be a confrontation. A shot of fear crossed his face, but he forced it to the back of his mind as he prepared himself for what was likely to happen. Donny's face was now white, devoid of any colour. His eyes became dead and he raised his chin a fraction. 'You've been under suspicion – and you've been making remarks.'

Hudson knew that if Donny wanted to deal with him it would most probably be in public, a display in front of other members. It was the way things were done, as a warning and also to show who was in charge and how things were dealt with. He had accepted that Donny had turned up to deal with something, and now he had to confront it.

'Oh, that's right is it?' Hudson said, 'Well, let me tell you some home truths here.'

He looked about the room, all eyes were on him and he nodded, now committed to continue. 'Let's say it in front of everyone –

cos everyone fucking knows – fuck me, Donny, we all know what you are. Look at you!'

He checked quickly across at Johnny Ferguson, glancing under his eyes. But Donny caught it. It was a look that asked for back up, and had been discussed beforehand. Donny looked over at Johnny Ferguson, watching him leaning against the door frame, and then he looked at Pauline, who looked as if she wanted to laugh. Hudson was staring at Donny, and a smirk ripened across his face into a disdainful sneer as he spoke, this time with more confidence as if thinking he had support from some people in the room, especially from Johnny Ferguson. 'When we were wee lads, just discovering our dicks, and we realised the wee girl from across the road had tits and hips, you were never there sharing your feelings – always hiding behind your hard man act – combat trousers – your knife collection – and the set of wee weights in your bedroom. You never looked at the girls – and we noticed this, all that time ago, and then we became family men – but you stayed the same – well, got worse – Jesus, you most probably wanked yourself off watching Marc Bolan on the television – sitting on your ma's sofa, while she made your tea in the kitchen…'

But these were the last words he said. Donny stepped forward quickly and hit him on the side of his head, a brightly shined knuckleduster glinted on the hand that delivered the blow. Hudson dropped heavily and directly to the ground, the side of his head covered in blood that poured from his temple in a pulsating thick trail. Donny stood over Hudson, grabbed his head and pulled him up from the ground. He looked at Dougie and laughed. Dougie grinned, and Donny looked into Hudson's face and then bit into his cheek. He spat out a chunk of flesh. Donny stared at the gushing wound as blood quickly filled the hole in the side of Hudson's face. Donny let him drop to the ground and turned, glaring at Pauline. She looked at him, her breathing fast and short. Donny looked around the room and then shouted, 'Out! Get out of here.'

As the group moved towards the door, Donny pointed at Johnny Ferguson, Pauline and Ian McClelland, instructing them to stay and for the others to leave, and all the while Hudson's intermittent groaning filled the room. Donny looked at Ian

McClelland, who gulped down any saliva he could muster in his dry mouth. He had been standing watching Donny earlier with his arms out to his sides, as if he was going to be involved in physical action, and Donny had noticed. Donny composed himself, an empty smile on his face as he put his hand with the knuckleduster in his jacket pocket and walked towards Ian McClelland. He said, 'You tell tales and run errands – here,' and Donny's hand flashed from his pocket. He was holding an ice lolly stick in front of the young man's face. Ian McClelland jumped back, and then steadied himself, puzzled, he looked at the lolly stick, his eyes darting furiously around the room in the shade afforded by the peak of his baseball cap.

Donny said, 'Here's a sweetie that I've been keeping for someone like you.'

Johnny Ferguson and Pauline watched Donny as he stood in front of Ian McClelland, nodding at him, his smile staying the same. Donny held the lolly stick away from his face and then quickly pushed it in front of his eyes. The scared young man was startled, and just as he began to relax a confused look showed on his face, but it was too late because Donny stabbed him in the side of his ribcage with a stiletto knife he was holding in his other hand. The young man's eyes froze before breaking into pain, and his mouth opened, letting out a cry that had no sound. He leant against Donny, who smiled, his hand holding the handle of the stiletto. Donny looked at the lolly stick while speaking to Ian McClelland who was losing consciousness. 'If you look on the side, there's always a joke.' He read the writing on the side of the stick. 'There's no joke on this one, things have changed – there's no fun anymore – just a safety warning.'

Ian McClelland started to choke. Donny read what was written on the stick. 'Be careful how you dispose of me – I am dangerous – children can choke and die.'

Donny looked at Ian McClelland and said, 'Now they tell me.'

Ian McClelland began to spasm and he groaned. The expression on Donny's face changed, his lip curled and his eyes deepened. He stepped backwards, letting him drop to the ground. Ian McClelland landed in a position of sitting upright, his back against a filing cabinet. He died, with his eyes open, staring in surprise and pain.

Donny looked from Johnny Ferguson and Pauline to Hudson. Donny suddenly became fired up, snarling, he reached down and grabbed the crotch of Hudson's trousers and pulled his trousers and underpants down. He punched Hudson in his face with the knuckleduster. Hudson's nose snapped and a small, dainty fountain of blood released itself from the bridge of his nose. Donny stood up and grinned. He looked at Dougie and asked, 'Dougie, may I have a cigarette please?'

Dougie lit a cigarette and handed it to him. Donny looked at the cigarette and then bent down, grabbed Hudson's penis and stubbed the lit end of the cigarette into it, forcing the burning tip under the skin. Hudson screamed and rolled around on the floor. Donny kicked Hudson unconscious, laughing all the while. He then positioned Hudson's head on its side and delivered an accurate blow with the knuckleduster into his temple. He punched him again, and again, the sound of bone splintering cracked out. The side of Hudson's head become soft and Donny's fist appeared to sink right into the skull.

Donny stood back from Hudson, breathing heavily he looked at Johnny Ferguson and Pauline. Donny and Johnny Ferguson stared at each other. Donny's stare penetrated right through him, and in Donny's mind everything became silent, as if entering a void. The music from the warehouse having gone, all sound had gone as he looked at Johnny Ferguson, except the voice of Malc, Johnny Ferguson's younger brother. That was clear in his mind from the time in borstal, and he listened to the words that Malc spoke all those years before. 'Oh yeah, my brother Johnny, he'll muller them so bad, and no one, and I mean no fucking one ever gets away with anything with Johnny.

'Cos my brother has a reputation see, and it's Johnny's thing. He'll always get you back. You'll do nothing to Johnny Ferguson and get away with it. Never. He'll always get you back.'

The voice trailed off and the sounds from the warehouse returned. Donny pushed past Johnny Ferguson, opened the door and left with Dougie walking behind him. Johnny Ferguson watched Donny leave, glaring at the space in the doorway left by him. Pauline looked from the body of Hudson to the dead young man, Ian McClelland, seated upright, the stiletto sticking out of

157

the side of his body and his eyes looking forward, as if waiting for an answer.

Thirty

The Range Rover drove slowly away from the warehouse. Dougie allowed the wheel to spin lightly through his hands, his manner relaxed and unhurried. It was like any leisurely day trip style of driving, at ease, content, as if time had been taken care of. Donny looked out of the side window, trying to make out the shapes of passing buildings in the darkness. He told Dougie to drive to a lock-up garage on the edge of town that had been used from time to time to store things. Donny watched Dougie as he drove, noting the easy manner about him, his workmanlike approach, a professionalism about his driving. Everything was correct and all procedures were adhered to.

'It's a one man band,' Donny said to Dougie. 'One man and his friend – no back up, no bastard is to be trusted – we'll take a spin out to the lock-up, I've had some hardware delivered, little gifts to take to the party tonight.'

Dougie's eyes left the road momentarily as he glanced across at Donny. Donny noticed this and went on to explain what he meant. 'I'm off to see those English fuckers, pay them a little visit – there will be four of the fuckers, in that old farmhouse they use to put their people up.'

Dougie nodded, his eyes not straying from the road in front of him.

The lock-up was one of a row at the back of housing on a new estate. Dougie waited in the car with the engine running while Donny unlocked the padlock, went into the lock-up and returned with a holdall. They then drove off in the direction of the old farmhouse. Donny knew the English contingent would be there, and he knew how many there were. It was part of the information that he had learned earlier in the day.

After driving for twenty minutes Donny told Dougie to pull over. It was dark, the only sound coming from a shrieking wild animal, probably a female fox, maybe a weasel or perhaps a stoat. Donny opened the holdall, his breathing now shallow and his mind focused. He turned on the interior lighting in the car and his eyes lingered for a few seconds on the contents in the holdall. He pulled out a gun, an MP5 and inspected it, pleased with what he was looking at he placed the machine gun on the dashboard and took a Browning pistol from the holdall, which was also placed on the dashboard. He eased out from the bag a sawn-off shotgun. Donny placed the sawn-off in his lap and pulled three hand grenades, one by one out of the bag and placed them carefully on the dashboard. He took out rounds of ammunition for both guns and cartridges for the sawn-off, and placed them strategically on the dashboard.

Without showing any emotion Dougie watched Donny take the contents out of the bag, and he watched Donny take a plastic coin bag containing amphetamine powder from his pocket. Donny licked his finger, rolled it in the powder and rubbed it over his teeth and gums. After repeating this a few times he then poured a little mountain of the powder on the back of his hand and snorted it. He went through the ritual twice, once for each nostril. He looked at the bag, and then to Dougie, offering him some of it. Dougie declined with a short shake of his head.

Donny went about checking the guns, loading them, putting ammunition and cartridges in his pockets and finally throwing the empty holdall onto the back seat. He put the grenades in his lap and nodded to Dougie to get going. The skin on Donny's face had tightened. He licked his lips. He was numb, buzzing, and excitement poured through his body in a charge that brought a nervous laugh, and in the pit of his stomach a dense tingling gave way to sharp pains that dulled to what he felt was a pleasant discomfort.

The lights of the Range Rover beamed onto the road in front of them, but also brightened the hedges at its sides. Donny's eyes were fixed on the blurring rush of hedges. His eyes widened. There were no thoughts, just a feeling, and they were now no more than two minutes from the old farmhouse.

Thirty-one

The Range Rover coasted to a standstill a stone's throw distance from the old farmhouse, the lights were on in nearly every room. The car was quiet and still as both men looked at the isolated building. Donny's tongue unstuck itself from the roof of his mouth, it was dry with the adrenaline rush and amphetamine powder. He fingered the button to unwind his window. Dougie saw what he was doing and turned the key one notch in the ignition, a red light appeared on the instrument panel and Donny's window unwound silently. An animal called out in the distance and music could be heard coming from the farmhouse.

Donny began to talk, his voice low and his eyes not leaving the farmhouse, as if he could see the people inside it. 'The man Connelly is a grass. He's come over here to burn us up – to monitor what's happening and then to set us up for the chop.'

Dougie's eyes drifted from the farmhouse to Donny, watching him, and Donny continued in his trance-like condition, his voice a dull monotone as he talked of conspiracies and of how he had to protect himself. He stopped in mid-sentence, staring at the farmhouse, and without saying anything he pulled the lever in the door, opened it and got out. The action was performed agilely and in silence. He handed Dougie the Browning and some ammunition. 'Follow me, as always, watching what I can't see,' he said, and Dougie nodded, looking at the gun in his hand, feeling its grip, weighing it. Donny picked up the MP5 and the grenades, and holding the sawn-off close to his chest he walked towards the farmhouse, leaving the car door open, and Dougie would do the same.

Donny stood thirty yards from the farmhouse. He knew the piece of ground that it was on and the inside of the building itself, having been there before on a couple of occasions to meet people who had been put up in the past. He continued to walk towards the back door of the house until he was standing a stride away from the door, his breathing eased as it always did just before engaging in a violent act. A warm feeling filled him, especially his stomach, and it spread throughout his body. His hands felt warm and strong, an involuntary smile appeared on his face and he had to resist the temptation to laugh. Donny was not nervous, but excited. He was enjoying himself, and a feeling of vindication filled him with pride because he saw his actions as deserved retribution. He was justified to do it because of what the people in the building were going to do to him.

Donny listened to the music, something about it puzzled him. The voice was not as it should be, and when hearing laughter he realised they had a karaoke machine in there. One of them was singing over Blondie's 'Tide is High.' Donny listened to the voice, trying to distinguish if it was Michael Connelly who was singing. The song ended and laughter and shouting erupted. Another song started, but this time it was not them playing around with the karaoke, it was the real recording. 'Reach Out I'll be There,' by The Four Tops started to play. Donny's attention was drawn to the music, listening to the start of the song, he frowned as he considered it not the sort of music he would have expected them to be listening to.

He stepped to the side of the door and tapped the barrel of the sawn-off against the window of the back room. The light was on with the curtains drawn, and he waited, again listening to the song. But there was no response, so he tapped again, the taps growing louder. He continued to tap, the glass nearly breaking, all the while his eyes fixed on any movement behind the curtain and checking the back door. Listening for sounds, he continued to tap the barrel of the sawn-off against the window, and without seeing anybody inside the room approach the window, a man's face suddenly appeared with the curtain flung over his head, but, just as the man's eyes started to adjust to the dark outside, he jumped back at seeing a person standing there. His mouth was just beginning to form a word, of warning maybe, when a shotgun blast took the top of his head off. Donny turned and fired two shots into the back door, at the places where the locks were fitted on the other side. He stepped into the kitchen, knowing that they would not come rushing into the room. His eyes passed quickly over the body of the man he had just killed, noticing the way the top of his head had flicked back and was now secured only by gristle and skin, acting like a flimsy hinge at the back of his head, and reminding Donny of sweets that were around when he was a young boy, and Donny wondered if they were still around. They came in a little plastic container and had a head at the top, you flipped the head back with your thumb and a little sweet appeared through the mouth. The heads came in various designs. Donny tried to remember what were they called, and as this thought passed through his mind his eyes glared at the open door that led to the hallway and the other two rooms that made up the downstairs of the house. The music was still playing and he noticed the volume had not changed.

Donny assumed they were hiding, and with an easy action he fired the sawn-off into the open doorway and threw the gun in the direction where he had fired. It bounced off the door frame into the opening of the living room. Before the gun had settled on the floor Donny had the MP5 ready. He stepped backwards, carefully, retracing his steps out of the back door. Donny took one of the grenades from his pocket and looked up at an upstairs window that he knew was a small bedroom. The light in the bedroom went off. He swapped the grenade into his right hand, lobbed it through the window and threw himself onto the ground. The explosion took the window clean out of the stone wall. The sounds of screaming and shouting came from inside the building. Donny was up on his feet and into the kitchen, all the while conscious of The Four Tops song that continued to play. As Donny reached the doorway in the kitchen he saw Michael Connelly's face at the bottom of the stairs directly in front of him, and in a fraction of a second Donny deduced that Michael Connelly had intentions of going upstairs, but the grenade had wrecked the staircase making it impossible to climb. Michael Connelly was shocked, his face seeming smaller than Donny remembered. Connelly gritted his teeth in anger as he raised a gun, a pistol, but before he could fire it Donny sprayed him with the MP5, aiming at his head and body. As Donny did this he dropped to one knee, making himself a smaller target. Michael Connelly was literally torn to pieces, parts of his head and face smashed through a window. Amongst the debris of flesh, blood, bone and clothing a gold medallion and chains were stuck onto the wall.

Donny stood up quickly, checking around himself, but also looking at the remains of Michael Connelly, remembering what he thought of Connelly the first time they met in England. A voice sounded behind Donny, it said 'D C.' Donny did not have to turn, he knew it was Dougie. It was what he had always called Donny when they were youths and had continued to call him that when they were on a 'mission.' Donny turned right into the living room, and saw a man sitting on the floor by the music system. He was a man in his early thirties and very overweight. Donny pointed the MP5 at him. The man squeezed his eyes shut and let out a guttural roar that climbed higher in tone until he was screaming. Donny walked towards the man, and then stopped as the song ended. He waited, as if for another song to start playing. But there was not one, and Donny checked quickly over his shoulder at Dougie standing in the doorway. Donny knelt down next to the man, looking at his vast belly and fat face. The man watched Donny. His face, that would normally have been red, was stone white, his small eyes pleading and having no control over his mouth, his teeth were chattering and his lips danced at angles. Donny placed the MP5 on the floor and from the inside pocket of his jacket took out the syringe containing the infected blood he had taken from the addict earlier in the day. He pulled off the safety cover from the needle and stabbed it into one of the layers of veins in the man's forearm. The man flinched, but Donny held him in place as he tried to pull away.

'A present from Ireland,' Donny said, and as he finished injecting the blood he looked into the man's face. 'Something to surf on – the best stuff – but you gotta be careful, because too much can make you lose weight – but then, fatso, there's no need to join a slimming club.' He grinned at the man as he pulled the needle out of his arm, dropped it onto the floor and picked up the MP5.

Donny stood up. 'Watch him,' he said to Dougie as he checked his gun and turned towards the doorway. Donny tried to climb up what was left of the stairs, clambering over rubble and broken wood, then stopped when seeing a foot on the floor at the base of the banister. Not able to climb the rest of the stairs, Donny jumped and grabbed the foot, pulling it with him as he came back down. The body of a man followed. Donny pulled it to the bottom of the stairs and stood over the dead man. It was the body of Duane Bishop. His face was blackened by dust and half his torso was missing. Donny looked at the remaining arm, the frayed threads of skin hanging from the body and the torn trousers. Donny thought about what a sharp dresser he was before turning away and going back into the living room.

'That's it – that's the lot,' Donny said, 'let's get rolling,' and he pointed the MP5 at the man's knees and fired off a blast of rounds into them. As the man writhed across the floor Donny said, 'Now don't you go running after us, and all.' He nodded at Dougie to get moving and the two of them left quickly, making their way back to the car.

Donny laughed, his voice dry and hard as Dougie drove in his controlled way. Donny pushed an old cassette of The Velvet Underground into the player, 'European Son' started to play. He raised the volume, as loud as the system would go and sat back in the seat. Donny bit the back of his hand as he stared through the windscreen, nearly gagging and letting the screeching sounds of the song wash through him.

Thirty-two

It was a busy evening in The Royal Bar. Donny entered through the door looking around the familiar surroundings. The atmosphere felt surreal to him, the noise, the shouting and the music merged into a jumbled distant sound. He stood at the counter, alone. A few people raised their glasses and smiled at him, but he barely acknowledged them. The television flickered and Donny looked up at it. He shouted at the barman to turn the sound up, Lord Roddy Harding was talking in the House of Lords. The barman fiddled with a dial on the wall and the music increased in volume. Donny shouted at him, 'Turn the fucking sound down – the music I fucking mean – turn the television up.' The barman rushed to do the correct procedure and the voice of Roddy Harding could be heard quite clearly. 'Drugs and the paramilitary – the feeding of perverse egos – fear and ignorance – money and power. These people see themselves as untouchables – an inconceivable idea, which sickens the stomachs of all decent people who live in the Province. We will never accept the hypocrisy, the proffering of role models that are beneath the gutter world of diseased rats. These self-appointed barons, who rule their grubby areas with bullying arrogance will not win the day for me.

'These individuals are to have a war declared upon them – by us, the decent members of our society – and I, personally, would like to turn the key in the lock of the cell door that slams behind these thugish, vile men.'

Donny looked around the bar. Nobody was taking any notice of Roddy Harding's speech, that was a recording from earlier in the day when there was a special debate on the 'Northern Irish problem.'

Roddy leant forward, playing to the camera and said, 'Trust me, when I say, I will fight with all the power that I have, and fight with the last breath that I have in my body to bring about normality, so that ordinary people can go about their lives.

'God help me – and God help us, for together we will lay down the challenge – and we will win, so that our children can enjoy a quality of life that they deserve.'

The picture on the screen changed to a news desk in the studio with a man and woman sitting behind it, both smiling.

Donny looked away from the television, gazing moodily at the bottle in front of him, and just as his thoughts were about to settle a voice caused him to look up.

'Donny, how is it?' It was the man who ran the karaoke. His sweaty face shook a nervous greeting at Donny as he paid for a cola, specifically asking for a can or bottle. Donny offered half a nod, his expression not changing as he looked at the man.

The man went on, 'We're all getting older.' It was idle banter. He usually made a point of avoiding Donny, and anyone to do with him, but he felt he wanted to say hello on this occasion. He had known Donny, or had seen him around, since he was a child, having been born and lived down the same road as Donny.

Donny could not bring himself to nod at the man's remark, his eyes averted to a point on the bar, then back to the man, taking in his dyed thinning hair and the weakness in the man's podgy face.

'Haven't said hello to you for a long time.' The man said, and he smiled, but despised himself for speaking to Donny Campbell. The reason why he had spoken to him was because he thought Donny might help him in some way. He was an influential person, with connections in clubs, and probably in the media. The man thought that as they came from the same place and went to the same school, there might, but only might, be a chance that Donny would introduce him to people who could get him bookings, and even a big break, maybe on the radio. Donny went to nod, but stopped himself. The man saw a glimpse of acceptance in Donny, so he said, 'Your ma and mine cleaned at the hospital, Donny – do you remember?'

Donny stared at him, like he was staring at a history that he denied existing. He was sickened by what he saw as a feeble, defeated man. Donny looked into the man's face, which led the man to mistakenly think that Donny was considering him, but Donny's mind was travelling back to his childhood. Donny remembered the man's mother, she reminded Donny of his own mother. She always did when he was very young, seeing her walking down the road, sometimes, at first sight, he thought it was his mother, laden with bags of shopping, head down, trudging tirelessly, threadbare and worn out, aware of her own disadvantaged position. Donny and other youngsters knew full well of their plight, of being poor and the limitations that went with it, and learned not to expect too much. This was something they were told all year round, not just on birthdays and at Christmas. Donny remembered that the man's mother and his own scivvied at the local hospital, both having that wearied look, holes in the elbows of their cardigans, hands deformed from hard work, it was as if their femininity had been worked out of them from constant kneeling, scrubbing with hot water and bleach, anxious about lack of money, their faces etched with eternal worry.

Donny's eyes focused on the man and he pushed back his thoughts of long ago. He wanted to smash the front of the man's face into the back of his head. He looked at the man's small, doughy hands, the expansive soft belly spilling over his belt, his short legs in unfashionable trousers and shoes that were in style many years ago, worn by provincial media types. Donny wanted to wipe him away, brush him aside with a sweep of his arm and in doing so hopefully remove him and all the memories from years ago out his mind. The man looked at Donny, realising that he was not going to speak and noticing the deep melancholy showing in his face. He did not want to upset him so he nodded and said, 'Well, take care of yourself, Donny,' and he slid away from the bar, breathing hard, pretending that he had something to do with setting up the karaoke.

Donny did not look at the man as he walked away. He turned, facing the counter and stared moodily at the bottle in front of him. A group of people were sitting at a table nearby. One of them was Pauline, Johnny Ferguson's girlfriend. She watched Donny as he looked at his reflection in the mirror behind the bar, his agitation growing to anger. Donny looked along the bar at a group of people, who were laughing at a joke one of them had cracked. He sneered at them and shouted, 'Fucking hypocrites – you're fucking hypocrites, and cowards.'

The group suddenly became silent, eyes looking anywhere but at Donny.

Donny glared at them and slammed his bottle of beer down hard. He turned and left the bar. Pauline watched him leave. She gathered her bag, said her goodbyes and followed close behind Donny.

Thirty-three

Donny entered the bedroom of his uncle's old house, and although he turned the light on the room did not brighten to a great degree. A piece of cloth was draped over the light shade hanging from the ceiling, giving the darkened room a splintered effect. Pauline followed Donny into the room and closed the door. She immediately laughed at seeing the room and said, 'This is one of your penthouse pads, is it then, Donny?' She laughed again, one of her knees buckling, she had been drinking heavily. Donny looked at her over his shoulder and pointed to a chair by the table for her to sit down. She negotiated her way to the chair in drunken steps, noticing there was polythene sheeting laid out on the floor. 'A secret place,' she said under her breath, the heels of her shoes piercing the polythene on the floor.

Donny placed a bag of white powder on the table. He took off his jacket and put it over the back of a chair, opened the door to a little bedside cabinet, took out a full bottle of whiskeywhisky and two tumblers and placed them on the table. Pauline watched him, excited, all the while suppressing laughter, knowing she had gone too far but was caught up in the fun she was having. She took a packet of cigarettes from her bag, put one in her mouth, lit it and looked at an ashtray on the table. Pauline looked up at Donny, aware that he was watching her, but she did not notice that he had turned on the video camera that was on the chest of drawers and pointing at her. Donny sat at the table. Saying nothing, he poured the whisky into both glasses and started to open the bag of powder. Pauline laughed loudly, crude laughter that gave her relief. 'C'mon, Donny, ease up a little – that was one thing Hudson was right about with you – needing to chill a little.'

She laughed again, causing Donny to look up from the superstore loyalty card he had edged into the powder. 'Fuck – he didn't stand a chance.' She blurted the words out, her excitement growing as her eyes probed Donny's face. Donny snorted in the powder, dropped the card next to the bag and gestured for Pauline to have some. As Pauline looked from Donny to the bag of powder, Donny stood up and pulled out the film projector that was standing against the side of the wardrobe, a film was loaded on top of the stand. He set the projector up, pointing it at the wall above his bed.

Pauline snorted some powder and laughed at what Donny was doing. The light of the projector lit the pattern of the wallpaper, making the little islands stand out against their background. As the film began to play Donny downed a glass of whisky and snorted a large amount of powder. Pauline watched him with an amused expression. She said, 'He was ready to take you on – Hudson, so he was – you should have heard the things he was saying like, and what he was going to do.'

Donny looked from the projector to Pauline. Sound from the film burst out and Donny quickly turned it down. Pauline was confused as she looked at images playing against the wall of a concentration camp in the Second World War and then of the German army marching their distinctive goose stepping march. She took a sip of whisky and looked around the room. 'Fuck me, Donny, you've split some fucking heads in your time,' she said.

Donny ignored her. Satisfied with the position of the projector he went over to the sound system. Pauline watched him pick up a cassette and inspect it. She said. 'Is this the place you bring some of them to get a – a confession?'

Donny did not answer as he inserted the cassette, pressed a button to rewind the tape and took out his uncle's Luger pistol from one of the drawers. Pauline continued to watch him, and just as she looked as if she was going to laugh she had another gulp of whisky. Donny sat in the chair and looked up at the flickering images. Pauline was not taking any notice of the film, she looked around the room and then at the gun in Donny's hand. A puzzled expression began to show on her face, it was as if she was regretting coming back with Donny, but Pauline was a woman who had lost most of her judgement. Her unstable mind had become increasingly irrational, clouded with delusions, a state brought about by years of lying, alcohol abuse, fear and paranoia. Her insecurity had rendered her quite helpless to make any sound reasoning. Pauline's eyes flitted up at the images on the wall. She shrugged, not knowing whether to snort some powder or have a drink. The decision was too much for her, so she quickly stubbed out her cigarette and asked, 'What you doing with the gun?'

'What do you mean?' Donny asked, levelling her a direct look, his stare remaining on her long after he had spoken. She shrugged and said, 'Don't you have any music in here, for fuck.'

Donny nodded, continuing to stare at her before speaking. 'Oh yeah, there's music, there's always music in here.'

She had another drink, wanting to speed things up. 'You know I'm Johnny Ferguson's woman?' she asked.

Donny did not answer, but continued to look at her. 'Johnny Ferguson,' she said, 'oh yeah, I'm his girl – we have a wee brat – no, love him really – Malcolm, his name is – named after Johnny's brother.'

Donny cast a thoughtful look down at the table. Pauline leant close to Donny, her voice lowering. 'But that doesn't stop a girl having fun.'

Music suddenly blared from the sound system. 'What's this?' she asked, her face contorted in disgust. Donny stared at her, saying nothing, and Pauline nodded at him to prompt him to speak, but he continued to stare at her. The music playing was 'Private World' by The New York Dolls.

'Arthur Kane on base,' Donny said, the features in his face coming alive. He grinned at her, but the grin turned quickly into menace. Pauline looked at Donny as he said, 'Arthur "Killer" Kane – The New York Dolls – the best rock and roll group in the world – ever!'

His eyes widened and Pauline looked unsure on seeing the weird look in his stare. She threw a playful punch at his crotch and said, 'Oh come on – Donny the dong, eh?'

She stood up and laughed, it was a mocking laugh and she said, 'Donny the dong – well come and show me.'

She stretched out on the bed, lifting her skirt and pulling down her knickers, her eyes closing, heavy with the drink, 'Show me what a hard man you are – or…' She stopped herself for a few seconds before saying, 'You can get hard, can't you?'

Donny got up, placed the pistol on the table and stood over the bed. He unbuckled his belt, looked down at Pauline and then up at the images moving against the wall. He stood looking at the images.

'What's fucking wrong?' Pauline asked, and she laughed loudly. It was a forced and strained laugh, and she only broke it to say, 'Some say, it's in your jeans – and that's where it stays – in your fucking jeans, when the girlies are around.'

She laughed again. She was deranged, becoming hysterical, shouting out, moving on the bed the action of being fucked as she said, 'Come on, Donny – Donny the hard man – use your finger to stir my honey – or is it the wrong flavour – not for your taste?'

Her laughing became uncontrollable. Stopping the fucking action she lay on the bed shaking and pointing up at Donny. He mumbled, without looking at Pauline. 'Don't look at me like I'm a lesser man.'

Donny looked up quickly at the images on the wall, snatching himself from what he was thinking and had just said. He went to the bedside table, opened the drawer and took out a spring loaded cosh. He slammed the handle of the cosh squarely into Pauline's face. She raised herself from the bed, as if hurling herself upwards, but Donny grabbed Pauline by her hair, and her attempts to protect herself were useless as he smashed the cosh down on the crown of her head. Speaking without opening his mouth, he said, 'Don't bleed in my bed, you whore cunt.'

He pulled Pauline from the bed, threw her face down on the floor, stamped on her back and then beat her head with the cosh handle. He pushed her onto her back and dropped onto her chest with his knees. She gasped, the lack of air pulling her from a semi-conscious state. Donny pressed a button on the handle of the cosh that released a rod. Donny rammed it into Pauline's open mouth, but her mouth was not fully open so he smashed the butt of the cosh into her mouth, breaking her teeth, and he slammed the butt of the cosh repeatedly into her mouth, making room to push the rod right into her mouth. He forced the rod down into her throat, grinding it in jagged circles, and pushing his knees deeper into her chest, wanting to snap her bones, break her into fragments, she had to be destroyed, this was in his mind, and the words he muttered were barely audible, 'She didn't care – they don't care.' He wanted to twist her body and smash her face out of shape. That was how he wanted to remember her. Stabbing into her eyes with the rod, sinking it deep into the sockets and turning and grinding, and as they cracked and splintered he nodded nonchalantly. He was aware that 'Frankenstein' by The New York Dolls was playing. And it was over.

Donny took a knife from under the bed, flicked it open and stabbed it into Pauline's legs, jabbing and twisting the blade, working from her thighs down to her calves, and all the while the faceless head moved from side to side with the stabbing blows. The eye sockets were massive gaping holes above a ragged hole that was the mouth area, now looking like a scarecrow mask in the splintered light of the room. Donny stopped stabbing the body, he was breathing heavily, as if exhausted. As he knelt over the body examining wounds a confused look momentarily glanced across his face. He stood up, went over to the video camera and turned it off.

Donny stopped the tape and picked up the remote controls for the sound system and the television. Turning off the light, he lay down on the bed and pointed the remote at the television and began to rewind the videotape. When it was fully rewound he pressed the remote button for the CD player. He breathed deeply and pushed his hand down the front of his pants and masturbated as the recording of the night's events played to the music of 'Santa Claus is Coming to Town.' After he ejaculated Donny drifted into a thin sleep, barely unconscious, but enough to remove him from the erotic violence.

An hour had passed when Donny's eyes snapped open. He looked around the room as though he had just arrived there. He zipped up his trousers, got off the bed, picked up his jacket and took a mobile phone from one of the pockets. Leaning lazily on the table, he pressed some buttons and held the phone to his ear. He looked down at the table, speaking into the phone in an even tone. 'Dougie, I'm down Millburn, don't ask questions, we need to make a final delivery, of the wasting kind – it'll be nearly cold when you get here. Dump it in their turf – if found it will be a distraction. I won't be here when you arrive – we'll talk later – thanks Dougie.' He put the phone on the table and looked at it for a long while in silence. He looked at Pauline's mutilated body without expression.

Donny went over to the window and placed his finger in a crack between the curtains, he slowly parted them and carefully opened the window. He looked out onto the street, his eyes tensed

174

to a sound in the distance, it was the sound of a baby crying. He frowned in concentration, trying to locate and decipher the sound. After realising what it was he listened to it, hearing it as a backdrop to the exceptionally still and quiet night in the surrounding streets. He stood looking out of the window, all thought frozen in the centre of his head, his mouth slightly open and conscious of the baby's tortured screaming. The sound absorbed him, having a cathartic effect in numbing his feelings and relaxing his body. And the sound amplified in his mind as he looked out at the rain soaked street.

Thirty-four

Out of eyeshot from the window that Donny was looking out of was the terraced house where Norman the Minister lived, the man whom Donny had spoken to at the civic centre. Norman was sitting behind a small desk in his spartan bedroom, his eyes staring through the open window. The room had not been decorated for years and only given a meagre, token clean every few months. There were no curtains and the room was lit from the street light outside. The open window let in a chill, damp air.

Norman was wearing an old white shirt, its collar and cuffs frayed. He was pale from lack of sleep and rest. The Bible was open on the desk in front of him. He had been reading a passage earlier, trying to gain comfort and forgiveness for the feelings he had felt all his adult life towards young boys. He was emaciated, burnt through with worry. The threat and warning that Donny gave him at the civic centre had built in his mind to an all-encompassing obsession.

The room had been silent, the only sound coming from the wooden sounding tick of a clock, but then Norman's eyes began to waver at the sound of a baby that had started to cry in a house directly opposite his own. His expression intensified as his features became more pinched as impending defeat weighed upon him. He braced himself as he listened to the crying. Norman believed it was a sign, a message, thinking that God had sent the cries of the baby. He understood it as a signal that was to bring about his punishment.

His fatigued mind was demented with guilt, depression and worry. The sound of the baby became louder and deeper in tone, and then it grew in pitch to a shrill screeching. A fine film of sweat glinted on his face, lit from the street light outside. He was totally absorbed in an inner confrontation that was taking place, but he was weakening and lacked the power to fight the battle. The baby let out a long screeching wail, as if driven by an intolerable fear, and then the sound flattened to a low, repetitive heaving and guttural squeal. It remained like that as a woman's

176

voice could be heard attempting to hush the baby, trying to soothe its discomfort. But the distress the baby felt was too great and it gave out a painful screeching cry. The concern in the woman's voice grew as all her efforts to comfort the baby failed, and Norman tilted forward in his chair, staring through the open window. He glared at the sound and barely opening his mouth enough to show his stained teeth he recited words from the Bible, speaking slowly, in a stage whisper, and as he spoke his eyes became wide, trance-like as he seemed to be drawn into the baby's screaming.

"'Listen to my cry for help.'"

"'Have mercy on me, oh God – blot out my transgressions – wash away all my iniquity and cleanse me from my sin. Do not cast me from your presence or take your Holy Spirit from me.'"

He began to shake, his face intensifying with the distraught screeching of the baby. The crying was hysterical. Norman fell to the floor, holding a scalpel in his right hand. Clenching his teeth he pushed the scalpel into his left wrist and twisted it, pulling it back and forth. A jet of blood spurted upwards, splattering the front of his shirt and face. He knew that he had hit the main vein and had planned to slash the other wrist, but weakness immediately overwhelmed him. It was as if he had hit a wall. A realisation of what he had done gave birth to rabid fear, but that was over in seconds. Norman fell on his side. Silent screams discharged his anger and resentment at a world that he despised. He stared in wonder at the pumping blood, and as his consciousness faded the screaming from the house opposite continued, and when Norman's eyes were shut and his body was still, his face twisted at an inner pain of what he was. The screeching in the house opposite reached a crescendo and then dropped to quiet burbling, as if all pain, discomfort and fear had left the baby.

Thirty-five

The telephone on the desk in Richard Piquard's study was ringing. Richard Piquard entered the room, sat behind the desk, deftly reached out his manicured hand and picked up the phone while admiring his neatly cut polished nails.

'Hello, Richard Piquard,' he said, and his eyes immediately narrowed as he listened to Geoffrey Stuart explaining how he had been told to contact him and discuss his concerns and plans. Piquard asked Stuart what his concerns and plans were, his manner guarded and thinking why and how those above had connected Stuart to him. Stuart told Piquard how Donny Campbell had rung and threatened him and his family, and that it was an open secret that Campbell had killed 'the English.' Piquard listened, one eyebrow arching as he schemed, letting Geoffrey Stuart talk, and giving him space to build confidence.

Stuart said, 'Campbell is out of control, turning on his own people. The structure that's just been put in place is now in pieces. It's obvious that we can't work with him any more.'

He went on, telling Piquard that Donny Campbell was not involved in a feud to settle any future outcomes or financial expectations, just that he was going it alone, waging a paranoiac vendetta against anyone. Richard Piquard nodded slowly, pursing his lips, his mind made up as he let Geoffrey Stuart continue to speak.

Stuart told Piquard of Stevens, the policeman, and of how he had been involved with Campbell. He said, 'Stevens has been in Donny Campbell's theatre of death, as it's called, where Campbell watches his own video nasties.'

He told Piquard that Stevens was a man of many persuasions and that he was of no value any more. He said that Stevens had been involved for years in collusion with the paramilitary groups, passing over names and addresses, giving confidential files over to the 'illegals' to do the dirty work and 'stir things up with the peasants and despatching innocent people.' Stuart said Stevens had overstepped the mark and that he was going to be dealt with by Donny Campbell.

He said, 'Information has been given to Campbell telling him of how Stevens has been plotting against him – so, the Royal Ulster Constabulary, will be missing one of their finest, very shortly.'

Stuart concluded, stating how things should 'pan out,' and as he wound up what he wanted to say Richard Piquard wrote down Geoffrey Stuart's name on a notepad and drew a firm line through it.

Piquard thanked Stuart, said goodbye to him and leaving his finger pressed down on the receiver he admired the manicured nail as he pondered his next move. It did not take long before he dialled a number and relaxed back in his chair, his voice was firm as he spoke into the telephone. 'Yes, Richard Piquard here, just had a phone call from the upstart Stuart – yes, the lawyer.' Anger showed in Richard Piquard's face as an irritation had boiled over and needed to be dealt with.

Thirty-six

The light in Donny's bedroom was splintered as before, the cloth remaining over the old lampshade hanging from the ceiling. Donny was wearing only his underpants as he stood over a man who was crouched on the plastic sheeting that covered the floor. The man was gagged and had his hands and feet bound, a cheese wire hung loosely around his neck. A fine cut ran around the man's neck and from it flowed blood that had soaked the front of his shirt. Stevens, the policeman, sat on the side of the bed. He was dressed in his police uniform trousers and shirt. The music coming from the sound system was a trance-like sound of a Jew's harp twanging the same note accompanied by the repetitive chugging of a didgeridoo. Donny looked at Stevens and said, 'Listen to me, Stevens, your bosses have little get-togethers with their farmer friends, and politicians – yeah – speaking nicey nicey to their nicey wifes, in the big houses they live in – all ever so civilised, with their children going off to some school to learn fucking Latin, or some shit – yet, they all ignore what and who has given them their privileges – if it wasn't for the foot soldiers...'

Stevens cut in while looking at the man on the floor who was staring at him, resigned but petrified. 'Foot soldiers! Foot soldiers!'

He smirked as he looked up at Donny. 'Am I hearing proper here? A talk of sanctimony! Now listen, Donny, this is Belfast, the language is Chinese whispers – that woman Pauline, they found her body in an area that isn't yours – the case on her isn't closed – morals might be fucked, but people ask questions when a person is murdered – and you're doing very well in having questions answered that have been asked about you, by the "nicey" set of people you're going on about – we all know what your game is Donny – for fuck's sake, man.'

Donny looked at Stevens as he continued, 'Fucking hell, how you'll get away with blowing away those boys from England, I don't fucking know – you've come a long way, as they say – but that cunt Stuart, the lawyer, won't be going away – this is his place, and he's going to fucking rule it – they'll be sending more over from England, killing the other ones isn't the end of it – it's all sown up – you must know that – take what you can – you've done very well out of it – everybody's got a place, they just have to learn to know where it is and to stick to it – or they'll get their head hammered from all bastard sides – Stuart is up there with them all, they weave the jacket – all we have to do is wear the fucking thing.

'Look at me for fuck's sake – I'm like you – from the same area – we might be bad cunts – but there's things for us to do here – we're lucky – but we've got to watch our backs – but fuck it – don't make it worse for yourself, Donny.'

Donny had heard enough and waved his hand as he said, 'Whatever, whatever. We've all got our fingers stuck in the candy jar – just you learn to take what you're given and keep your hands under your hat.'

What Donny had said confused Stevens. He looked at Donny, and Donny was looking at him. 'As I say,' Donny said, 'just keep it under your hat, and we're all laughing – and, Stevens, things are being said about you – you're lucky that you've got me on your side.'

He grinned at Stevens, who returned an equally insincere grin.

Donny pushed the man's back with his foot and he slumped forward.

'Is this fucking cunt dead yet, or what?' Stevens asked.

Donny leant over the man and tugged on the cheese wire. The man grunted and Donny said, 'Not yet, but doing nicely.'

Donny lifted the man up, draped him face down over one of the chairs and pulled down his trousers. Donny stepped back and grinned. He took a bag of powder from the table and spread a thick line on the back of the man's collar. Donny turned to Stevens, still grinning, and said, 'I think I'll have a bit of fun with this one.'

Leaning over the back of the man he snorted the powder and pushed his hand down the front of the man's underpants. Stevens watched him, and stood up, but losing his balance he reeled to one side. He pulled a face of mock disgust at what Donny was doing before breaking into laughter.

Stevens pulled off his shirt, picked up a police truncheon and staggered towards Donny and the man. Donny stepped back from the man and walked around him. 'I'll fuck the fucker's fucking face.' He told Stevens as he picked up a hypodermic syringe that was next to the sound system. He injected his own penis as Stevens pulled down the man's pants and pushed the truncheon up his arse, he then snorted the remains of the powder from the collar of the man's shirt.

They laughed at each other's antics. Donny pushed his penis into the man's face and then began to grind his penis into his mouth and eyes. Donny's face was a meltdown of hate and ecstasy.

Donny pulled away from the man, his arms raised in triumph, and wiping his hands in the man's blood he then smeared it over his own face and body.

Stevens was shagging the man's arse. Donny watched him momentarily before picking up a scalpel from the table. He leant over Stevens, simulating the movements he was making. Stevens turned his head, grinning at Donny, but his eyes suddenly froze as he saw the scalpel coming across his face and down to his throat.

Donny pulled the scalpel through the skin and blood instantly spurted out, Donny liking the feel of it hot on his hand. Stevens was locked in his position, but then stumbled backwards and fell to the floor with hardly a sound coming from his open mouth. Donny urinated over Stevens' head and body, watching the blood wash from his neck onto the polythene sheet. Donny crouched down, and using the scalpel scored the word GRASS into Stevens' back. He stabbed the scalpel into his back and left it sticking out. Donny stood up and looked at the scene that was presented in front of him. His mouth opened slowly in lust as he roared a venting of approval and satisfaction. He turned and faced the video camera that had been recording, and all the while the Jew's harp, with the accompaniment of the didgeridoo, continued to play the repetitive trance-like sound.

Thirty-seven

Donny contacted Roddy Harding through a complex system of communications. At first Roddy Harding offered resistance at seeing Donny, but that quickly weakened as his mind pondered the enjoyment he would have with him. Donny told no one of his trip to London, except Dougie. He booked a room in a small hotel, not far from Roddy Harding's flat, travelling light, intending to stay just the night or maybe two.

When letting Donny into the flat the preliminaries were cut short as both men understood what the visit was about. Roddy Harding knew it was risky, to say the least, but his excitement drove all reason from his mind. Once fuelled with alcohol and powder the two men indulged themselves in acting out their interests. Roddy Harding wanted to cut Donny across his body with a knife, scald him with hot water and burn him with cigarette butts, but Donny made it clear that was not for him and it was he who would be doing any beating or burning. As the night wore on Roddy Harding spoke of his attraction towards the abuse of young boys, but his excitement was put on hold because Donny did not show any interest in what he was talking about.

Donny was losing control, the drugs had an hallucinogenic mix and the alcohol heightened his emotions, creating a complete mental delirium. It was late into the night when he found himself in another room, lying on a bed. It was a large bed with silk covers and large pillows. Roddy Harding scrambled about the room on his hands and knees, operating a video player and playing tapes that did not make sense to Donny. For Donny, the room, the videos and all of it just seemed surreal. He was unsure if it was actually happening. All speech as a form of communication with Roddy Harding had finished, mere grunting or imagining what the other person wanted or was thinking was now in place. At one point Donny's eyes concentrated to focus on what was being shown on the television screen. It looked like a children's party, but out of the chaotic images there was a scene of a young boy, a child, screaming, his body covered in blood.

Donny thought he looked a half-beast half-boy creature. Donny stared at the boy-beast as he pulled himself along the ground, screaming as he struggled, and Donny screwed his eyes up, focusing, and he saw that the boy was being skinned alive. Donny looked over at Roddy Harding who was watching him expectantly, and then Harding burst into hysterical laughter as Donny looked at him, his voice dry with dehydration. Donny turned his soporific gaze back to the screen, the boy-creature was now motionless, dead, and the skin was being pulled over his head.

Donny closed his eyes as a red darkness swarmed around him. The music being played was a classical piano piece, light and tinkling in sound, evoking images in his mind of silver glinting on running water in a tranquil brook. And Donny felt himself being drawn deeper and deeper, and just as he lost consciousness he was dragged out of it by Roddy Harding who had jumped on top of him. Donny found the strength to twist his body and shrug Roddy Harding off, throwing him onto the floor. As Donny eased his back against the coolness of the silk bed covers, a mass of fleeting dark clouds descended upon him, and he lost consciousness.

Thirty-eight

The following evening Richard Piquard was sitting behind the desk in his study. The room was fairly dark, but with enough light from the table lamp to show tension in the cheek on one side of his face. Piquard was holding the telephone to his ear. He was frowning. His eyes darted around the desktop in front of him as if looking for answers to what was being said to him. Roddy Harding was the person on the other end of the telephone, the panic in his voice could clearly be heard from the other side of Piquard's study.

Richard Piquard spoke in an even tone, trying to calm him. 'Nice and slow – nice and slow – don't get yourself excited, old thing – that's it, Roddy, that's the way now – there you are Roddy, and control yourself now, old man.'

The features in Richard Piquard's face darkened as he listened, sometimes holding the telephone from his ear when Harding broke into hysterical screaming. He soothed Harding by repeating words to comfort him, but all the while nodding with a growing severity in his expression. His voice deepened, maintaining a deliberate control in choosing his words he said, 'Listen, Roddy, listen to me now – you try and get some rest, old thing – do you hear me? Fine, that's fine – take something to give the old mind a rest – and just leave the whole thing to me – we will take the appropriate action – don't worry, old thing – just don't worry yourself about anything.'

He listened as Harding's voice quietened and whined in self-pity. Nodding slowly Piquard interjected in a neutral tone. 'We will have to talk though, Roddy, old dear – but for now, it is important for you to rest and leave the messy little puddle for me to mop up.'

He waited for a reply, his eyes turning to the ceiling. 'Do I hear yes? That's it – that's the man – old Roddykins, because listen, there are plans to be laid – so you just get your head down in Bedfordshire – and we will talk in a few days – okay, old thing? Do I hear okay? Bye now.'

A click sounded to signify that Roddy Harding had put the phone down, but Richard Piquard kept the telephone to his ear. He was deep in thought as he stared at the opposite wall, but his concentration was broken as he cursed desperately, 'Stupid, stupid – fucking stupid.'

His mind jumped into gear, punching out numbers on the keypad he braced himself as he waited for an answer. A muted voice sounded on the other end and Richard Piquard spoke in a crisp, determined manner. 'Hello, yes, it's Richard here – high security please.' He swallowed and shifted in his chair, his bearing purposeful as he waited, and on hearing a voice he spoke quickly and concisely.

'Yes, it's Richard Piquard – we have to talk, and there is action that has to be taken, quickly. Now, let me explain more when I see you, but it concerns dear old Roddy Harding – he's been having a bit of fun with a circus bear – that's right – that's him – anyway, poor old Roddy has been telling tales, I'm afraid to say.'

He listened intently, nodding carefully to the voice on the phone and then answered dutifully. 'That's it – that's right, he has told of them, and us – the parties – he showed videos of the orphanage – that's it – yes, of the boys – he told him of the knowledge – of our world – he gave him insights.'

He listened to the voice, nodding thoughtfully before continuing.

'I'm sorry that I have to draw this to your attention, but it is – fixable. Certain journalists are talking – they can be contained, but questions are being asked, and we don't want that leading to questions being asked in the house.

'Yes, just some minor pruning – if one collects shit for one's garden, one does not want the stuff in the house. So, we'll take some rubbish down to the dump.'

He listened to the voice on the telephone, nodding in agreement to what was being said to him before saying, 'But we also have to – downsize our operational team?

'There are those on board, who will have to be pushed overboard – yes, yes, in the usual fashion, of course – by the old enemy – the media will be reeling at the horror of it all – yes, yes all that is in place, we foresaw what might happen and contingency plans were drawn – Murray tells us that the whole

186

bunch of them come from a time of idealism, and that two from our side, from the operational team, are to be despatched. One is the obnoxious little lawyer chappie Stuart, Geoffrey Stuart, and the other is the pious bore Alexander, Philip Alexander – yes, that's right – he has been led to believe that he's in the frame for a top position, and we've left him a nice long piece of rope – and like all stupid small-minds who think that they can separate greed from other parts of life ¬ will duly hang himself.

'I actually spoke to him a short while ago – the bait was laid to test his loyalty – of course, he hasn't any – and what with the circus bear Campbell knocking over the table at the tea party we've been setting up over there, some of the new upstarts have been asking for his head – but dear old Roddy wouldn't sign his name to such a thing – although now, of course, what with Roddy being a messy boy, it has all become very different. So, now we can let them have their wish – and in doing so let them believe it is with our blessing to turn against their superiors – yes, Murray is an old hand, he can play them like a children's song – yes, yes, our boys will do the deed against the upstarts – it will be a doddle.'

Richard Piquard frowned at what was said to him. 'No, I said doddle,' he said, 'it will happen the same night that Alexander does away with his old foe, the bear Campbell.'

His conversation came to an end, and putting the phone in its place on the receiver he studied the back of his hand. Richard Piquard checked his wristwatch and spoke in a satisfied manner to himself. 'He will be sitting in the warm bosom of his family – excellent.'

Thirty-nine

The telephone began to ring in Philip Alexander's house. His home was pleasant, nothing ostentatious or grand. The telephone was on a small table in the hallway, at the bottom of the stairs. Amanda, Philip Alexander's thirteen-year-old daughter, answered it. 'Yes, who is it please?' She asked, and listened intently to the voice of Richard Piquard telling her that it was a matter concerning Mr Alexander's work and asking if it was possible for him to come to the telephone. 'Yes, one moment,' Amanda said brightly. She put the phone down on the table and went into the lounge, calling as she entered the room, 'Dad, Da – it's for you.' Philip Alexander came out of the lounge and closed the door. He held the telephone to his ear and said, 'Yes, hello, Philip Alexander here.'

Richard Piquard was leaning across his desk, the telephone held closely to the side of his face, his expression was very serious.

'Yes, Richard Piquard here again.'

Philip Alexander gave a short intake of breath, licked his lips and prepared himself for what Richard Piquard had to say. 'Any thoughts of putting in place a plan of action, since we last spoke?' Piquard asked.

Philip Alexander looked around where he was standing, as if checking to see that nobody was standing near him. The anxiety was plain to hear in his voice as he spoke. 'About Chief Constable Murray, do you mean?'

'Yes, that's what I was thinking about,' Richard Piquard said.

Alexander nearly faltered as he answered, 'Chief Constable Murray does not play the game that way, Mr Piquard. As I have told you, he is old school, very old school.'

He said 'old school' derisively and in a way as if he believed that Piquard had shared feelings with him on the matter.

'But...'

'But, what? Mr Alexander?' Piquard cut in.

Philip Alexander steadied himself as he said, 'I have given this a lot of thought, and as you've said, kept everything to myself – it could very well work out as you mentioned – I'm certain it will, that there will be a successful outcome to the plan we have discussed.'

Richard Piquard spoke slowly into the phone, knowing that the man on the end of the line was hanging on every word.

'I'm sure you will handle it professionally, and we know that you are capable of doing it – and believe me, Mr Alexander, it will not be if it is successful, but when, and that will bode very well for you, very well, Mr Alexander. For a man of your age to reach the position of Chief Constable would be an unprecedented achievement, Mr Alexander – and one that would not go unnoticed by Crown and country – and that is my first priority and duty, the interest of Crown and country.'

Philip Alexander gripped the telephone tightly as he began to speak. 'Why have things changed? There has been a change of mind hasn't there?'

He gained confidence as he continued. 'I have been talking with Geoffrey Stuart, he was telling me how he had contacted people about getting rid of Campbell, but his proposal was shelved and it came to nothing, and now we have a change of thinking, with more added to it.'

Richard Piquard flexed his jawbone to a point where it bulged and looked as if it was going to burst through the skin of his cheek. He explained to Philip Alexander that orders had changed from 'above' and that he was simply passing them on. He went on to tell Philip Alexander that his ideas had been considered by 'those above,' and the contributions that he has made had not been overlooked.

'Who knows where you'll end up, old boy,' he said in a lighter tone.

Philip Alexander liked the cosy closeness of 'old boy.' It made him feel as if he was being invited in, into an inner sanctum that he desired and had always very much coveted.

Richard Piquard asked for his advice and opinions, and for his ideas of getting rid of Donny Campbell. Philip Alexander's ego had been massaged and a sense of relief came upon him as he felt accepted and important. He told Richard Piquard. 'I know, we know, a man who has offered his help – his brother fell foul of Campbell – his name is Johnny Ferguson, a known figure – it's safe, he's just another piece of scum – an expendable.'

Richard Piquard smiled inwardly at this last remark, and he asked if it was, 'secure.'

'It's secure,' Philip Alexander answered dutifully, 'They use the word respect here, but it really means fear – and they all want a little less fear.'

Richard Piquard's voice lowered and Philip Alexander detected the change of tone. The warm cosy feeling had disappeared. It now felt ominous and any confidence that had built up drained from him. Richard Piquard's voice held a cruel, clinical edge. 'Nothing personal, with you and Campbell, I trust old chap?'

Philip Alexander gently traced the scar on the side of his face with his fingertips. 'Not at all,' he answered, 'purely professional, a duty to Crown and country.'

After a pause, Richard Piquard began to speak, his voice dropping lower and more deliberate as he became detached and cold.

'You deliver this, Mr Alexander, and we will be grateful, and when we are grateful, we are generous.'

Philip Alexander noticed that sweat had formed on his upper lip. Richard Piquard continued, his voice quieter. 'Who was that who answered the telephone?'

Philip Alexander frowned and offered his words tentatively, 'My daughter, Amanda.'

Richard Piquard took a short while before speaking. 'A nice sounding and well-mannered girl – you must be proud. You're lucky there – doing well with her studies, is she?'

Philip Alexander was concerned, 'Yes, yes, she enjoys her work, and a challenge.'

'How old is she?' Richard Piquard's tone made what he said sound more of an order than a question.

'Thirteen, yes, she's thirteen now,' Alexander said, trying to force a smile in an attempt to lighten the feel of their conversation. 'Thirteen going on twenty-one.'

He waited for Richard Piquard to speak. The length of the pause made him very uncomfortable.

Finally, Piquard spoke. 'Yes, yes – you have to watch them at that age – once they're out of your sight – anything can happen – I don't know, the things they can get up to once they are out on their own – get themselves in all kinds of jams, and trouble – just have to be careful – and always vigilant to keep them from harm's way – to be a parent, Mr Alexander, the worry of it all – of what might happen to them when one isn't around to keep an eye on them – and it happens so quickly, and easily, once your back is turned, and you're not there – well – who knows what can happen – and it does – even to those coming from the most respectable families and backgrounds.'

Philip Alexander gripped the telephone tightly as Piquard said, 'I'll be in touch, Mr Alexander – and hopefully, next time we speak this little bit of business will be finalised.'

Another pause passed before his voice returned. 'Goodnight now – have a nice evening.' The telephone clicked as Richard Piquard hung up, not giving Philip Alexander a chance to say anything. He slowly replaced the telephone on its receiver and looked at it anxiously for several seconds before drawing an uneasy breath.

As he turned to enter the lounge Amanda came out of the room making for the stairs. He stopped her, and taking hold of her shoulders he kissed her forehead. She went to pull away, but he drew Amanda to him and hugged her firmly. Amanda was startled, because her father had never done this before.

Forty

A week later Katie Preston had confirmation that the house David and she wanted to buy had been accepted. The mortgage was in place and everything had worked out. The body of Ian, David's brother, was discovered in a ditch with Hudson's body a couple days after Donny had killed them. Katie did all that she could to support David. He cried as she held him in her arms and he listened to her loving words of comfort. He grieved because of the way his brother had wasted his life and felt anger that he lived in a place where gangs, fear and murder were the way of things. The first words his mother said after being told was, 'They've killed one of my sons, how long will it be before they kill my other one?'

She had joined the legions of relatives in that part of Ireland who believe they shared a grief that is not shared or understood outside the confines of where they lived.

David McClelland struggled to come to terms and accept what had happened, but was not going to let the situation destroy him. He wanted to build a good life and it was going to be different for him and Katie. They lived in a place full of bitterness and hate, but they had plans. He knew that the two of them together were unbeatable and that they would realise their dreams.

The day after Ian McClelland's funeral Katie and David visited the house they were to live in. Katie was excited and wanted to do something to mark the occasion, but unknown to Katie, David had booked for them to stay in a country mansion set in its own grounds up on the coast. It was a special weekend deal that he saw advertised.

That evening David went round Katie's house and talked to her mum about buying a house and setting up home with Katie.

At the end of the evening David and Katie went for a drive in David's car to spend a little time together. It was inclement weather, the rain was thrown to the ground by a hostile wind that seemed as though it was trying to break away from itself, and the unrelenting wind and rain, that had lasted since late afternoon, began to rage as the storm had now fully arrived.

They drove across the city, passing over the motorway and out of the urban sprawl. A roaring clap of thunder exploded less than a second behind a wall of sheet lightning that lit up the streets around them. Katie screamed and then she laughed as she placed her hand on David's leg for comfort. The rain grew, as if in anger, hurling itself in wrathful vengeance down onto the concrete, steel and glass that had been constructed upon the earth. Again and again the whitening flashes of lightning licked at the ground, accompanied by thunder and the fury of wind and rain.

The windscreen wipers had lost the battle to provide clear vision so David reduced his speed, negotiating the road that climbed out of west Belfast and up the dark brooding Black Mountain, standing massive and resolute, fearless yet quiet, as if waiting, watching over the city and its inhabitants that over the years have scarred the mountain as they gouged and cut into its sides in their pursuit of profit. While keeping a mindful eye on the road, David reached out his hand and smiled warmly as he gently stroked Katie's cheek with the back of his fingers, and Katie smiled, relaxing into her seat with her hand resting on his knee. A feeling of peace and security travelled through her body, and a flash of lightning illuminated the windscreen, as if hit by the force of a thousand juggernauts driving at them with full beams blazing.

They climbed higher and higher, slowing in speed as an occasional car passed, but continued climbing until they reached a lay-by cut into the side of the road. David pulled over and switched the key in the ignition to turn the engine off, but to leave the radio on. From where the car was parked they had a view over and across the whole of Belfast, a city that was built in the basin of hills where the sea intruded into its heart.

David turned off the radio, which was tuned into a station playing bland sounds, and sat back in his seat. Katie and David held hands as they looked down and over Belfast, sitting quietly, saying nothing. David was thinking about his brother as he looked across the city and thought about its history and all the people who had made it what it was today. Katie played with her imagination, seeing the landscape that lay before her as like Los

Angeles. She had seen night-time photographs of that city, and although larger, it reminded her of Belfast, brightly lit and sprawling at the foot of valleys and hills.

Katie leant forward and turned the radio on. The flat monotone voice of a male newsreader was reciting sombre news. 'Police are appealing for witnesses as this murder is particularly nasty and disturbing for a number of reasons. There has been an acceleration in paramilitary violence and murder as an internal struggle for power is taking place. This has had…'

Katie turned the radio off, sighed and sat back in her seat. David held her hand, gently and slowly tracing each part of her fingers, touching over the knuckles and running across the tips of her fingers and the palm of her hand. He leant across and kissed the side of Katie's forehead, sensitively, keeping his head there as he looked at her for a few seconds before sinking back into his seat. The inside of the car was silent and peaceful, but gave to one side as a hefty gust of wind shifted the car slightly. David leaned forward and turned the radio on once more and changed the radio station. The Beach Boys song, 'You're so Good to Me' was playing. He listened to the words and turned to Katie. He smiled, and she smiled back. They sat quietly, listening as the song played. When it finished David turned the radio off and switched on the interior light in the car.

They sat in silence looking out at the panoramic view that was set out before them. Even though the storm raged, a comforting tranquillity filled the two young people as they looked from the dock area, across the city centre and to the residential dwellings that had spilled out of the town. Thunder erupted and they watched forked lightning stab downwards from the heavy skies and pierce the blackness beyond the city that was the sea. The dock area lit up and then another flash lit all around them, illuminating the part of the mountain where they were parked, and Katie thought she caught a glimpse of a wild animal, scurrying into the undergrowth, escaping the exposure caused by the sudden light. She thought what type of animal it could have been, and then fear ran through her as she felt the danger and vulnerability that the animal must suffer. She breathed out, calming herself, gripping David's hand tightly. The rain pounded the roof of the car with an extra vigour and when a violent crack of thunder raised Katie from her seat, they fell into each other's arms and another flash of lightning lit the car and its surroundings. They held each other and laughed, murmuring soft gentle words, and there they remained, holding each other tightly.

A sound grew, at first sounding like it was part of the storm, but then it was apparent that it was a car approaching at a speed much too fast for the conditions. Katie caught sight of the car over David's shoulder as it roared past them. There were two men in the front of the car, and one of them was Donny Campbell.

Forty-one

Donny's eyes passed over a car parked on the side of the road, noticing that there were two people hugging each other in the front. An image nearly formed in his mind, but it vanished before he could construct anything vivid. He averted his gaze to the nearby hedges being blown to all sides and the road disappearing under the car, as if sucked up by the blazing headlights.

Dougie stared out of the windscreen, his head fixed slightly forward in concentration, reflections from the road flashing across his dark eyes. But they did not distract him, because he was set determinedly on his course. Cool Water played quietly in the car. Donny had bought the CD in a garage late one night. It was a cheap production of a collection of 'cowboy songs.' On the cover a photograph of a young cowboy, leaning lazily forward in his saddle, his horse standing by the edge of a creek, head stooped, drinking water, the young cowboy exhausted, mopping sweat from his brow with his hat pushed to the back of his head. Donny stared absently out of the side window, his voice distant. 'It always seems to be this kind of weather when we go and see Little Willie.'

Dougie did not respond, his eyes not straying from the road ahead. Donny glanced over at Dougie, and realising he was not going to answer returned to gazing out of the side window, thoughtful and feeling deflated. He nestled into the seat, like a child. Looking at the distorted reflection of his face in the window he began to speak while watching great big dirty rubber bands move around that were his lips. 'I have to see Willie – I need to see him.'

Again, Dougie did not respond, his eyes narrowed as his full attention was given to managing the car at great speed in the risky conditions.

Donny looked sadly from the dark canyons that were his eyes to the rain pelting on the side of the car. He sighed deeply in reflection, his mind folding backwards in time, once more going back to a time when he was a very young boy, leaving the present and returning to that time. It was clear in his mind, the sounds, tastes, the place and the people. It was a wedding reception in the back room of a pub. Donny was nine years of age, dressed in a cowboy outfit, complete with hat, waistcoat, leggings, clip on spurs, two holsters on the belt and six-guns. It was one of the only outings he had as a child. His mother bought the outfit on hire purchase from a catalogue. It was a special treat because he had been ill. He had spent a couple of stays in hospital to discover why he kept fainting, but nothing was concluded and the episodes of fainting passed. Everything was happening in slow motion as young Donny took the six-guns from their holsters. 'The Streets Of Laredo' was playing. A man approached Donny, smiling, using his fingers as pistols he shot at Donny, and Donny shot back. But the man shot again and widened his eyes in a gesture that told Donny he had shot him. Donny fell to the floor, dramatically rolling onto his back and played dead. The man mouthed the words of the song in time with them, 'and the young cowboy died.' He then blew imaginary smoke from the barrels of his imaginary pistols. Young Donny closed his eyes, and when he opened them he saw the man turning and laughing as he walked off. Young Donny looked to his side and saw that his uncle Alan was watching him. He was nodding, but he was not smiling...

Donny caught his breath as he returned to sitting in the car with Dougie. He was trying to control his breathing. The rain hammered the roof, and for a split second Donny found relief in the sound of the rain pounding on the roof of the car. And as Donny became conscious of that feeling of comfort he immediately hurled it away, outside of the car, to the rush of speed and the frenzied storm, to be left grazed and crushed on the road they were leaving behind.

Donny lit a cigarette, blew smoke down onto the dashboard and stared in front of himself, his eyes narrowing. Donny and Dougie were both staring forward, and they would not speak until they reached the little coastal road that took them down to the edge of the sea where Little Willie lived.

It was a deserted area of coast. The rain had not relented and lightning flashed over them, lighting up the tiny old caravan that was Little Willie's home. A light was on inside the battered caravan.

Donny and Dougie sat in the car looking at the lonely habitat for a while before Donny picked up a bottle of brandy from the floor. He opened the door and told Dougie that he would not be long. He shut the car door, pulled up the collar of his jacket in a futile attempt to ward off the elements and walked towards the caravan. Dougie watched Donny negotiate his way to the caravan, carefully placing his feet on an uneven path that had subsided long ago and was now mostly under water. He watched Donny bang on the door of the caravan and enter. Light spilled from inside the caravan onto the grass and sand, but only for the few seconds it took Donny to open and shut the door.

Forty-two

The inside of Little Willie's caravan was cramped, ramshackle and claustrophobic. Miscellaneous objects that had been collected over the years cluttered up any amount of space that the small caravan had to offer. Little Willie was sitting in an old armchair listening to a radio that was wired up to a car battery. Watching Donny enter he turned the radio off, his voice small and metallic sounding. 'Donny – ah, welcome.'

Donny did not answer. He put the bottle of brandy on a table, after pushing aside bits and pieces to make room for it, and placed a bag of white powder on the arm of Little Willie's chair. Little Willie did not look at it. Donny looked around the inside of the caravan, taking in Little Willie's life. He looked at Little Willie, looking closely at his face. It was chalk white. Donny thought that Little Willie looked older and wizened, reminding him of a character in a Charles Dickens tale. Then it dawned on him that Little Willie was just like a character in a Dickens tale, and nothing had changed and it never would. Donny looked at little Willie's one eye that was dropped lower than the other, and in doing so pushing down that side of his face, which pulled the corner of his mouth down at an angle, giving the impression of eternal sadness, like a theatrical mask depicting the suffering felt by those who are grossly disfigured and different. Little Willie's tiny body had become weaker and shrivelled, and Donny considered that there will be a time when he will be too small for the armchair. His mouse-like hands were dirty, nearly the same colour as the grime on the front of his trousers that had legs so short they looked bizarre. The trousers were made of rough cloth and they were cut well above his ankles, showing bruised and scabbed skin and frayed socks. His feet were pushed into worn bedroom slippers, feet that were small and narrow, the left one turned inwards, as if twisted at a painful angle. Donny looked at the filthy shirt he was wearing beneath his shabby cardigan, and the wisps of hair on his head, still brilliant white. Donny studied his physicality in detail, and then thought about the whole of this solitary man. Willie was an albino and Donny thought of how his abnormalities had shed him aside. He was with all the other unwanted waste that was cast on the shores of the seas.

Donny looked down at Willie's bed that was no bigger than a child's cot and sat down on it. Little Willie looked at the bag of powder with a stony expression. Donny watched him as he spoke quietly. 'Here – always alone.'

'You or me, Donny?' Little Willie asked, looking directly at Donny.

Donny shrugged tiredly and looked down at the floor. Little Willie continued to look at him. 'I've told you all this before Donny, I stay away from others. Fearful and feared – no room for us Donny.'

Donny looked at him in a sad and reflective way. Little Willie watched Donny. When they spoke it was not as equals, Little Willie was the teacher and it was his sermons and wisdom that Donny sought. Little Willie began to speak, maintaining his position of Donny's mentor. 'You don't have to be physically different – yet the defining principles are not subtle – loneliness – to be alone – Donny.'

Donny stood up and leant against the door frame. He looked down at his feet to the top of the door frame and then to the ceiling with the paint peeling in sheets. Donny spoke, seemingly to no one, but it could have been to someone or something that was next to him or a thousand miles away. 'Why am I so fucked up?'

Little Willie watched Donny for a long while before speaking. 'There has to be people like you – and me. There are those who are frail, old, alone and scared – yet, will give to others for they see a need – and in turn, they are pounced upon, beaten and killed by the young, who fear the painful loneliness that the old and weak represent – victims and aggressors – it's not a perfect balancing act – maybe it was never meant to be.'

He watched Donny, and Donny stared at him. Little Willie looked through Donny, right through him and the wall of the caravan to a distant place that held up the words that he was to say. His tone was solemn and his speech deliberate. 'You've come here to speak to me, Donny – but you haven't really – you have come to speak to yourself. You, Donny, do not ask questions of that kind for others to answer.'

After a long pause Little Willie carried on in the same tone. 'When people are setting dinners at Christmas, getting together for birthdays, it will be with people like you in their minds that brings them to clasp each other's hands, and to say soft words of love's intention – for they need protection, from what you are – so they can be what they are, wanting to feel safe and to be together.'

Another pause followed before Little Willie continued, and all the while Donny stared at him. 'It is because people are scared that they gather together – they can't bear to face a world that presents fear – and you – Donny – are that fear – it is just the way of things – the order – your presence is needed to show others unlike you how to love – and when they hold hands, in a show of affection, at a celebration with others, or in private, being alone, just two people – they hold each other because of fear – it is a fear of you – of what you are – there are no questions to be asked – and if questions are asked, then there certainly are no answers – for such reasoning is a thing, artificial, an invention – having no place in the natural order – in which we, and everything belongs – from fear comes malice – and hatred is fear – and to accept it is to love – but the likes of you and me Donny, and the others like us, stand alone – that is our place in the order of things – there is no conscience – it just is – and again, don't ask why – we do so that others can stand together – and that is all they need – they don't want truth – that is invented, and it's given to each other just as a present might be – its wrapping changed with the seasons – they are who they are, because of what we are – and they ask no other questions – they just pray that you don't come knocking on their wee small door in the middle of the night – they don't want to catch their reflection when they cast their eyes upon you. You – of all people, should not be asking questions of the sort that you have just asked me – for it is to do and not to ponder why – reason, is a successful contrivance – but misused Donny.'

He stopped speaking and looked at Donny rather than through him as he had done so before. Donny continued to stare at him.

Little Willie pointed his finger at Donny. 'You are not able to speak to others – this place...'

He stopped speaking and looked around the squalor that was his home and life, and his eyes settled in a place called nowhere. He was listening to the wind and rain. A crack of thunder broke and lightning lit the inside of the caravan. His eyes moved slowly up Donny's body as he said, 'This place is like all places for people like us – wherever it might be – whatever it might look like – this is a place of loneliness – not a home – for the lonely do not have a home – but on that odd occasion when they settle in themselves long enough to ask who they are – it is to places like this that they come to – we're all the same.'

His eyes drifted down to the bag on the arm of his chair. He opened the bag, wet his finger and dabbed it in the powder, and as he sucked it his eyes roamed all over Donny until he finally spoke. 'Broken people who feel how imperfect it all is.'

He closed his eyes tightly and he shook a little before opening them again. He dabbed his finger into the powder and sucked it, leaning forward in his chair he looked directly into Donny's eyes. 'Kill – maim – gore – Donny – the stage is set – the costumes are ready – and don't think that you've written your script. You will force your touch upon the world of feeling.'

The two men looked at each other for a long while, saying nothing, staring into each other's faces, as if time had been suspended, holding an hypnotic gaze as thunder rumbled and crashed, their faces, at times, momentarily illuminated by the lightning, and beneath the rush of wind and rain the deep swell of the sea roared and shrank back as it dragged away from the shore. There were no other sounds, no shrieking, barking or calling from creatures of nature. All sound was of wind and water, the gale and the sea, as one, clashing, a conflict, exploding and breaking in upon itself, and all else, matter or other, was weak, insignificant and meaningless.

Donny snapped out of it, snatching himself from his stare. He turned away from Little Willie and looked down at the floor, but only fleetingly before standing erect and looking at Little Willie. He then opened the door to leave, but Little Willie's voice stopped Donny in the doorway. He turned, looking at Little Willie, the door open just a little.

'Don't shut the door, Donny – for I need to hear the rain.'

Donny looked from Little Willie to out of the door into the darkness, and then he left. As Donny shut the door his face was suddenly lit by a brilliant light that stopped him dead.

Forty-three

The telephone on the desk in Richard Piquard's study was ringing. The darkness in the room was split open by light as Richard Piquard entered and walked over to his desk. He answered the telephone, his voice calm and controlled as he gave his name. His whole body relaxed and a playful smile opened on his face as he spoke. 'Roddy, hello old thing – yes, that's right – well we know you don't like a mess – we know your fastidious little ways – and that's right, there is a bag of rubbish ready to be cleared away in Belfast – mission accomplished, old thing – brawny bender is dead – and you continue to watch all the fun on your telebox – Roddy, you just sit there and make yourself nice and comfy.'

Roddy Harding was sitting in an armchair in his lounge watching the television. He was wearing a dressing gown and covered by a duvet. The light from the television blinked on his face. A newsreader read out information in a contrived voice that expressed solemnity and importance. 'It has been, even in the bloody history of the Troubles in Northern Ireland, a considerable period for murder and upheaval in the Province, and some of the victims who have been murdered in the last few days were people occupying important positions. Last night, a significant figure in paramilitary activity, Donny Campbell, and the high ranking Acting Assistant Police Constable Philip Alexander were murdered. This has accelerated the intensity surrounding the post-peace era and gives a new dimension and proportion to the carnage taking place in the Province. The Prime Minister has been told about the murders and he said that questions will be asked at the highest levels, and the matter will be discussed in the House of Commons today under emergency meeting status.'

An old news item showed Philip Alexander shaking hands with a visiting public figure, and then it cut to live filming outside his home. The newsreader told of how long Philip Alexander had served in the force, the work he did for charities, his involvement with community projects and of how he had a special interest in the young people of Northern Ireland. The newsreader said that Alexander had always valued the contributions young people make to society and believed that all possibilities of change for the better rested with them. A snapshot of a church Alexander went to every Sunday popped up on the screen and the newsreader told of how Alexander was an active participant in the activities of the church. The date was given when he got married and that he had two children. A family photograph appeared on the screen and the newsreader said that his family are now together sharing their grief.

The newsreader explained that Philip Alexander was called out from his home very early in the morning, saying it probably had something to do with the recent rise in murder and violence, and what happened after that was confusing. But a coded message was received by the security forces telling them that his body along with another policeman, Sammy Stevens, were trussed in bags and lying in a ditch ten miles outside of Belfast.

The face of the lawyer Geoffrey Stuart sprang onto the screen. The newsreader told of how a knock on the door of Geoffrey Stuart's family home signalled the last seconds in the life of a reputable lawyer whose career was growing. The newsreader said that Stuart had been asked to take part in Government inquiries, and he was known for the work he had done in high profile cases in the Province. His clients had included notable figures from the political, business and entertainment world. When Stuart opened the door he received several gunshot wounds to his body and head. It was reported that a car screeched away as he lay dead in his doorway.

As the information was read out live coverage outside his home was shown, and again dates of significant events in his life were given with family photographs and details of his children. His wife was too distraught to speak.

The newsreader spoke to an 'expert' in the studio and discussed whether this signalled the end of peace, or could the terrorists finally be defeated. The 'expert' spoke of concerns for the image of the Province, of how Northern Ireland was perceived by people in other countries and that connections with the other murders that happened cannot be ruled out. He talked of the bodies of three men that were found in an isolated old farmhouse, and that there were investigations to discover whether they came from Northern Ireland and that it was a mystery who they were, what they had been doing and who killed them. The 'expert' spoke of an 'evil conundrum' and that the security forces, with the full support of the Government, were determined to resolve the matter and allow the positive road to peace and financial betterment continue in the Province. He added that, 'We are in a state of change, and there is always conflict before a new beginning – it is inevitable that there will be painful episodes in the process of change, and it is that which we are experiencing.'

The newsreader thanked the 'expert' and looked straight into the camera, his voice slipping back into a sombre tone. 'Two nights ago the bodies of two men were found, one, a man who has been described as a hermit, William Whitman, the other was Teddy "Dougie" McCracken. They were found trussed up in a burned out Range Rover car on a barren coastal road, both men had been shot in the head.'

A clip showed the Range Rover cordoned off by police tape. Two policemen were standing next to the car, grim faced, holding machine guns and bracing themselves against strong winds.

Back in the studio the newsreader was staring into the camera, cued ready to deliver his lines. 'And now let's go to Belfast where two bodies were found this morning. One of the men killed was the infamous paramilitary leader Donny Campbell, the other was Johnny Ferguson – investigations are piecing together a possible connection between the murders.'

A shot of an alleyway tripped onto the screen. Police tape had cordoned off an area and armed police stood in front of the alley. A Northern Ireland newsreader talked over the scene. 'The body of Johnny Ferguson, a member of the same notorious paramilitary group as Donny Campbell – and the largest in Northern Ireland, was found in this alleyway by a paper boy on his rounds this morning...'

The voice whined out details of Johnny Ferguson's known life of crime. The picture cut to a construction site, and then to a shot of the hoarding on the parameter of the site. It zoomed in on the words, BELFAST IS CHANGING. The shot drew back and focused on a police investigation tent that had been erected. It had been cordoned off with police tape and within the taped area people were standing around, some in white jumpsuits the forensic team wear. The bleating voice continued as the camera searched for any clues around the construction site. 'The other body found this morning was that of Donny Campbell – his body was found here on the vast construction site that is to be a showpiece in the future Belfast, where there will be a hotel with helicopter pad, restaurants, a conference centre and shopping plaza. The murder bears all the hallmarks of a terrorist gangland killing, probably committed by feuding gangs vying for power.'

Chief Constable Murray appeared on the screen, he was standing by the side of the tent. Wind caught the microphone that was being held in front of his face, giving his voice a distorted muffled sound. Murray was introduced and he explained in a brusque, confident tone the reasons why the murder had taken place. 'It is an internal struggle for power by those who have gutter morals, but unfortunately, their evil intent and actions influence and shape our society...'

And he carried on, his face set hard and determined while the man interviewing him nodded. The interview finished and the camera shot panned back, giving a view of the construction site and the surrounding area, and as it did so the camera picked out a pigeon and followed it as it swooped over the construction site. It was as if the pigeon was watching the human activity on the ground. The pigeon flew in an easterly direction, which would be over by the dock area, flying higher and higher until it was just a dot, and the people on the ground would also appear as merely dots if viewed from the height that the pigeon was flying.

The light from the television screen reflected fast dancing shadows on Roddy Harding's face. He pressed the button on the remote control and the channel changed to a children's programme. He muted the sound, stretched languorously and looked vacantly at the screen. Sighing with relief he settled himself in the armchair, making himself comfortable under the duvet.